Under a Thin Moon

Livi Michael

Under a Thin Moon

First published in Great Britain in 1992
by Martin Secker & Warburg Limited,
Michelin House, 81 Fulham Road, London SW3 6RB

Copyright © Livi Michael 1992

A CIP catalogue record for this book
is available from the British Library

ISBN 0 436 27883 9

The author wishes to thank Jane Rogers
for her invaluable advice.

Phototypeset in 12/15 Perpetua by Wilmaset Ltd, Birkenhead, Wirral
Printed in Great Britain by
Clays Ltd, St Ives plc

To my son Paul

'A sense of beauty, although mutilated, distorted and soiled, remains rooted in the heart of man as a powerful incentive. It is present in all the preoccupations of secular life, it is present in all human pursuits and relationships.'

Simone Weil

'Beauty is power made visible.'

Eric Gill

It is very simple. She is afraid.

There is a ring of greyish scum around the bath. Wanda stares at the greyish ring, the mottled stains near the plug. She washed it out two days ago. It is like the scum is always there. It disappears for a moment when you wash the bath, but comes back again when you stop. Wanda traces a section of the ring with her finger. I will wash it out, she thinks.

As Wanda walks into the kitchen the greys and oranges of the winter afternoon pass by through the windows of her flat and are reflected in the painted doors. Her kitchen is painted in shades of airforce blue and cream. Every kitchen in the tower block is painted the same, over two hundred of them. They say the council did a deal with the firm that provides the paint, giving them permission for a lorry park and getting a job-lot of paint in return. Windows and doors all over the estate are airforce blue and cream. Wanda thinks it is very ugly.

She never minded when she first moved in. She walked from the window of one nine-foot-square room to another and could hardly wait for the social worker and the housing officer to leave.

You haven't even got a kettle, the social worker says.

Wanda says it is alright, she's got a pan. The housing officer looks bored and waits by the door with the key. Coral begins to kick and whimper under Wanda's arm.

She's tired, Wanda says.

But she hasn't anywhere to sleep, says the social worker.

It's alright, Wanda says. She'll sleep in her trolley for tonight. And I've got my sleeping bag. It's only for one night. Tomorrow I'll get things sorted.

Can we get going, says the housing officer. But the social worker is not ready to leave yet, not without impressing on Wanda all the things she has to do. Wanda stops listening. She finds the small pan in her bag and takes it into the kitchen. She fills it with water from the tap and puts it on the cooker to boil, ready to heat Coral's bottle. Everything works. It is the best place in the world.

At last they are gone and Wanda takes Coral into the front room for her bottle. She goes to the biggest window, the one with the glass door onto the balcony. She cannot get over the view. It is evening already, and a thousand windows facing west reflect the sunset like a fiery ball. There are glittering ribbons of lights from the main roads into the city, and as Wanda and Coral watch the night deepens and more lights appear in the city centre itself: some flashing neon, others shedding long beams across the new motorway, the football stadium. There are lights from restaurants, discos and private clubs. Nearer home there are the domestic lights of windows in which, if the curtains are not drawn, Wanda can make out people moving, eating, watching telly. It is like a free show for her and Coral. Out there, she feels, is life, excitement. Things are happening.

Look Coral, she says. The whole of the great big shining world out there, just for us. The dark eyes widen momentarily but the rhythmical suction carries on. Wanda shrugs Coral into a better position on her hip. She cannot stop looking at the windows of the opposite flats, Trafalgar House, or further down the block she is in. It is like being able to enter people's lives unnoticed, into the lives of real families, with a father and mother and children. She squeezes Coral. They are a family too, her and Coral, a proper family in a proper home. People might be looking in on them, wanting to be part of their family. This is our home Coral, Wanda says. Ninety-two Blenheim House. Coral coughs and turns her face away from the bottle. A small posset of milk runs from the corner of her mouth. Wanda pats it industriously with the edge of her sleeve. She will be like one of those mothers on the adverts, who is always worried about whether or not to boil her whites. She lifts Coral up to give her a better view. The moving lights reflect in Coral's eyes. Black eyes. Black as the buttons on Wanda's coat.

*

Once you get up it is generally alright.

Coral sits at the kitchen table with her back to the window and both hands round a cup of tea, for though it is August it is always cold inside.

Outside, the streets are maggoty with children, their screeches fill the air. Some whirl bottles round and round on the end of a rope until they fly off and smash on the garage walls. Others play football, kicking the ball time and time again against the outside wall of Coral's flat. Even in the kitchen she can hear the thudding and juddering of the bedroom wall whilst the cracks in the plaster lengthen and deepen and the little clock rattles on the bedside table. This will go on all day, almost till midnight in June. For this reason Coral looks forward to winter.

Now it is August. It seems like it has always been August, the light like an old tobacco stain and the occasional spatter of rain, not enough to make the kids go in.

At least the pounding on her walls makes her get up and that is a good thing. Every morning she wakes up feeling the print of Larry's body on hers but when she turns to him he is not there. She lies a while staring at the mottled ceiling with the yellowish stain from Larry's smoke. This is always the worst time. But if she can get up she will be alright. In the kitchen there is always the floor to be swept or a pot to wipe, and she does these things edging round the parts of the kitchen which are not near the window because she does not like to be seen from outside. Coral knows that Mrs Whitcombe, who lives below her, is the same. From the outside you would never know she was in, but for the occasional twitch of a curtain and the whisking of a narrow face quickly out of sight.

Coral finishes her tea and rinses the cup, standing to one side of the window and using just a little water so it will not attract attention to the pipes outside. Though she has just wiped the draining board she wipes it again. She does not know what she will do today. There are the envelopes of course, but she is tired of envelopes. She does not know what she will do tomorrow. She walks to the lounge and stands still, as if any time now it will come to her what she must do.

When she was with Larry it was different. They had always known what to do, or at least when they did not know it didn't matter. They would stay in bed, eating their meals there, and neither the pounding on the walls nor the rain streaming in through the cracks in the window frame bothered them at all.

*

Is it jaundiced, her visitors at the hospital ask, one after another. Her mother says nothing at all. She leans over the cot then straightens, taking her glasses off and putting them back inside her bag. She does not look at Wanda, though Wanda cannot stop looking at her, at the fairish greying hair in a stiff perm, the lined face, and the lips that look like more of the lines on her face. She clips her bag shut. Then she turns and walks away, past the other beds on the ward and through the swing-doors at the far end, her heels making clicking noises on the polished floor. Wanda wants to call out to her but she won't. Later she gets a letter from her father. They are decorating, it says. She had better not come home just now. He encloses two ten-pound notes. Wanda reads it with a mixture of triumph and terror. She crumples the notes up in her hands.

Everyone tells her she must give Coral up for adoption. She is only seventeen, they say, and she has nowhere to go. But if she gives Coral up she will have to go home. That is all she can think about. Without her baby she will not have the courage to stay away. So she will not give her up. In the end they call the social worker and she finds Wanda a place in the hostel.

It is time to change Coral's nappy. Wanda turns away from the glittering city. For a moment she is afraid of the shadows which gather strangely in the corners of the room. She remembers being a child, afraid of the darkness and always just out of reach of the light switch. It's alright Coral, she says. She walks boldly to the other side of the room and presses the switch. Light glares from the bald bulb and hurts their eyes. Coral begins to struggle and whimper. She rubs her fist into her face. She is ready for bed but first Wanda has to change her nappy. She sits cross-legged on the floor and unbuttons Coral's baby-gro. The shadows in the room are huge with soft blurred edges. The windows are blind black squares. But Wanda will not be afraid. She makes herself concentrate on taking off the nappy, on smoothing the nappy-rash cream round the creases of Coral's skin with her hanky. No matter how much cream she puts on, the skin is red and flaking here, and in the crooks of her elbows and knees, the creases and folds of her neck. There are so many creases and folds. It is like she is wearing a suit that is too big for her. The skin slides and bunches as Wanda picks Coral up. She is going to try washing her down in the sink.

Wanda does not like the shadows which follow her silently down the hall. But it is their first night together on their own. They will be happy in their new flat. Warm water runs instantly from the tap and Wanda splashes Coral. Coral makes gurgling and coughing noises which are loud in the silence. Wanda goes back into the lounge for her toothbrush, then cleans her teeth and sits on the toilet keeping Coral with her all the time. She does not like the noises from the cistern. She goes back to the lounge again, puts on Coral's nappy, fastens her into her trolley, and then unrolls the sleeping bag on the floor next to it. A picture of sunflowers falls out. It is from her bedroom at home. Mary brought it to her at the hospital along with the pan and some clothes and other things she might need. Over by the window there is a nail in the wall and a pale square where another picture once hung. Wanda hangs her picture on the wall. The room looks better already, more like her own. She stands back and looks at the room with the picture. Coral looks at Wanda and sucks two of her fingers. Wanda takes off her shoes, then her coat and jeans, folding them neatly on the floor. Then she switches the light off. Instantly the room is full of strange half-lights and the moving beams of cars. Wanda eases herself into her sleeping bag. The floor is very hard. And the flats are alive with noise: groanings and creakings from the lift shaft, the sound of voices below and the television next door. Occasionally there is the sound of footsteps thudding up the stairs and shrieks of laughter. In the flat itself there are the clicks and creaks of strange joinery; a hissing noise in the pipes. Wanda cannot get to sleep. Coral is not asleep either. From time to time Wanda hears a small sigh and the intermittent sucking of fingers. Wanda will never get to sleep. When she closes her eyes the noises get louder and there is a moving pattern of lights against her eyelids. I must get some curtains, she thinks.

*

Today in the class-room Valerie feels the familiar churning of her stomach; her shoulders and neck seize up.

Stop it, she tells herself. Her leg trembles beneath the desk. As the voice at the front of the class-room drones on about sheep farming in New Zealand, or the national deficit, Valerie stares slowly round the room: at the clock, the globe, the window. Her eyes blur, then focus, then blur again.

Pay attention Valerie, the teacher snaps. Valerie wants to curl herself into a tight ball. Instead she stares at the scarred wood of the desk and tries to breathe properly.

When the bell goes Valerie is first to the door, blundering past desks and chairs. She must get some air.

Outside, near the big bins Valerie leans against the wall. She presses her fingers to her forehead, expecting a migraine. It is a free period but the field is empty because of the soaking drizzle. The dripping trees, the reddish houses on the drive, the solitary pedestrian walking a bedraggled dog, are all seen through a fine mist of rain.

Valerie feels the wetness on her face and thinks of going home. There is another lesson later on, geography, or economics, so she should stay. Already she is walking towards the drive.

Valerie lives further away from the school than anyone else. Her mother fought for years to change her council flat, but the move came through at the wrong time for Valerie, who had just started her A-levels and did not want to change schools. Not that she liked her school, she just didn't want to change. So her mother put on make-up, squeezed herself into corsets and an old suit and, looking like a shocking caricature of her former self, went to sort things out at the school. Something of the old assurance must have returned, because Valerie was told she could stay, and now she has to catch two buses to school each morning. It is too far to go home, unless she doesn't mean to return that day.

Valerie kicks a twig and notices all the fat shiny slugs on the drive. It is strange how you never notice them crawling towards the path, but one day they are all there, as if they have grown out of the gravel itself. And they sit so still, with a terrible patience, as cars and bikes wheel over them, and feet trample them into the autumn mould.

Valerie avoids the slugs. At the back of her neck she feels the fear of being seen. But at the end of the drive she sees the bus stop, and her strides lengthen into a loping run.

*

The first night in the hostel a fight broke out in the crowded stuffy room and someone drew a knife. Wanda sees the blood spatter up the wall. She is nearest the door. As quietly as she can she grabs her cagoule and Coral and the push-chair and manoeuvres them out of the room. She bumps the trolley down one stair after another, scared that Coral will cry, that someone will hear the trolley and think she is going for the police, that they will not get out in time. At last the door clicks to behind her. She cannot get back in.

There is nowhere to go. After the initial hurry to get out Wanda realises this, but she walks quickly as if she has somewhere to go: through the darkened streets, trying not to see the huddled shapes in doorways, remembering all the tales her mother told her about little girls who go out at night alone. She sees the headlines, mother and baby murdered, and almost cries out when someone brushes past her as she turns the corner. But it is only an old woman carrying several bags. She does not even look at Wanda as she jostles past. Wanda goes on, carrying Coral under one arm. She is too young for her trolley, the health visitor says. It could damage her spine. Wanda ought to buy her a proper pram. Instead Wanda carries Coral around under her arm, only using the trolley when her arm is aching badly.

All the streets look different in the dark. Everything looks different. Wanda walks more slowly now and the trolley rattles gently over the cobbles. These are the streets no one ever uses, even in the daytime, except for parking. They are not on the direct route to the shops or pubs. Although they look strange in the small light they are not very frightening. As Wanda pushes Coral past the big bins which are overflowing with litter she realises there is nothing much to be frightened of at all. The streets are empty except for the silent ghosts of cats flitting in and out of alleys. Is this it, Wanda thinks. Is this what she has been frightened of all her life? A thin moon glitters on the broken glass. Wanda takes her time to look around. She walks behind the backs of stores where newspapers and cardboard boxes are stacked, across the empty market ground where orange peel and cabbage leaves are slippery underfoot and chip papers get entangled in the trolley wheels, then past the sewage works where the brownish water foams and spills in little waterfalls to the sluice.

There is no one to see her at all, but as she walks Wanda imagines she is being filmed, as part of a true-life documentary about the homeless. Down every alleyway invisible cameramen record her progress, sympathetically appreciating her plight. They cannot let her know they are there as it would spoil the realism of their documentary. Even so the thought of it makes Wanda walk with a certain consciousness, hunching her shoulders in an oppressed way. She imagines the narrator hurrying after her along the narrow streets, speaking into his microphone in hushed tones, but with a perfect accent . . .

. . . *In Britain today the number of the unemployed and homeless has increased yet again. Here you see one of the faceless millions: a young girl, fresh from the maternity ward of the local hospital, onto the streets. What does the future hold for this young woman? Where will she go next . . .*

The narrator is very moving. Wanda feels tears pricking her eyes. It is hard to believe she is homeless, that such a thing could happen to her so easily. She feels the tears rolling down her cheeks and rubs at them with the back of her hand. Perhaps she will be found dead after all. Her mother will be sorry then.

Even as she cries Wanda is conscious of the reaction of the cameramen, their desire to comfort her checked only by the greater desire to show the world her pain. She does not know if she is crying for their benefit or her own. But when Coral wakes up and begins to kick and wail it becomes hard to think of outside eyes watching her sympathetically. She has a sense of hostile eyes following her but she does not want to think of that. She joggles Coral gently in her arms realising too late that she has left too many things at the hostel: Coral's bottle, blanket, and the cover for the trolley. Coral is hungry and will not sleep. Wanda is hungry too but she has no money, anyway nowhere is open. Rockabye baby, she whispers, on the tree top. The buildings around her loom enormous, their darkened shapes and blind black eyes press in on her. She is very tired. All the buildings begin to look alike. Wanda knows they are all different really, in the daytime, but in the darkness they all look alike. Street after street is the same to Wanda because none of them has any meaning. There is nothing for her to recognise in them. As she walks through street after street of terraced houses all shut against her Wanda realises that this, all the time, is what people are really afraid of in the dark. Everything loses its shape and becomes unrecognisable. You could be anywhere at all. Wanda's footsteps echo on the cobbles. Without a sense of place it is hard to remember yourself. You could be anyone at all.

Wanda stops crying. She has to comfort Coral who is drawing her feet up and making sharp little moans. Besides there is no one to hear. She is losing her sense of audience. She feels like she is becoming invisible. All she wants is to find somewhere to stay for the night. Under her arm Coral whimpers and kicks. Wanda wishes she had remembered her bottle. When the wind blows, she says, the cradle will rock. She is leaning too heavily on the trolley, looking round all the time for a sheltered bench or a bridge where she can stay the night. She will not be allowed back in the hostel in the daytime either. No one is allowed in between nine and six. But maybe she can sit in the library if they will let her in with the trolley and Coral doesn't cry. Wanda doesn't know how long it is till morning. A bell rings and she counts three or four chimes. Time has no meaning in the darkened streets. It is all gone, along with the sense of place, and self.

There is a thin rain in the air. She must find a place to shelter. In the park the pavilion bench is occupied, there is someone beneath the railway bridge and the toilets and waiting room are locked. But on the platform there is another bench which is partly covered by the overhanging roof. Wanda sits down. She is aching all over. There is more than one person beneath the railway bridge but she is beyond fear. For the first time in her life she is beyond fear. She could die here in the night but she is not scared of that either. She wishes she had brought Coral's blanket. Holding her inside her cagoule for warmth she lifts her jumper and presses Coral to her breast. Coral chews hungrily at one nipple then the other, then cries sharply because there is no milk, ever since Wanda's illness in the hospital. She sucks again and cries. Wanda hums the lullaby to her. When the bough breaks, she hums, the cradle will fall. The ridges of the bench are hard against Wanda's back. Overhead the pale curving moon passes in and out of clouds, briefly illuminating the scrawls of graffiti on the platform pillars. It is the kind of moon where the white bit is new and keen, but you can see the rest of it, round and full in its darkness like a round dark plum. Her mother used to say that the moon was a bowl of cream, and the sky was a big black cat licking away at it each night until there's nothing left. Wanda could never see it, because if you licked cream it would run all over the bowl, but her mother said it was double cream, whipped up thick.

The floor of the flat is not so hard as the bench that night. And tomorrow Wanda can start to look for curtains, and for the other things for her flat. Everything will be alright now, or soon, when she can get some things of her own. All she has to do tonight is to get to sleep.

As Wanda lies on the floor, her coat stuffed under her head and Coral's breathing hoarse in the empty room, she has a sense of watching herself, on the floor of the strange room, near the trolley, trying to sleep. Then she has a sense of watching herself being watched. She shifts slightly and shuts her eyes.

*

Now it is evening but not yet dark. Coral stands in the lounge rubbing the toe of one foot against the carpet. Soon she will be able to go to bed. The cries outside are fading as mothers call their children off the street. In an hour or so they will all be gone except for one or two stragglers waiting for parents to come back from the pub.

Coral crosses to the side of the window and sees the street-lamps lighting. If she listens she can hear the faint buzz of traffic from the main road off the estate but that too is fading. In the lamp beams she can see fine sprays of rain and the dull metallic glow of garage roofs. Tarpaulin flaps and scrapes, flaps and scrapes in a broken window. It is almost an inorganic world.

It has always been like this, Coral thinks. She can't explain it but she knows it will always be so. But there is no one to see it with her, to look as she does at the glittering concrete and spouting gutters. Larry would have seen it that way, she would not have to explain it to Larry. Other people looked at them with strange or hostile eyes, as if Coral and Larry were not like them, as if they could have nothing to do with Coral and Larry. Coral and Larry saw each other differently, but sometimes when they were together and the police or neighbours looked at them that way their own way of seeing slipped and they could only see themselves the same way, you couldn't help it somehow. But the strange thing was that, whoever they were, police, social workers, DHSS, your way of looking at things didn't affect them. They never saw you the way you saw each other.

Now it is quiet enough to go to bed and Coral moves around that little flat closing curtains. She goes towards the bedroom and her slippers flap softly down the hall.

From time to time Larry would look for a job and occasionally find one. Coral was miserable then. From the time the door shut in the morning she waited for him to come home, storing up everything that happened in the day so it would be like they had shared it, like the outside world had not divided them. They never had more money – with so many out of work the bosses could pay what they liked and sack the workers after each job. There were always plenty more men to be hired. One place the boss had commented loudly on Larry's appearance, his split shoes and ragged jeans, and then grinned broadly round the room seeing that everyone joined in the joke. Larry laughed too, but then the boss leans over Larry's desk so that his big red face is close to Larry's own:

People like you, Parker, he says, are born losers.

Coral was furious when Larry told her. She wanted him to leave right away but Larry wouldn't. She said he was a million times better than that slimy red-faced wanker, but Larry only laughed a bit and said nothing. Coral knew he did not believe her and this struck her as being important. All her love and her high opinion of Larry counted as nothing beside what a red-faced boss had to say.

*

Outside there is tremendous energy in the jagged skyline, the flaming sky.

14

You could almost believe in God, thinks Laurie, a god of industry, grime and power.

In the daytime it is all spread out before her like the crumbling remains of a picnic, cooling towers, factory chimneys, warehouses, scrapyards, tower blocks and terraced houses stacked tightly together, block after block, but now at evening it takes her by surprise in its magnificence, like the silent God she half believes in.

Laurie is a thief. For her it is a social occupation. She goes to one of the local supermarkets where there are always crowds of people and moves amongst them as they plan their weekly meals and budgets, struggle with toddlers and discuss the neighbours. Then she picks out a shop assistant and strikes up a conversation. It is Laurie's theory that store detectives ignore people who are talking to shop assistants. Of course some will not be talked to at all. With others a simple remark like, I bet you'll be glad when it's closing time, is enough to set them off about their tired feet and aching legs and the hours they have to put in before Christmas for the kids.

It's all want want want, says Joan on the cooked meats.

Sometimes Laurie feels bad, taking the stock from right under their noses. More commonly she feels excited, the more daring she has been. She walks out of the store with frozen peas, candles, fish-net tights and pot noodles, buzzing with energy. And it is not as if she is not interested in their lives. Joan on the cooked meats has varicose veins and an ailing mother. Sue on dairy produce has food problems. She once ate a 4lb slab of blue cheshire she was supposed to be selling and had to put the money in the till herself.

I'm in the wrong job here, she says.

Laurie pours a third of a pint of milk into a pan and looks at the day's takings. She has a bag full of exotic fruit. Savemore is doing a run on exotic fruit – guava, pawpaw, passion fruit and mango, which lie in ignored heaps at the end of the vegetable section. Tonight Laurie is having a guava, pawpaw, passion fruit and mango salad, with custard. She pours milk onto the custard in the jug. Her diet has never been so varied and interesting.

For a while Laurie used to twine rather than shoplift. She would exchange her dole money at a bank for a ten-pound note and a twenty. Then she would pick her shops carefully. Bigger stores are better. Smaller shops don't always have change and there is more chance of being recognised. She buys something small, maybe polo mints, with the twenty-pound note, ignoring the disgusted look of the girl at the till, and begins her patter. She comes out of the shop with thirty pounds change from the twenty-pound note. In the next shop she buys a biro with the ten-pound note and emerges with fifteen. She can earn quite a lot on a good day. And it is hard for anyone to prove you have been doing something wrong. You do not have a 2lb bag of frozen peas inside your anorak.

Twining has its disadvantages however. Some people notice what you are doing and then you have to leave the shop with as much haste and confusion as possible. And it is not wise to visit the same shop twice in case they cotton-on immediately after you leave, or in case the whole process has been filmed on a shop camera. You spend days trudging round town centres looking for likely victims. And you know, because you once did the work yourself, that the shop assistant will be in big trouble at the end of the day when the till is cashed. If it happens often enough she will be sacked. It is never the people you would like to hurt who really suffer.

But this is not the main problem with twining. When you twine you cannot strike up a proper conversation. It is not like talking to Joan on cooked meats or Sue on dairy produce. Laurie pours custard onto the bowl of chopped fruit. Before she took up 'lifting she never got to talk to anyone. She would look at someone at the bus stop or in the Cozy Caffy and think, I could talk to her. She would think out what she could say – I hate waiting for buses, or, the coffee here's much better than the tea. She would sit quite still, feeling the suffocating pressure to speak, until the bus arrived, or the other person left the café.

When she steals she is a different person. She never has so much to say as when she is lifting food. She is bright and witty, sympathetic. People's eyes light up at her approach.

The fruit salad is good. Today has been a good day. There are days, she thinks, making patterns in the custard, when even the stains on the wall, the holes in her socks, seem part of a larger, more meaningful pattern, and she rides freely on the world's shoulders. Other days the world sits firmly down on hers. All her thoughts and actions drop like litter in her wake and everything seems shrunken, shrivelled, except for (of course) the holes in her socks and the stains on the walls. She cannot always tell the reason for these sudden shifts and changes. Yesterday for instance the world seemed sour and maggoty, though nothing in particular went wrong. She had gazed out of the window with an inhuman eye and was surprised by her own malevolence. But then yesterday was Sunday and the shops were shut.

Laurie sucks thoughtfully on the mango and pawpaw. She looks forward to her shopping tomorrow, the next day. It has made a great difference to her life, giving it meaning and shape. It has made a great difference to her, enabling her to see beauty in the scuffed edges of the Manchester skyline.

Valerie no longer lives with her mother.

I can't stand you any more, she screams.

Well get out then, her mother screams back. I'm sick of the sight of you.

Then when she found the flat her mother got very drunk. Blinking, she watches Valerie pack, with the stupid fixed expression Valerie hates.

You can take these tablecloths if you like, she says, holding a crumpled bundle in her hands.

No thank you, Valerie says. Her mother drops them anyway.

And all this bedding, she says, dragging the sheets from her bed behind her.

No mother, you need the bedding, says Valerie. Her mother hauls a chair into the lounge.

You'll need a chair, she says.

Mother, says Valerie, the flat's furnished. It's got chairs.

Her mother disappears into the kitchen. Valerie hears the crash of dropped cutlery and broken plates. She comes out again with a mixing bowl and whisk and drops these on the floor with everything else.

Valerie sweeps the things aside to clear a space and goes on packing. More junk is dropped on the floor. Stop it mam, says Valerie.

Valerie's books are next, half thrown, half dropped onto the pile.

You may as well have these, says her mother, trampling over them into the bathroom. Valerie sorts them into bags. When she turns to go into her bedroom her mother is in the way, clutching towels this time, and the bath-mat. Valerie brushes violently past.

She checks her bedroom several times. It is hard to concentrate. When she returns to the front room her mother is looking through her bags.

I want my little clock, she says thickly. You can take anything else, but just leave me my little clock.

Valerie pushes past her so hard she nearly falls, then struggles to gather up all her bags at once. But her mother is in front of Valerie, still blinking in the same idiot way.

You can't ever come back you know, she says.

Get out of my way, says Valerie.

I want my little clock, her mother says.

Valerie drops her bags. She feels her arm rising, fist clenched. She strikes her mother hard in the chest and stomach. Her mother staggers back. She leans heavily against the wall, breathing noisily, eyes half shut. She is waiting for another blow. Valerie drops her arm. Grabbing her bags she hurries away.

But before she is out of the square her mother is outside, dressing-gown flapping open, showing the stains on her night-dress.

Don't let her go away, she begs a man who is crossing the square. She clutches a woman's coat – Don't let my baby leave.

She runs from one passer-by to another. Soon there is a crowd in the square.

Valerie hates them all. She hauls her bags to the top of the steps leading out of the estate. But at the top is Tracey, a tall scrawny girl, staring wildly ahead.

Whatever shall we do mam, she moans, staring into space. It isn't yet, it isn't time. She wrings her hands and twists the material of her skirt.

Valerie gets past Tracey and is out of the estate at last, on the main road. She struggles towards her new flat, wondering why she can't be left alone, to slip through life unnoticed. As a child she was dragged hunched and glowering into the limelight, where she failed miserably to perform. Her mother is a performer. She used to sing in clubs. Even now, running round the council square in her stained nightdress with no teeth, she sees not the empty faces of her neighbours but an audience, not the concrete playground but a stage.

*

A long time ago Coral is looking for her mother. Up and up the stairs she goes because she can't reach the lift button, and as she climbs higher and higher all the old anxiety returns. The stairs seem to go on and on but then she gets to the door and calls out mam, mam but no one answers. The door is open as she pushes it.

Coral must run down the hall very slowly, calling and calling for her mother. She runs into the lounge but her mother is not there. Then she runs into the kitchen but her mother is not there. Now Coral must go into the bathroom. As she pushes the door she remembers that her mother does not like her running into the bathroom when she is there. As she pushes the door she knows that she mustn't push the door open any further. But there is just the door and Coral, and the door keeps on opening. And there is her mother sitting up in the bath, staring at Coral. And there is the blood curling all around her like scarlet smoke in the bath-water. Mam, mam, screams Coral, but no one answers. Her mother is staring straight at her like she doesn't know her at all.

*

Wanda shakes the powder round the bath. It is Flash, which cleans baths without scratching. The powder is white, turning blue where the bath is wet. Wanda takes a cloth which is part of a ripped-up sheet and rubs it round and round with the powder and the water in the bath. Round and round she rubs the cloth, with strong, repetitive strokes.

She was always such a pretty girl. Show aunty your new dress, her mother says. Show everyone what you learned at dancing class. And Wanda goes round and round, the pink flouncy dress flying up and showing the pink frilly knickers beneath. Ringlets of hair whip her cheeks as she twists and turns and the red shoes make clicking noises on the floor. Her hair is fair and naturally straight but every Friday night after her bath her mother puts it all up in clips, ready for her dancing class on Saturday morning. She is such a pretty girl. Complete strangers stop her mother on the street to tell her so. She is always the prettiest girl in school. But she has not had a pretty baby. No one says anything about Coral at all.

Every mother thinks her baby is the most beautiful in the world, the health visitors say. But when they hand her to Wanda after the birth when she is drugged and sick from the pain, she cannot bear to look at her. Coral is bluish-brown all over like a bruise, mottled and blotchy. She is slippery with blood and mucus. Wanda turns her face away, but they prop Coral up on her breast, to see if her mouth will attach itself to Wanda's nipple. It is the latest way in all the books. Coral slithers around on Wanda's chest like a slimy creature from a pond. Wanda's arms flail uselessly at her sides, she will not take the baby. All the faces in the ward blur and tumble into one another until they make one many-headed animal bending over her, trying to make her take hold of her child. They have her arms, but Wanda twists and turns her head from one side to the other. She is crying like she will never stop. No no, she says. No no no no no no.

Even now she cannot think of it without feeling sick. She feels pangs of sickness at the sight of pregnant women, or new-born babies in their prams. Coral never had a pram. Wanda bends over Coral in her trolley. Come on Coral, she says. Let's look for something else.

It wasn't easy getting money from the DHSS. She had to queue all day in the stuffy office, fill in forms, take them back and queue again. Then she has to get the lowest estimates from all the second-hand shops. In the end they give her a cheque for the cheapest items. She can only have floor-covering for instance, not carpets, so a white oilcloth with blue and green blotches is fitted. It makes Wanda bilious, and the neighbours complain if there is too much noise when she moves around, so she beats a dealer down over a single bed and mattress and an old wooden wardrobe with a mirror in front and buys two pink rag rugs for the lounge and bedroom. Next she buys a set of drawers and some plants. These are not on the list of things she is allowed to buy but she can't resist them for the balcony and window-sills. She wants to be able to look out at something other than the grey slate roofs and factory chimneys. One of the plants will grow tall and leafy. She stands it in the corner of the room. Her flat will be like one of the New York apartments you see on telly. Wanda buys a telly, a black-and-white one for five quid, though she cannot afford the licence. She dreams of Habitat fabrics, or Laura Ashley, like the ones in the adverts, but instead buys some oddments for the curtains, hoping to sew them into something stylish and modern later on. Next Wanda buys a table, two chairs and an old pink sofa which is also a bed settee. Because the sofa is badly sprung and some of the stuffing is coming out the dealer throws in a bathroom cabinet with a mirror. Wanda buys a screwdriver and puts it up herself. So far she is doing well. She needs a fridge, and some pots and pans and crockery, and the money has almost run out, but then she sees two framed prints. One is a misty painting of London Bridge, the other a black-and-white photo of a street scene in Paris. In the foreground there is a man in a trilby hat leaning against a post. There are people sitting at an outdoor café and prostitutes in darkened doorways. One of them wears a short skirt, and is Oriental-looking. This picture grips Wanda's imagination though it is almost too big for her to push home on the trolley. She imagines she is part of the scene, part of the street life in Paris. As she walks past the stalls of the flea market she feels like she is being followed by the slow glance of the man in the trilby. It makes her walk differently, with style. The new pictures look great in her flat, she cannot be sorry she bought them though all the money is gone. They look right in her flat. It is right for her to have them there. And the next week she sees a cheap fridge and buys it anyway, though they have to spend three days on white bread and sterilised milk.

The truth is she does not want to stop spending the money. In spite of the drizzle of the dull spring days she cannot wait to get out in the mornings. It is the happiest time of her life. She does not buy the things she needs any more. She buys a lacy cover and cushions for the sofa to hide the stains, and a tablecloth with a jazzy pattern to cover the scratches on the table. She needs cutlery and crockery so she and Coral can stop eating out of the pan, but she picks this up a bit at a time. Then she finds a carry-cot for Coral with a small, pretty quilt, and a duvet for her own bed. There is the gas bill, but she buys it anyway. She will have to pay off the gas bill a bit at a time. She spends a long time looking for sheets and a duvet cover. The thing is, she cannot bring herself to buy the cheapest. It is plain and common. The one next to it in the window is twelve pounds dearer, but it is more like what Wanda thinks of as being herself. Without spending money she cannot have an image of herself. It seems right, and necessary, to buy the things which seem beautiful to her. She cannot contradict this feeling, it is too powerful. She returns every day to look at the duvet cover, hoping it will not go. Finally she buys it, and hurries all the way home as if hunted. She does not know how she will get through the rest of the week.

The sense that all this is forbidden to her makes it worse. Sometimes she tries to stay in. She sits by the window stitching the oddments into curtains and watching the world drift by below, though she hates sewing and nothing she makes hangs right. But sometimes she is taken by a kind of fear, a pressure in her chest, and she drops everything on the floor and hurries out as fast as she can with Coral. It is only on the market or the precinct that she really feels alive. As she walks around pushing the trolley and carrying Coral under her arm she feels like a character from one of the sixties films she loves to watch – 'The L-Shaped Room', or one of the other black-and-white ones with Rita Tushingham. Life is decadent, and a little seedy, but very artistic. Soon she will get to know all the other characters in her tower block. There will be unemployed artists, and homosexuals, trying to make an alternative lifestyle for themselves. Soon she will meet them all. Meanwhile she has to get her flat looking the way she wants it to look, so that when the people visit they will be able to tell that she is like them. She doesn't know yet exactly how it will look when it is finished, but each day when she buys something, no matter how small, a little bit more of the room and of herself is revealed to her. A small vase and a stained-glass sticker for the window add the finishing touches to the lounge.

Then suddenly she stops. The electric bill has arrived, and both Wanda and Coral have stomach-ache from the tinned soup, and she has run out of baby food. She is feeding Coral on white bread dipped in milk but she is worried because Coral cries all the time and is sick in the night. Wanda doesn't dare call the health visitor. She sits up all night stroking Coral's forehead and wiping up the mess. She will not buy any more things. She will not pay either of the bills tomorrow, she will get Coral some proper food. Coral moans and cries and sweats in her cot. Wanda is nearly crying too. She wipes Coral's face down with the flannel. I'm sorry Coral, she says. I'm sorry I'm sorry I'm sorry.

Wanda stops shopping. It is an empty feeling. On wet days she wanders from the window of one room to another, pushing back the lop-sided curtains and watching the people below. On fine days she sits with Coral on the market ground watching all the people as they shop in twos and threes, with children, pushing prams. It is a social occupation, spending money. Without it you do not belong in the world.

*

Laurie is woken by the shrill fluting of a bird above the cooling towers. Although she is wearing all her clothes she is stiff with cold. She lies very still, staring into the blackness of her room. She feels stillness creeping over her like stone, the urge not to move at all, until everything fades away.

Her mood blackens as she pokes her nose into the biting air. She wishes she knew the time but her clock broke some weeks ago and has long since been crossed off her list of 'optional extras'. But she knows she must get up. It is fatal not to move, to gradually lose the desire to move. She begins to insult herself for lying around, for wallowing in bedclothes and self-pity. Get up you stupid bitch, she says into the stillness of the room.

Suddenly she thrusts back the bedclothes and jerks her body into the thin and freezing air. Even through tights and socks the

25

bare floor numbs her feet. She tugs on jeans over the tights and zips an anorak over multi-coloured layers of T-shirts and jumpers. Finally she pulls on the fingerless gloves Shelagh made. Today she will not allow herself any sympathy for the darkness and cold. Today she despises herself and the world. She shuffles into the kitchen and switches on the light. Seconds later it flickers off again.

Fuck, curses Laurie. Shit, goddamn, bastard. She hobbles round the kitchen muttering curses like a creature from *Macbeth*, lighting one match after another and dropping them when they burn. Propped on the window-sill is the large mottled fragment of a mirror. In it as she passes her face appears like a ghostly triangle, the eyes shaded, almost shut, the lips a straight thin line. Then she strikes a match and the reflection leaps into life, orange, weirdly pockmarked because of the stains on the mirror, shadows sculpting the bony hollows of her face. It is like Shelagh's face as she best remembers it, propped up on her hand as she lies on the bed in the flat they shared, lamplight shaking orange lights from her hair, making the angular face almost beautiful.

Laurie stubs her toe and swears softly, fluently. Then she stops herself, thinking that she is beginning to sound like Jean in the bottom flat, a belligerent cylinder of a woman with a blueberry nose and hairs sprouting from unexpected places on her face. She never goes out except on her twice-daily trip to the off-licence in her nightie and sheepskin jacket, bottles of cider and brandy tucked inside. She sits behind the curtains of her window and as the day wears on people at the bus stop outside are startled by the abuse rumbling out invisibly. Laurie does not want to end up like Jean. She manages to light the cooker and set a pan of water on the boil. The kettle also broke, two weeks ago. She flicks on the radio, but there is only a noise like bacon frying which makes her hungry so she switches it off again. Perhaps she can get batteries out of this week's dole.

Laurie remembers the recent publicity stunt of an MP who said he would try to live for one week off the same money as the unemployed. It was hard, very hard, he said to all the local papers. Unbelievably hard, he said. For some reason it has made him very popular, though it has never done much for Laurie. And of course no one asked him about his freezer full of food, his wardrobe full of expensive clothes or the free travel he gets. Laurie wishes she had been there. She would have smacked his stupid lying face. She imagines herself digging her fingers into the fat lard of his face and dragging them downwards leaving marks like a fork in dripping. She smacks her mug down hard on the table then she sits down suddenly, wearily. She knows she would do nothing of the kind.

Outside in the haloes of the lamps the street glows a dull orange. There is still no sign of traffic but Laurie can hear a faint hum and buzz from the main road off the estate. She sits hunched over a steaming cup of tea. She is thinking of her giro which is due in the morning post. She is thinking of all the things it will have to buy – toothpaste, washing powder, though maybe soap will do. But the soles of her boots are flapping open in the rain though she only bought them six weeks ago from the flea market. She should really get some new ones . . .

The first car passes on the street below and a ray of light travels across the kitchen ceiling. Then Laurie hears noises from the flat below, the dull clump and thud of Mary's movements, the scraping of a chair. If Mary is awake soon everyone else will be. There is a terrific crash from her kitchen. Mary is a stout young woman with wispy blonde hair and a flat face like a round pink moon. At twenty-two she has been through eight pregnancies, though some were terminated and none of the children live with her. People shake their heads as she walks past. Something should be done, they say.

Now there is a shrill wail from the flat next door. The kids are up and so is their father, hurling orders and abuse. None of them speaks if Laurie sees them on the landing. They flit past like a family of shrunken ghosts, so the amount of noise they make inside is always surprising to Laurie, the snarls and screams and moans, the bumps and bangs which rattle her own flat. Sometimes the woman cries out to Laurie through the door, help me, she cries, help me. So one time Laurie waited for the safest moment and then sneaked out down the stairs. The nearest phone-box was vandalised, there was a long queue winding round the next one. Finally she went into a pub, ignoring the staring men at the bar, and called the police. They want to know who she is, and her address, and her exact reason for believing they should be called out. Then in about an hour they call round. This time they want to know how old she is and whether or not she is working. She begs them not to let her neighbours know who phoned and they promise not to say. Then she hears them on the landing, warning the man to keep the noise down. He keeps asking who called them out. We're not allowed to tell you that, they say. Then they knock again on Laurie's door, making it obvious to everyone who called. Call us if you have any more problems, they say. When they are gone Laurie turns off all the lights in her flat and barricades the door. She sits in her bedroom waiting for the man next door to batter his way through to her flat. She does not go out for three days.

Outside the sky is greying into dawn. Everyone is up except for Sharon who lives below the family next door with her daughter Paula. Nothing wakens Sharon or Paula before eleven, and they are always the last to bed. Below Sharon the flat is empty. A

28

stream of people have come and gone too quickly for acquaintance, but for a while it has been empty.

So here they all are in this crumbling heap of concrete, plasterboard and cement. The walls are so thin they are aware of all the small private details of one another's lives, and in many ways their lives run on similar lines, yet they are all encased in small apartments so that each is absolutely alone.

At the bottom of the flats the door swings open and shuts again. Laurie tenses, but there is only the clink of bottles.

Grey light seeps around the room, exposing the cracked pot sink and the large stain which is oozing on the wall. She has reported it a hundred times to the council. Laurie thinks of a life lived entirely in suspension, waiting for the approach of a postman who never comes. She yawns and runs her fingers through her hair.

And today's problem, children, says the schoolmistress voice in her head, is how to get forty-three pounds' worth of goods out of thirty-two pounds. Laurie runs through everything again in her mind, ticking off all the things she can possibly do without, but it still comes to thirty-nine pounds. Where the hell is the postman anyway? If he doesn't come there is nothing she can do at all but wait.

The door at the bottom clicks again. It is certainly the postman this time, bringing something for Sharon and (Laurie hugs herself as the steps ascend the stairs) the family next door. Then there is a pause. Laurie is out of her chair peering at the front door from the kitchen doorway. The postman shuffles through his bag. Then something in a brown-paper envelope is flipped through her letterbox and Laurie pounces. She has half torn it open when she sees it is a bill.

The postman's steps are retreating down the stairs. Laurie hurries onto the landing and hangs over the stairwell. Hey, she shouts, too loudly. The postman looks up in surprise. Laurie feels foolish. Is there – I mean – have you – the words come tumbling in a rush – are you sure there's nothing else for flat 8B?

I'll have a look, says the postman, rifling through his sack.

Nope, he says, and walks away.

*

At last the bus pulls up. Valerie can go home to the new flat. She feels better already, lurching to her seat.

Why didn't you move further away, says Marcie at the meeting. Valerie settles herself into her seat, hugging her school bag. She gazes gratefully out of the window.

Why didn't you move further away, Marcie asks. Valerie blinks around the lighted room. She does not expect the question. She expects approval of her decision to leave home. But everyone is looking at her, wanting to know why the flat she has chosen is only ten minutes down the road from her mother's.

Well, she says, it just came up, you know.

For the flat belongs to the father of her best friend Ros.

Come on Val, Ros urges. It'll do you good.

Val is not sure. It might well do her good to get away from her mother. She might even get some work done. But how can she stand not knowing from one minute to the next what her mother is up to, not paying the rent, getting herself arrested, setting herself on fire.

You think you can keep tabs on your mother, says Sheila, but you can't. You can't take responsibility for someone else's life. Valerie denies she is trying to do this, but at the meeting they cry her down.

I've got no money, she says to Ros.

You won't need any, says Ros. Look, my dad's not going to charge us rent, and I'll see to the bills. I'd have to anyway. You'll only need a bit for food. You can get a Saturday job like me.

Just like that, Valerie thinks. For Ros things do happen just like that. She gets pocket-money from her father and models hairstyles in her sister's salon on Saturdays. Valerie does not get any money. She loves Ros with a bitter, resentful love, because all the time they spend together is shadowed by this fact.

But Valerie does have a little money, from Christmases, birthdays, bus fares on the days she misses school. Her mother doesn't know about it or it would soon disappear. She hides it in a different place each day. It will not go very far though.

You can work at Alison's with me, Ros says.

And frighten all the clients, says Valerie, but Ros insists and she is used to getting her own way. Anyway, how else will Valerie ever get to move without any money? They don't think of that at the meeting. So after a while Valerie gives in.

She does not go down well at the hairdressing salon. Alison gives up trying to style her thick rough hair in a becoming way and the clients complain when she shampoos them. Ali gives her five pounds for brewing up and sweeping the floor. It does not go very far. But Ros insists on paying for them to go out, and even tries to buy Valerie some clothes. Valerie resists this. All the clothes she has are black and shapeless. She likes them that way. Ros is an art student. She wears brightly coloured sweaters over flimsy skirts and leggings, and silk scarves she has painted herself. One day she says she will give Val a new image. Valerie has to sit still as Ros back-combs her hair and drapes different materials around her. As Ros brushes on dramatic make-up, stroke by stroke, Val feels very strange. She feels like she is being brushed away. Soon she feels like she does not exist at all.

*

Coral flings her bottle onto the pavement. Wanda picks it up and wipes it and hands it back. Coral flings it down again and Wanda picks it up. Coral flings it down again. My life is meaningless, Wanda thinks. She pushes Coral past the advertisements on the side of the market hall, Christian Dior tights, Yardley make-up, sports cars. She has to go slowly because Coral keeps taking off her shoes and socks and dropping them in the street. Sometimes it seems to Wanda that she is becoming very small whilst the rest of the world has become enormous. Everything she does is difficult and takes a long time. Before she can go out in the mornings she has to pack a bag for Coral, with a nappy and a plastic bag for the dirty one and extra clothes in case she makes a real mess. Then she packs two bottles, one milk, one fruit juice, and a teething ring and some cream for Coral's rash and the blanket which Coral has to have with her everywhere she goes. Then Wanda manoeuvres the trolley through three sets of swing-doors to the lift but Coral starts crying for her doll. When Wanda ignores her she begins to scream. Back they go through the three sets of swing-doors. Wanda picks up the doll but as she is locking up she remembers the rain-cover for Coral's trolley. It will rain later the weather man said. Back she goes leaving Coral on the landing this time. But as they get through the first set of swing-doors there is a bubbling noise from Coral's nappy. Wanda bends over to examine her. She has shit over everything she has on. Because of the way she sits it is oozing up the back of her baby-gro almost to the neck. Wanda turns round again. Sometimes she feels like she is on a film and someone keeps pressing the rewind button so that she never gets on.

Inside she takes off Coral's clothes. Coral begins to kick and scream. She clenches her fists and doubles her arms up as Wanda tries to get the baby-gro off. Wanda forces back one arm and then the other, pinning her down as she prises the arms of the baby-gro over her hands. Coral's screams get louder, but Wanda tugs off the bottom of the baby-gro and the nappy and goes to wash her in the sink. Coral's screams are so loud now they are tearing Wanda apart. She is digging her nails into Coral's flesh. When she releases them Coral's head slips and bangs against the sink. Wanda leans heavily down on Coral to get the new nappy and baby-gro on. Coral's screams are fast and regular, staccato, her face is almost purple. Wanda bends her limbs one way then another, tugging her this way and that. Her head is full of screams, she cannot think. Finally she zips the kicking legs into Coral's outdoor suit and straps Coral tightly into the trolley. She locks up carefully and pushes her way through the three swing-doors to the lift. Then she turns back again. She has forgotten her bag.

*

It is quite dark now and a thin sliver of moon passes in and out of clouds. The windows are covered with fine silver globules of rain. Coral pulls off her clothes and climbs into bed, lying on her side with her knees tucked up. She always slept this way with Larry, her body tucked into his, knees in the crook of his knees, his buttocks pressed into her stomach.

A beam of light from a passing car slowly crosses the ceiling.

Another time Larry worked at an all-night garage. The hours were long and the pay worse than he had ever earned. The boss always had him doing overtime, saying there'd be plenty to do it if he wouldn't, but somehow the money for it never came. Also if the till was down at the end of the day it came off Larry's pay, but if there was extra the boss took it home. More and more the till was down. At least the boss said it was and he did the reckoning.

Larry couldn't understand it, and took to keeping his own accounts, but still the next day the boss would say the till was down. He didn't like Larry arguing. Larry knew he would soon be sacked. You're just not that good, lad, the boss says when telling him to go. Larry took it hard. It was a crap job, nothing to it, but they needed the money since their dole had stopped coming through. He might at least have been able to keep a crap job like that.

Coral argued fiercely. She told him the job was nowhere near good enough for him. The boss was as bent as a nine-bob note; he only sacked Larry because Larry was on to him, she said, but it was no good. Larry was not that good, the boss had said.

And that was the way of it with people in power, Coral knew. She had felt it herself with police and social workers, teachers or the social. It was like they put a frame round you and in that frame everything you said or did seemed wrong somehow, out of place. But it was funny, the way they looked at you and you couldn't help seeing yourself that way. It made you feel strange. Larry and Coral learned to keep themselves to themselves and to move around a lot so that hardly anyone ever saw them at all. They passed rapidly through squats and derelict houses, stretching brightly coloured cloth over boxes and rolling up at nights until someone complained and they were moved on again. By the time they got the flat and might have had visitors there was no one to visit.

Coral is tired of watching the beams cross and re-cross the ceiling. She shifts position slightly and shuts her eyes.

*

Laurie remains hanging over the stairwell. There is always the second post. She walks slowly back inside her flat trying to think

34

methodically. Second post may not arrive before midday. If her giro doesn't come then she will have to walk the four miles to the DHSS office since she does not have 10p for the phone. Anyway they always piss you about on the phone, so it costs much more than 10p. Then she will have to sit and queue. The office closes at 3.30; they will not get round to her in that time. But if she sets off before second post they will ask her how she knows it hasn't come. In fact she should probably wait until tomorrow. But there is not a penny in the house . . .

Laurie's new digital alarm tells her it is time for the shops to open. It is good to have time again. A time to be born, a time to die, she hums zipping on her anorak. She pulls on the nearly-new green suede boots, picked up from a fleamarket stall, and the fingerless gloves. She feels tight like wire. Today she is going to Marks and Spencer's. It was always her ambition to shop there. A time to give, a time to take, she sings, sorting out a large stiff shopping bag and two plastic carriers with the M&S logo. Then she is off, skipping down the two flights of stairs to the bus queue.

The air sings and snaps with cold. Even the sky looks pinched and red. Laurie stands in the queue stamping her feet and rubbing her hands. She recites all the titles of Shakespeare's plays in her mind to pass time. Her education has not been wasted after all.

On the roof of the flats opposite a row of gulls stand in precise formation on the very edge. Laurie bets you could measure the space between each of them and it would be the same. Twenty or thirty of them stand motionless, identical, except for one, who balances on one leg only as if defying the wind to blow her off. She sways and teeters on the roof edge, waiting for the very last moment before falling on the wind. Watching, Laurie wants to laugh out loud.

She thinks of an Edinburgh square on another stormy windblown day with birds, yes birds, even in the rain, for Shelagh is feeding them with her arms flung wide and chanting –

> Western wind when wilt thou blow
> the small rain down can rain.
> Christ if my love were in my arms
> and I in my bed again.

The birds don't seem to mind. They flock round eagerly, pecking at the crumbs from Shelagh's sandwiches. Laurie sits quietly on the steps beneath the war memorial, eating hers. They have skipped a lecture together. It is getting to be a habit.

It's just you and me kid, Shelagh says. Everyone else's fathers own shares in the fucking place.

The first time she met Shelagh, Laurie was sitting in a corner of the English foyer, but Shelagh was in the middle of a crowd of students.

Christ Jesus, she is saying, does everyone in this place have a double-barrelled name? Shelagh is nearly six feet tall with bright, shaggy hair. Most of the tutors are relieved when she sits down. They all know who she is, though none of them knows Laurie.

Soon Laurie and Shelagh spend all their time together, in coffee bars all round the campus. They will be fucking experts on coffee bars, Shelagh says, even if they don't learn anything else. In Laurie's second most characteristic memory of Shelagh she has her hands cupped round a steaming cup of coffee as she holds forth on the meaning of sex and power and God.

Sometimes they go to the lectures to see if they improve.

The underlying metonymic of the act of reading is in itself fundamentally phallic, says the lecturer. Eighty or so female students stare back at him. Can't tell his phallus from his fundament, whispers Shelagh.

Or shall we rather suppose, as has been provocatively suggested, that author, text and reader *reciprocally constitute* each other in a kind of narrative invocation? That, or the notion of passive text, awaiting phallic entry . . .

Listen to him, says Shelagh, wanking himself off at our expense. And us all sitting here like cream-faced loons. This strikes both of them as being irresistibly funny. Their silent laughter shakes the bench so that the students at the other end jiggle up and down and stare at them, which makes things worse. And Laurie or Shelagh has only to whisper clotted cream at appropriate moments to set themselves off again. It is a relief when the lecture finishes and they stagger almost tearfully to the nearest coffee bar. Shelagh buys coffee and biscuits for them both. Slowly she dips a chocolate finger into her coffee. There, she says. How about that for an underlying phallic metonymic.

Mmm, she says, biting into the moistened biscuit. You can almost taste them reciprocally constituting one another in a kind of narrative invocation.

Then gradually they become serious, almost moody, about the whole thing; their place in the university, the number of essays they have to write, their prospects of advancement within this particular system.

It seems to me, says Shelagh, that the whole damn thing boils down to sex in the end.

Power, says Laurie.

Sex, says Shelagh.

*

Val and Ros eat regularly at Ros's house. Ros's father is a butcher and a lay preacher at the local church. Valerie is atheist, and vegetarian.

Want to get some good red meat down you, he booms, every time he sees her. Put some roses in your cheeks. He pinches his daughter's pink cheeks. Valerie smiles her thinnest smile. While she is eating their meat and two veg, without the meat, she must be polite. But she dislikes any comments about her appearance.

You look a sight, her mother says. Valerie smiles and mentions that this makes two of them. But this was not always true of her mother, whose clothes used to be the talk of the 'Bridge. Before she had Valerie all her money went on clothes. She bought a dress from *Vogue* magazine, a dark blue chiffon with sequins. There was nothing like it in any of the clubs. She bought tailored suits with silky blouses for the office jobs she did in the daytime.

At last the bus pulls into the station. Valerie sees the other bus waiting by the next shelter. She gets on and takes a seat towards the back. There is no going back now.

She is thinking of calling in on her mother.

Checking up on her eh? says Sheila's voice. Looking for a row?

I just want to see how she is, Valerie thinks. She leans back and shuts her eyes. When she opens them again someone is nodding and smiling at her. Quickly Valerie looks away. It is Ellen Durkin who used to live next door to Valerie's gran. The last time Valerie was on a bus with her mother Ellen Durkin sat down with them and talked all the way about her discoloured toe and her husband Alf's bowels which had been the death of him in the end. And Valerie's mother just listened, not stopping her at all.

So this is your young un, Ellen says at last.

Aye this is Valerie. Sit up Valerie, her mother says as if she is two.

Eee well she has grown. And she's the spit of you Jean, when you were young. Though of course, she says to Valerie, your mam were a real beauty when she were young.

When it is Ellen's stop her mother helps her off the bus.

Well that was stimulating, Valerie says, as her mother returns to her seat.

What, says her mother, surprised.

The conversation. Thrilling. If only she'd stayed on a bit longer. We might have got to know all about the insides of her bowels too.

Her mother just says they might all be old and lonely one day, which silences Valerie. Her mother can be like this sometimes, unexpectedly soft. It always infuriates Valerie who knows she only does it to make her feel bad.

But today Ellen stays in her own seat and does not look at Valerie again.

Valerie thinks about visiting her mother. Just thinking about it makes her feel bad. She will have to let herself in. And when she calls out no one will answer, though her mother will be there, slumped in a chair, head lolling backwards, teeth out. She has learned to leave her teeth out when drinking since she nearly choked on them once. She will be in her nightdress and dressing-gown as she always is. Even when she goes out she just puts on a battered sheepskin jacket over them both and a woollen headscarf. All round her chair there will be bottles, glasses, beakers . . .

Stop it, Valerie tells herself. Going over it all like this. But she has decided to go.

You need a bit of muck in your life, K.T. says.

K.T.'s bedroom is a midden, her mother says. You have to climb over things to get to the bed which is almost buried under heaps of clothes, magazines, records, old biscuits and crackers and unwashed laundry. K.T.'s mother does not know what she has done to deserve a daughter like Katherine. She is a small, neat woman, very fussy about her weight. K.T. is large and lumpish, plain. She sits in a lot, in the dirty stinking compost heap she calls a bedroom. K.T.'s mother tells Wanda's mother that she doesn't know how lucky she is, having a neat, pretty daughter like Wanda, who couldn't be more different from Katherine. It's no wonder Katherine stays in such a lot, her mother says, though it's a shame, because she has a nice personality really. K.T. has a nice personality until she discovers Punk. Then she has her hair shaved into a green mohican and safety-pins inserted into her nose, ears and lower lip. She uses chalk-white foundation cream and smudges of red lipstick near the safety-pins to look like blood, and great black rings round her eyes. At least now people'll look at me as well as you when we're out, she says to Wanda.

She is preparing to go to a church fête with her mother. She has drawn a grinning scar round her throat and pinned a sanitary pad to the outside of her jeans. Maybe this time she'll spontaneously combust, she says.

When Wanda thinks she is pregnant K.T. buys the gin, then sits on the toilet seat drinking it herself as Wanda lowers herself into a scalding bath. She reads from a punk magazine about call girls having acid thrown into their faces, and how to achieve this effect yourself. Wanda gasps and sobs for breath. Her face is wet with tears and steam. K.T. hands her the bottle. She can hardly see it through the steam.

Here, K.T. says, take a good swig. It must have worked sometime.

Wanda gropes blindly for the bottle. She drinks till it runs down either side of her mouth then K.T. takes it from her. Steady on, she says. You're not trying to kill yourself. She keeps on talking whilst Wanda doubles up with pain. She feels dizzy, light-headed. K.T.'s voice seems to come from a long way off. Then she bends down and turns Wanda's face up to hers. Come on love, she says, get out. Wanda grits her teeth and shakes her head. Right, K.T. says. Get a load of this. She lifts her T-shirt high above her breasts. Wanda looks. She is almost sick.

Through the steam it looks like K.T.'s nipples have been cut off. There are safety-pins through each breast. K.T. twists and turns in front of the mirror in the bathroom cabinet. Great, aren't they, she says.

What have you done, says Wanda. K.T. laughs, pulling the T-shirt down. You know Alf, she says, at the Comfy Club, the one who's always gawping at all the girls?

Wanda nods.

Well last Friday, when I were in, he leans over the bar and says go on love, show us your tits. So I got this gear from the joke shop – blood and pins – and Tuesday I went in again and I said Eh Alf – Da-Da! You should've seen his face. I thought he were going to throw up. Then I went and shoved them at Jim at the bar, and he threw me out. Funny – he always said he wanted a topless barmaid.

Wanda takes another swig from the bottle. The pain is going away. Doesn't it hurt? she says. Christ no, says K.T. It's all stuck on. She peels off a blackened scab and a pin to show Wanda.

Wanda lies back in the bath. It is bearable now. But all her body is throbbing. She drains the last drops from the gin bottle. Her reflection swims in the misted mirror tiles round the bath. Even pink and sweating it retains its porcelain prettiness. She does not know how K.T. can walk around the way she does. Sometimes the way she looks appals Wanda. Though they are friends she does not always want to be seen with her. But sometimes she remembers looking at her own face in the mirror and thinking it looks exactly like a mask, one which has grown so tight she can hardly breathe. She wants to tear it off. And she remembers how, as a child, before her dancing class, she would fall so she would damage her face, or rub it into the bricks at the corner of the house, and how mad her mother would get, and slap her beneath her dancing dress, where it wouldn't show.

K.T. is still talking and reading from the magazine but Wanda isn't listening any more. Thoughts are floating in her mind like water, she begins to close her eyes. It is like all the steam from the bath is filling her head. Then K.T. pulls the plug out of the bath. Come on you, she says, get out. She pulls at Wanda's arms. Wanda clambers out and K.T. wraps her in a towel. She almost carries her through to the bedroom. Wanda sinks down onto the bed. She is blazing pink all over and she begins to sweat. She can hear the blood pounding in her ears. She rolls from one side of the bed to the other. Her teeth are chattering so she can't speak. Even K.T. is frightened. She gets onto the bed and rocks Wanda like a child. It's alright Wanda, she says. Everything's alright.

*

At last the bus arrives. Laurie sits upstairs, right at the front. It is her favourite seat. Sitting here gives her a sense of journey, of beginnings, of having somewhere to go. Downstairs the driver plays the radio. Caught in a trap, goes the song, no going back.

Laurie taps one foot to the music. She has the whole top deck to herself.

The bus pulls off, driving past bright flapping rows of winter washing and the common, where the dogs forage and prowl. Then it pauses on the brink of the steepest hill in the area so that for an instant Laurie has the sensation of riding straight into the sky. She braces her feet high up against the panel in front as they begin the downward haul.

She is not left alone on the top deck for very long. At the next stop two old men get on. They are discussing the proposed new shopping precinct.

It's a complete waste of time, says one.

I couldn't agree more, says the other.

And public funds, says the first.

You're right there.

They've only just shifted bus station once and now they're mucking about with it all over again. They don't know what to do with their money.

That's just what I say.

Laurie is only half listening. She is going over the possibilities of the day ahead, the moves she might make, how much she can possibly get away with. As always she imagines herself being caught, and how she will act. She will offer no resistance. She will walk proudly with the store detective back into the shop, smiling at the astonished faces of Joan and Sue, or maybe Phyllis or Marje. Yes, her smile will say to them, I have been taking stuff from this store, the store that's been robbing you for years. Just think what would happen if we all did the same thing – a secret sisterhood of shop assistants and the unemployed, doing what has been done to us for years. For when the rich rob the poor, she can hear herself saying, they call it free enterprise.

Then with the police she will be self-possessed, explaining to them the logical inevitability of her actions, and the theory behind them. After all, she will say, saving money on food allows her to spend more on gas and electric. And by removing the more exotic produce from the shelves she is actually helping to create a demand. You could argue, in fact, that people like Laurie give the system a boost.

She can imagine the reaction at the station. The police will admire her cockiness and wit. At least a few will be instantaneously converted.

Two women sit on the seat behind Laurie and begin smoking, interrupting her thoughts, for she hates people to smoke on the front seats where there are stickers requesting people not to smoke.

They are discussing the Charles and Diana diet. Course it's a bit expensive like, says the younger woman. Keeping up a stock of smoked salmon and mange-tout . . .

The older woman says she prefers the grapefruit-and-egg diet herself, or the high-fibre diet which is nearly all beans. It saves you having to think when you're buying-in.

Any minute now, Laurie thinks, she will turn round and politely request them to change seats, since the smoke is bothering her. Mentally she prepares her speech. After all, she will say, these seats are here for the benefit of non-smokers who wish to enjoy the view . . .

Of course, says the older woman, I never lost an ounce on either, and I'm fatter than ever now.

At least, Laurie thinks, she will register her disapproval by moving to the opposite seat . . .

There is the thundering of many feet up the steps of the bus. Laurie flinches as a gang of schoolkids stampede up the aisle shouting and cheering. They whistle and howl and hammer on the windows at the people below. They are spitting down the length of the bus. Below, the driver turns the volume of the radio up.

Laurie glances backwards. The people on the bus sit stiffly, holding themselves in, noticeably occupying less space than before. The air is tight.

Laurie imagines she is in the middle of an epic battle. Any moment now she will step forwards and take control, not by force but by the sheer commanding presence of her personality. Get back in your seats, she will say, or, get off this bus *now*. She will seem tall and terrible, despite the smallness of her build. She will be celebrated in the local papers. Woman routs rabble single-handed, they will say.

The sudden thud of a briefcase hitting the window in front of Laurie jars her out of her thoughts. She has been retreating into fantasy. She looks behind her once again. The other passengers have fallen silent. They have stopped looking resentfully over their shoulders and are gazing glassily ahead as if nothing is happening. Laurie wonders what fantasy they are withdrawing into; the re-organisation of local-authority spending perhaps, or the moulding of a body into a perfect replica of Princess Di's. At any rate they are retreating further and further inside themselves as the noise increases. It is no longer a group of people riding on a bus but a collection of isolated worlds. Like the rest of society, Laurie suddenly thinks, on retreat into a fantasy of control.

The yelling and spitting do not stop. A lad roars as he is slung to the front of the bus. Then they are all trampling to the front and down the stairs. You fucking gits, screams the lad they are trampling over. He picks himself up and grasping the steel rail propels both feet into the back of the boy in front.

At last they are off the bus. For a few moments no one speaks, then one of the old men says eee, kids today, and with these words everyone is able to relax. Soon they are talking and joking as if nothing has happened.

Laurie gazes out of the window as the bus approaches the town centre, once more noticing the scene around her. There is a big poster on the side of a building advertising a new make of car. It's a steal, the caption reads. Laurie smiles. But not as much of a steal, she thinks, as what she is about to do.

*

There are always dogs hanging round the estate, sniffing through the litter, baring long yellow teeth at passers-by. The square is covered in dog shit. There are dogs hanging round the kids on bikes who are roaring up and down past the entry to her mother's square. The dogs run after them, leaping and barking themselves into a frenzy. Valerie lowers her eyes. There are lads on bikes and others watching. With them is Kelly, in her short skin-tight skirt, black hair hanging down her back. One of the lads puts an arm round her and tries to pull her off the steps and she laughs a shrill, screaming laugh. She is half mad, they say. She does not live on the estate any more. So many of her mother's children died she was put in care, but wherever she goes, hostels, bed-and-breakfast places, she is always thrown out because she cannot keep the rules. So she hangs round all the lads on the estate where she used to live. And she gets into terrible fights. Valerie remembers one night when the whole square is out watching. Kelly is screaming in quite a different way, lower-pitched, snarling, like she will never stop. She flies at the lad she

46

is with, tearing at his hair and face with her hands and teeth, spitting his blood back at him. He is crying as he tries to fend her off. You're mad you, he cries, fucking mad.

Valerie does not want to pass this group. The noise from their bikes tears the air. She keeps her eyes carefully downcast. Everyone stares as she approaches. No one makes way for her. As she pushes past someone spits accurately at her feet. In spite of herself she glances up. She sees Kelly's red mouth open, laughing the same piercing laugh. Then she is past them and down the stairs leading to her mother's flat.

She lets herself in. Her mother does not answer when she calls out. Valerie treads through the washing, crockery, papers scattered about the floor. What is it with the women round here, she thinks. Wrecks all of them. Through the window she can see Tracey wandering around the square with her loping, uneven stride, still wringing her hands and muttering.

Valerie checks in every room but her mother is not there. The smell is very bad. It is a sweetish smell, of old alcohol and decomposing rubbish. Mam, she calls. Her own room is piled high with junk. She can hardly open the door. Of course she does not want to come back. But she feels annoyed about her room.

All the curtains in the flat are closed. Her mother does not like the light. Besides there is a bus stop near her window and at times the whole queue can be found staring idly in, or using the glass of her window as a mirror for fixing hair. Valerie opens a window a chink, to the roar of bikes and the frenzied yelping of dogs. Through it she sees Alex, trudging from door to door with his stack of socialist leaflets. He limps badly ever since Jed, who patrols slowly round the square with Rottweilers straining at the ends of his tattooed arms, released them one day in Alex's direction, and no one helped for a while. NF is sprayed all over the outside of Alex's flat but he doesn't stop delivering the leaflets.

Valerie shifts the stack of papers and greasy plates from her mother's chair and sits down.

Perhaps it is not a good idea for her to live so close to her mother. These days her mother does all her shopping at the mini-market beneath Ros's flat. She says she might as well, rather than lug all the shopping back from the 'Bridge. She turns up late at night or early in the morning and stands rattling the iron network at the windows. One time she is brought there by the police. Valerie and Ros quarrel for the first time.

Can't you do something about her, says Ros.

What do you suggest, says Valerie.

Ros doesn't know, but she does know it is Valerie's problem. Valerie feels very cold. She clenches her teeth to stop them chattering. Something'll have to be done, Ros says. I just hope my dad doesn't get to hear. She doesn't look at Valerie. She shouldn't be allowed out in that state, says Ros. Anything could happen. She should be put away. I know she's your mother, but honestly she'd be better off, taken care of.

Valerie says nothing. She has nothing to say. It is Ros's flat. Soon Ros changes the subject. She says that when she goes to Brighton Poly Valerie can keep the flat, at least for a term. She will sort it out with her father. And if Val gets a job after school she can take over the flat for good, or at least until she comes to the Poly too.

Ros is off on her favourite subject. She links Valerie and prattles on about the good time they will have in Brighton. Valerie does not listen. She is three months younger than Ros, in the year below her at school, but she feels much, much older.

A long time ago Coral's mother is doing her hair. Every Friday night she does her hair though she hates it, Coral can feel how much she hates it. But Coral's hair is very straight and Coral's mother must have it curly. She sticks clips all over Coral's scalp, digging them in hard. Coral must keep her head very still.

SLAP on the side of Coral's head to teach her to keep it still. JAB goes the comb, hard into Coral's scalp, then it is torn backwards through all the tangles. Coral's mother shoves her head forwards and drags the comb backwards.

Coral sits with her face screwed up tightly. Her breath comes out in sharp gasps.

Suddenly Coral's mother sags forwards, all her rage gone. She puts her arms round Coral. I'm sorry Coral, says her mother. Baby baby I'm sorry, I'm sorry, I'm sorry, I'm sorry . . .

*

Once Wanda knew she was still pregnant she began to be afraid she had hurt the baby. She began to dream she was giving birth to a monster. Of course as far as everyone she knows is concerned she *has* given birth to a monster. Wanda leans over the trolley to tuck Coral's blanket in more tightly. It would all be better if Coral was pretty, she thinks. Wanda tries to make Coral look pretty. Every Friday night she does Coral's hair, washing it first, then twisting each strand round her finger, then clipping it into place for the night.

Coral does not like this at all. She twists and squirms on the chair. Wanda stands behind the chair. She can hear the groans and creakings from the lift shaft, the howls and shrieks of the lads who are messing about in the lift. Up and down the floors they go, banging on the metal doors, and in the morning MUFC,

Gaynor is a slag, will be smeared all over the walls in their shit. And the lift won't work. Again.

Coral tries to get down off the chair but Wanda pulls her back on. Don't you want to look pretty, Wanda says.

No, says Coral, I don't, I don't.

Wanda knows she is not any kind of a mother unless she tries to make Coral look pretty. It makes her angry that Coral doesn't want to look pretty. She smacks Coral's legs to make her sit still.

From the lift shaft there is the sound of smashing glass and laughter. Music blares from a higher floor, electric guitar, drums.

Wanda pushes Coral's head forwards and drags the comb backwards through her hair.

Don't mam, says Coral, stop it.

Wanda smacks Coral's legs. She twists the strands of hair very close to Coral's scalp and drives the clips in hard. When Coral whimpers she smacks her again.

There is the pounding of many footsteps up and down the stairs, whooping noises and more bottles smashing. Above, the amplifiers are turned up to the fullest extent and a man's voice screams over and over again.

Wanda digs her nails into Coral's scalp to keep her still and rips the comb through the tangles of her hair.

Coral sits with her shoulders hunched. Though her eyes are screwed up tightly tears roll down her face. Her breath comes in short tight gasps.

Suddenly Wanda drops the comb. She leans forward over Coral and grips her tightly. Coral begins to cry in earnest and Wanda is almost crying too.

O God, she says, I'm sorry Coral, I'm really sorry. I'm sorry, I'm sorry, I'm sorry . . .

Valerie goes into the kitchen. Her mother is plainly not going to return. She is out somewhere, doing God knows what. The smell in here is worse, from the teeming bin. There is a pile of broken dishes in the sink, brownish droplets stain the fronts of drawers and cupboards. There is not much food. Her mother has stretched her credit to its limits with all the local shops. The fridge is full of tablets and there is an opened tin of cat food for the old grey cat who sometimes hangs around the square.

Valerie finds a tin of dried milk, the end of an old white loaf, arrowroot biscuits and a few tea bags. She stuffs these in her bag. Then she pauses. She is thinking of searching the flat for drink.

Every time she goes to a meeting they tell her not to do this. You're wasting your time, they say. Valerie stands still. Then abruptly she leaves the kitchen with the food she has taken.

Ros was very shocked, the time she caught Val stealing from her mother.

It's stealing, she says.

Valerie is angry. She didn't ask Ros to come. But Ros has asked her to the ballet. I'll pay, she says. Valerie knows Ros will pay. For some reason it annoys her tonight. Without a word she leaves the flat, but Ros hurries after her. What's wrong, she says. I'm sick of being broke, says Val. They walk on in silence. Then they come to her mother's flat and Valerie lets them in.

No one is in this time either. Ros perches on the edge of a chair. She looks uncomfortable at the mess and the smell. Valerie looks at her scornfully. There is nothing to say.

On top of the fire under a round wooden box there is a ten-pound note. Valerie looks at it and waits for Ros to look away. But as she takes it her eyes meet Ros's eyes. Ros looks at her and quickly looks away. Valerie will not put it back. You don't need it that much, says Ros. No. Okay, says Valerie. I'll just ring my Swiss bank account instead. It's stealing, says Ros.

Ros will never understand. When Ros says she is broke she means something entirely different from Valerie. Why should Ros break the rules when they work so well for her?

Ros is very shocked. She wants Val to be one of the deserving proletariat, worthy of better things. Valerie feels the need to justify herself, to explain. She feels that in some way her mother should still support her, she owes Valerie this much. And she is annoyed at her mother for being out, where Valerie can't know what she is doing. Further than this however, deeper and more obscure, she feels that Ros's rules will not do for her. She feels that where she is there are no rules.

Valerie can't explain any of this to Ros. They trudge back in silence. Valerie thinks she knows the reasons for what she does, she thinks she has good reason for doing it. Yet when she thinks of Ros's eyes meeting hers at that moment what she feels most clearly is a piercing sense of shame.

*

The memory is very vivid, like it is happening now. Wanda is sorry now, bending over Coral and stroking her hair, so that Coral looks up with her mottled ugly face and smiles. Wanda wishes more than ever she could make her pretty. She looks at the big adverts on the side of Estelle's and the bookie's; women with exotic jewellery and shiny cars, men holding out flowers to them or smoothing oil into their suntanned skins. This is what she wants for Coral, Wanda thinks. Money, a glamorous lifestyle, power. She lowers Coral gently down a kerb, then raises her again as a car whizzes past, spattering them both with gravel. To be pretty is to have power, she thinks.

Wanda pushes the trolley. She walks bent over all the time because the trolley handles are too low for her though she is not very tall. It's not nice to be too tall, her mother says. If she was too tall her back would ache a lot more than it already does from pushing the trolley. Her right arm aches too, because the trolley always leans to that side, so she has to push harder with her right arm to keep it straight. And she can only push the trolley on its back wheels because Coral dangles her feet on the ground and gets them trapped when the pavement is uneven. She has to stop every few yards to pick up Coral's shoes and socks as she kicks them off. Finally she stuffs them into her pockets, leaving Coral's feet bare. It's not as if it's really cold. Poor little girl says a woman passing by. It's not as if it's really warm.

Wanda is warm. The air is damp and steamy. There are roadworks everywhere holding up the traffic. A yellow machine tarmacs the road, and thick smoke belches out behind. There are long lines of cars. Some of the drivers press their horns but all they can do is wait. Wanda is able to weave in and out of the waiting cars as she crosses the road, but the fumes from the exhaust blow straight into Coral's face. Coral turns away and coughs. You'll have to do something about that cough, the health visitor says. You should try a Wright's Coal Tar Vapouriser and some Olbas Oil and a rub, and honey-and-lemon cough mix. Coral's room oozes damp and the window frame leaks. You'll have to do something about that window, the health visitor says.

Maybe Coral will be rich when she grows up, Wanda thinks, like the woman on the shampoo advert who lives in the wonderful flat – no, apartment – and turns down one date after another. And the man she finally accepts drives up in a Porsche and takes her to a posh restaurant. This is because she is beautiful, Wanda thinks.

The men working by the side of the road stop and stare as Wanda passes.

Look at that, they say.

Very nice.

Give us a smile love.

What are you doing tonight darling.

There's room down this hole for two.

Maybe Coral will be beautiful when she grows up, Wanda thinks. Lots of babies start off ugly and grow up beautiful. Things will happen for her then. She will have a different kind of life.

The air is so still that the fumes from the cars rise a little but do not move. They hang in the air like a choking blanket. Wanda is damp and sticky, her back hurts. The women on the adverts, for l'Oreal and Yardley and Persil, look like they are never sticky. Maybe Coral will be like them when she grows up.

Her father was nice-looking, though he was dark-skinned. His name was Sim. He was always on his own but he never seemed to mind, like he was sure of himself in his difference, and he knew where he was going, though he never had a job. He used to hang round street corners in his black leather jacket, rolling his own cigarettes. Wanda could never say she fancied him, and he would never ask her out. Maybe she wouldn't have gone out with him if he had asked. But she felt him looking at her even when he couldn't have been, like in the class-room. Whilst Mrs Owens was going on about the conjugations of yet another French verb, Wanda could feel his gaze pricking the back of her neck, or settling all around her like fine gauze. She carries the conscious-ness of him everywhere. In some way everything she says and does is said and done for him even when he isn't there. He follows her around like a lens.

She begins to think she is in love with him. She can't tell this to anyone, not even K.T., and especially not her mother. Wanda is going out with Gary Buckley, who is a nice boy, with a good job at the post office.

Gary buys her a lemon and lime. Do you want some crisps, he says. Wanda says no. Behind them someone turns on the juke-box. There is a woman taking short panting breaths in time to a disco beat. Oh, says the woman. Oh, oh, oh, oh . . .

Wanda remembers what it said in *Jackie* about being a good listener. Anyway there is nothing to say. She looks at the rings of spilled drink and the scattered ash on the table. Gary stares at the video games. There is a long silence. Ohhh, says the woman on the juke-box. Je t'aime, je t'aime, ohhh.

The article in *Jackie* said you should be interested in whatever your boyfriend is interested in but she doesn't know what Gary's interests are. She thinks of his job at the post office. Do you ever collect stamps, she says.

Ohhh, says the woman on the juke-box. Ohhh, ohhh, ohhh.

Wanda has asked the right question. Gary has over four albums full at home and only that week he swapped a Yugoslavian one for a really exotic one from Bengal.

Oh yes, says the woman on the juke-box. Oh yes, ohh yes.

And I had one from Ireland last week, Gary says, that the boss offered me ten pound for.

Yes! says the woman on the juke-box. Yes! Yes! Yes!

How long have you been stamp-collecting then, Wanda asks. Nearly seven years, Gary says.

Oh, says the woman on the juke-box. You made me do it, you made me, you made me do it . . .

Wanda gets up, pushing her stool backwards.

Let's go somewhere else, she says.

Wanda and Gary walk through the streets. Gary offers to buy her another drink but Wanda doesn't want one. She never thought dating would be like this. She used to watch her older sister Mary come out of the cigarette factory on a Friday night in her overalls with all the other girls and get a big fish-and-chip tea for her and Wanda and their mam and dad, and then, whilst Wanda was still licking the HP sauce off her fingers she would disappear upstairs for her bath. Wanda used to watch her putting on her best underwear and heated curlers and lipstick. When she went downstairs again she was transformed. She was off dancing with the other girls, or with a boy. Wanda is ten years younger than Mary. She had to go to bed. But she always used to watch them go, her face pressed to their bedroom window. She used to think it must be very exciting. But now here she is with Gary, walking across the croft in the rain. Gary tries to hold her hand and she pulls it away. She slips and stumbles in her high-heeled shoes over the stones of the croft.

The lights from the Roxy Bingo flicker on and off. Wanda's mother might be at bingo with Aunty Evelyn. If she goes home with Gary and no one is in they will have to sit in together, alone. On the other hand, if her mother is in when they get back she will make them both cocoa and keep them up late talking. Wanda does not want to go home with Gary. She must get rid of him somehow. She lets him walk her to the end of her street. Then she lets him kiss her. His mouth is soft and wet like a wet marshmallow. As soon as she can she pushes him away. I don't feel that good, she says. Gary is concerned. He wants to see her home. I'll be alright, Wanda says, I just don't feel that good. I'll be alright, honest, I just want to be on my own for a bit. You'd better go home. I'll see you tomorrow if you like. I'll be alright. Honest.

She has to let him kiss her again. Then he goes away. Wanda watches as he disappears through the streets, then she turns away from home. Although it is dark there are bands of blue and greenish light in the sky. Wanda does not want to go home just yet. She wants to walk through the dark streets where she is not supposed to walk. She wants to go somewhere she has never been at this time of night, somewhere she is always being warned about. She wants to go to the canal. Little girls should never go to the canal on their own after dark. It is one of the places Sim might go and stand quietly watching her, his long lean fingers rolling a cigarette.

The canal banks are muddy and the canal itself is choked with weeds. In between the reeds and rushes the rain makes dark circles on the water. Wanda can make out dark shapes amongst the rushes, an old pram, a bike wheel and a few ducks, their heads turned backwards into their wings. The sides of the banks slope steeply and long grasses wave in the breeze. The air is fresh but the rain is easing off. Everything is very quiet, Wanda has never known such quietness. She stumbles and slips along the canal path. She should never have come out in these shoes. But she is glad she has.

Wanda remembers there is a footpath by the old tunnel, she can get out there. She treads carefully on the rocky path and pushes the wet grasses aside with her hand. She is thinking of Sim. She imagines she is walking through the rain on a busy street. It is nearly Christmas and all the shops are lit up. Suddenly Sim is there, running through the traffic in his leather jacket, holding an umbrella. He has been attracted all the way across the street by her perfume. He opens the umbrella and though they are strangers they laugh and talk as if they have known one another for years. Whilst everyone else trudges through the rain they are almost running, lightly, with linked arms through the crowds. Over a bridge they go to an enormous old house where he lives in a bedsit in the attic. The attic has pictures of Bob Marley and arty type posters in it. They rarely go out except to the delicatessen down the road. And Sim paints a picture of Wanda and becomes famous only no one knows where they live . . .

As she nears the tunnel Wanda skids sharply by the path. As she steadies herself a shape moves out from the darkness of the tunnel. Even without looking Wanda knows it is there. Retribution. She is sorry she ever went down the canal path after dark but it is too late now. Her mouth is very dry. Slowly she makes herself look up. It is Sim.

He is frightened too, she can tell. She can see the whites of his eyes. He is smaller than she remembers him, and skinny. She will walk past, she thinks, as if nothing is happening. But when she is right next to him she skids on the stupid shoes, and he puts out an arm to stop her and he grips her arm tightly. Wanda holds onto his jacket. She can hardly breathe. It is just like a film. There is only one thing they can do. Without meaning to Wanda moves a little closer to Sim. He puts his arm round her. Then they are kissing, really kissing, just like they do at the pictures. Sim's lips are not at all like a marshmallow. They are slim and cold and hard. They kiss again. Wanda keeps on kissing Sim because if she stops they will break apart and look at one another and have to speak. They stand there with their lips fastened together in a slightly awkward position like they have been glued by someone who is drunk. Even as they stand and kiss Wanda is aware of the scene around them, the dripping eaves of the tunnel, the moving grasses, the darkness which seems to seep upwards from the canal itself. They cling together completing the picture. It is like there is nothing else they can possibly do. Then Sim presses Wanda backwards awkwardly, onto the stones of the footpath. The stones are wet and slimy with moss. Wanda is worried about her skirt. Her hair tangles in the bracken. She is worried about her hair. There is a sharp stone in the middle of her back. But she doesn't think, even once, of stopping him. It is like the film is rolling now and there is nothing she can do to stop it. Sim helps her to adjust herself on the stones. Then he pulls her skirt up. He has pulled her blouse out of her skirt and tugged her bra aside. He is rubbing away at her nipple as if trying to rub it out. Wanda remembers the woman on the juke-box. Oh, she says, oh, oh. Sim props himself up on one elbow. What's up, he says. Nothing, says Wanda, and she buries her face in his jacket, where the smell is more of plastic than leather. Sim goes back to rubbing at her chest.

Wanda is afraid of being seen. She wonders how long it will take. She thinks that any minute a troop of boy scouts will come by on a late-night pathfinding mission, or worse, her mother and Aunty Evelyn will decide to walk home from bingo the canal way. Wanda tries not to think about this. She shuts her eyes. She thinks about a film she has seen in which a woman crosses her legs over the man's back but when she tries it they slide forwards towards the oily waters of the canal. She can only keep them in position by pressing one foot against the wall of the tunnel and the other against a wooden stump on the other side of the path. This is not comfortable. She is beginning to get cramp.

She wonders if it will hurt. The stories she has read suggest oceans of pain and blood, but when it happens there is a bit of pain and soreness, nothing more.

Wanda expected to feel more than this, after all the gigglings and whisperings at school, the dirty bits underlined in books. One heroine lost consciousness in ecstasy. Perhaps they aren't doing it right. She wonders if he has done it before and if so whether he is comparing her to anyone else. Perhaps there is something wrong with her. She can only feel the pain in her back, the cramp in her leg. She shifts slightly but they pitch forwards another few inches towards the canal. She knows you must never interfere with a man's animal passions so she remains lying stiffly in the grass and bracken. She does not feel like she could interfere. She doesn't feel like she is really a part of what is going on. It is like she is part of a film that is being directed by someone else.

Wanda wishes she could see the moon, it would be more romantic. When she remembers this night by the canal she always puts the moon in somewhere. Sometimes it is huge and yellow, sometimes a pale paring. Sometimes there are huge birds waiting in the shadows of the grasses, and when she and Sim fall together into the long grass they rise flapping into the air, so that all around them there is the beating of great wings against the moon. Of course nothing like that happens really. All that happens is that Sim mumbles something and sags forwards over Wanda, and Wanda thinks *at last* and shoves him off. She stretches her legs and rises stiffly to her feet.

The walk back is the worst. Neither of them have anything to say. In fact they are hardly walking together at all, though they are going the same way. Wanda thinks nothing can be worse than this. At last Sim turns off in a different direction. See you then, he says. Wanda says nothing. She hurries round the corner onto the street where she lives. She is frightened about the way she looks. There are grass- and mud-stains on her skirt and tights, leaves and grass in her hair. She hurries limping to her house, raking her fingers over and over again through her hair to get rid of the bits of grass and leaves.

Wanda turns in to her estate. There is Kelly with a group of lads near the entrance to her flats. The lads are mucking around and Kelly is laughing her horrible screaming laugh. Wanda does not like Kelly. She is a slag, she thinks.

Wanda pushes the trolley with lowered eyes. As she gets near, one of the lads, Pete, with the red hair, pulls up Kelly's skirt at the front. He is doing it to Kelly, but he is doing it for Wanda. Kelly screams, laughing, and pushes her skirt back down. Mikey pulls it up at the back. Piss off, Kelly screams, get lost. As she pushes the trolley past Wanda is trembling with rage. She yanks the trolley through the swing-doors to the lift. She presses the lift button several times and smacks the metal door when it does not come. Bitch, she is thinking. Stupid fucking bitch. Cow slag bitch . . .

*

Laurie leans over the bridge, looking down at the foaming brown water of the sewage works. Tin cans and planks of wood bob and roll in the water, tumbling down little waterfalls to the sluice. It is dark, though only late afternoon. The sky has deepened to a metallic blue, layer upon layer of clouds obscuring the moon. Far away there is the muffled roar of traffic. Laurie has avoided the main roads. She has come the back way, through winding terraced streets without a light, to this place, here. She has lost all sense of time but the place is real enough. As she leans over she feels the power of the water as it pulls and sucks at the stone banks.

At the DHSS offices she began to lose her sense of time. She began to forget why she was there and the faces of the clerks all blurred into one.

I'm sorry there's nothing we can do.

You'll get back pay.

You should have waited for the second post.

Laurie wanders up and down identical corridors and wonders where they get their paint from. Everywhere is painted the same pale, bilious green. The numbers on the doors are disorienting – B.11, C.13, C.H.1.7. In every room she insists that if they can't help her she must see someone who can. The clerks sigh, or shrug and offer her more room numbers, D.29, A.6. Up and down the corridors she goes, up and down the steps. And in each room there is a pale-faced clerk, with or without glasses, who says,

It must be a computer error,

or

Someone must be running a check

and

You'll get back pay.

In each room Laurie explains clearly and earnestly that back pay won't do, as she doesn't have a penny in the house to live on, and each time the pale-faced clerk looks blank as if he or she is not equipped to deal with such data.

Finally Laurie begins to see that there is something going on beneath the surface of the conversation. She is saying one thing but they are hearing something else. She listens out for the switch, the shift that occurs between what she says and what they hear. She begins to pay special attention to what is unsaid.

I can't wait for back pay.

(You'll manage somehow)

There's not a penny in the house.

(That's what they all say)

Please, can't you just write out a giro to tide me over and then knock that amount off the back pay . . .

(This isn't a charity)

How can I manage a full week with no money and nothing in?

(They always manage to buy fags and booze)

Look, I haven't a penny in the house. What would you do?

(They're all the same)

Eventually these unspoken words seem louder to Laurie than what is actually said. The pressure of trying to break through the barriers in the conversation gives her a headache. She pays less and less attention to what the clerks actually say and they begin to treat her as if she is slightly mad. Laurie too wonders if she is going mad. She cannot find the thing she must say to make them hear. She feels a kind of numbness creeping into her mind and the palms of her hands are sweaty. She forgets which room she has just been in, which one she must go in next. The endless corridors lined with doors, the airless rooms and the whirring of the air-conditioning combine to send her into a kind of stupor.

You should have waited for the second post, says a clerk.

It'll probably be there when you get home. No use waiting here.

And Laurie believes him. Yes, she must go home. There is no point hanging round here, it is no use at all. She wants to leave, to get back to her flat.

And she is about to leave, her hand is on the door handle, when a thought flutters faintly in her mind. She pauses, turning. Suppose it isn't there, she says.

The clerk's glance slides away from her like she is no longer there.

Come back again tomorrow, he says.

Laurie leaves, hurrying down flight after flight of steps to the door which takes her out of the building. She stands still a moment, feeling the fine rain on her face, breathing the air. As she walks away from the building towards the lighted windows of the town centre she feels like she is emerging from a dream. Her steps quicken. She feels new sensations of clarity, the sole of her boot flapping in and out of puddles, the hunger in the pit of her stomach. There is the metallic taste of the rain. She has only been in the offices five hours, but it feels like weeks. She feels better, lighter, just for leaving. Soon, however, the consciousness of the empty flat awaiting her, the certainty that there will be no giro behind the door, that tomorrow she will have to begin the whole process over again oppresses her and her steps drag once more. She avoids the glare of the town lights which hurt her head and winds her way instead through lightless terraced streets to this place, here, an iron bridge above the sewage works.

As Laurie leans over the water her mind is full of the echoes of her day, long empty corridors and voices behind innumerable closed doors. She rubs her hands up and down the iron railings of the bridge and looks at the rust marks on her palms, but she cannot get the words and voices out of her head. She looks downwards at the swirling water.

Laurie never knew before you needed money even to speak. Now it seems obvious. She listens to them on their terms, they translate her into theirs. There is no common meeting ground, just this displacement. Laurie pushes the toes of her boots between the iron railings and leans out further towards the rushing water. The air is cool on her face. Below her a plastic bottle and a tin canister dip and turn. She feels the power of the water, pulling and sucking at the stone banks.

None of that seems to matter now as Wanda rinses water round the bath. She sits on the edge of the bath watching the water spill and churn into the bowl. There are grey and white splashes on the cream-coloured tiles round the sink. They need cleaning. Again. Wanda stares at the tiles until her eyes go out of focus. She is remembering the pink splashes on the cream-coloured tiles the first time Di came to her flat. She remembers it like it is happening now, the pink-coloured splashes and the back of Di's wispy blonde head as she hangs over Wanda's sink.

There is a terrible banging on Wanda's front door. Wanda is jolted out of a half-doze. Her heart is pounding like the banging on her door.

Let me in, shouts the voice. Open the fucking door.

Wanda cannot move, she cannot think. There is only the pounding on the door.

Let me in for Christ sakes, the voice shouts. There is more hammering.

Very slowly Wanda pulls herself to her feet. Her legs are trembling. She doesn't know who it is, what it might be. She only knows she wants it to go away.

You bastard, screams the voice outside. Just fuck off you bastard. You'll be fucking sorry. More thudding on the door. She will wake Coral up, Wanda thinks. It is a woman's voice but this does not make Wanda feel any better. She keeps screaming at someone else out there, outside Wanda's door.

Wanda pulls herself slowly along the corridor with sweating hands. She wants to get to the door to tell the woman she has to go away. But it is like a dream where she cannot get to the end of the corridor, and the door is further and further away. At last she is facing the door but she cannot speak. She is sweating lightly all over. The woman hammers on the door again and kicks it.

Stop it, Wanda whispers. Go away.

Wanda never opens the door of her flat to anyone. Twice she has had it kicked in, the glass panel in the top half smashed once, and once cut out. She has fitted an extra lock herself and a chain. When she gets in from shopping she locks the two locks and draws the bolts and puts the chain on. She does not go out again even if she has forgotten something, even when the silence in the flat is deafening. But now she stands facing the banging and rattling door not knowing what to do. If she doesn't open up the woman might not go away. Wanda will not be able to go out with Coral in the morning. She will be stuck inside the flat for ever with the woman outside.

Through the mottled glass panel Wanda can see the woman's face, blurred, featureless, looking at Wanda with no eyes. Wanda wants to run away and hide. Her fingernails are digging into the palms of her hands.

Go away, she whispers, go away go away go away go away.

Go on, the woman says outside, let us in, please.

There is exhaustion in her voice. Her forehead drops against the glass in Wanda's door and slides a little downwards. Wanda thinks of her opening the letterbox, of her eyes staring suddenly through at Wanda. Without meaning to she steps forwards and draws back the bolts on the door. Wait, she says. Just wait a minute, please. She goes into the bedroom for the keys. They will not turn in the lock. Wanda struggles desperately. All the time she is thinking she mustn't open the door to a stranger but it is like she cannot stop. The woman bangs again wearily with the flat of her hand. Come on, she says. Open door.

At last the door opens and the woman stumbles past. She is covered in blood. Wanda cannot see her face. There are splashes of blood on the hall floor. It is a good job there is no carpet. She has disappeared into the bathroom. She is hanging over the sink of it now. There are pink splashes in the bowl of the sink and up the cream-coloured tiles. Wanda can only see the back of the woman's bleached blonde hair and hear her breathing, which is hoarse and ragged.

I'm Di, she says without looking up. I live two floors down. With a bastard called Kev.

Wanda, Wanda says.

Wanda, the woman repeats. You wouldn't pass us some toilet roll would you Wanda?

Wanda passes her some toilet roll.

More than that, the woman says. Wanda passes her some more, and more again. Di stuffs a wad of it up her skirt. Wanda is shocked to see blood running down her legs.

You need a doctor, Wanda says.

No I don't, says Di, and sags forward again over the bowl of the sink. Wanda is about to say again that she thinks Di ought to see a doctor, when Di makes a harsh gurgling sound. Wanda thinks she must be crying but then she lifts her head and Wanda sees she is laughing, with the blood running into her mouth from her nose and eye.

Eh, she says. I got my own back this time. Give him some of his own medicine. Got him right in balls. That were what made him mad. She presses more toilet roll to her face and looks at Wanda over the wad of paper. Haven't I seen you before, she says.

Then Wanda remembers. Searching back in her mind she remembers the day she spent recently in the DHSS offices. She sat there all day in the end, with Coral getting angry and fretful, throwing herself onto the floor and kicking the legs of the riveted-down benches. They have cut her money without telling her why. When they lock up the offices for lunch Wanda still hasn't seen anyone. She is determined not to lose her place in the queue so she waits outside. She is determined to sit it out, to get a straight answer from someone. She has brought a packet of custard creams and some orange juice for Coral. Coral is happier now they are outside. She plays on the steps with the iron railings. After a while the people Wanda recognises by now begin to drift back in twos and threes with meat pies or chips and cans of coke. Then a couple with a double buggy, one older child and a baby in a sling join the queue. They were there before too, about an hour before lunch.

The man has a bullet-shaped head, close-shaved, and a tattoo of a snake wound round a cross on his cheek. The woman has a smaller one on hers. She has fair, fizzy hair, permed and dyed so much it is wispy like baby hair, but her face is very old. The man stamps his feet against the cold and rubs his hands. He spits at the wheels of the nearest trolley but some of it catches the wheels of Coral's trolley. He looks at Wanda and grins, showing blackened, stumpy teeth. Sorry, he says. Wanda looks away. The man turns back to the woman and claps his hands together rubbing them hard. Well, he says. It's a good job it's not Russia. Or we might have to hang around in queues all day. The woman does not smile. Her gaze flickers briefly over Wanda like the tongue of a snake then she is still, staring into the distance. Wanda is fascinated by her stillness. The man is not still, even for a minute. He runs after the children and they stumble away from him screaming. He chases them, making his legs bandy and his arms long like a gorilla. Then the woman and the man light cigarettes and the woman draws deeply on hers, her cheeks sinking right in as she inhales. Coral begins to play with the younger children. They clamber on and off the bottom steps on all fours whilst the eldest one jumps from the top. Six, he yells as he lands on the concrete paving and six, yell Coral and the others climbing on and off the bottom steps. The man looks at them and laughs but the woman seems to be looking at nothing. She remains where she is, one bony jointed hand on the baby in the sling, the other holding the cigarette. The ends of the fingers are yellow and blunt.

It is the fingers Wanda remembers now as they grip the edge of the sink. The tips are wider than the rest and they are bent back and creased with the pressure of her grip.

Suddenly Di cries out and doubles over. There is a rush of blood down her legs onto the bathroom floor. Wanda steps forward. I'll get you a doctor, she says. Di shakes her head. Get me on toilet, she says. Wanda pulls her backwards, flipping the lid up just before Di crashes down onto the seat. After a moment she raises her head. I don't suppose you've got a fag, she says. Wanda shakes her head. Di leans back closing her eyes as if this is all she needs. Then she opens them again. How about a cup of tea, she says.

Wanda does everything she says. She goes into the kitchen and fills the kettle. As she gets the things she needs, two mugs, a teaspoon, tea bags, sugar, milk, she notices out of the corner of her eye the yellowish light of evening, clouds like bruises swelling and gathering together, an occasional drop of rain spattering down from a congested sky. As the tea brews she notices crumbs on the unswept floor, a sticky patch beneath her feet. When she turns round, mug in hand, she is frightened by the sight of Di's ravaged face in the doorway. Do you have sugar, she says quickly and turns away, her heart thumping unevenly. Two ta, says Di, and remains leaning against the frame of the door, watching Wanda. Wanda stirs sugar into the mugs of tea. Shall we go into the front room, she says, then, I'll get a towel before Di sits down on the pink sofa covering it with blood. She spreads the towel across the sofa and Di sits down. Wanda perches on the wooden chair near the table. Di's gaze takes in everything in the room, the framed prints, the woven rug on the floor and the big plant in the corner. Eh, she says, it's a bit posh in here.

Wanda does not know what to say. She hopes Di will have her cup of tea and go, but Di does not seem to be in a hurry. She leans back on the settee. How long've you been here, she says. Bit by bit Wanda tells her story. She does not know why she is talking to this strange woman on her settee, but somehow it all comes out, about the hospital and her mother and the flat, and furnishing the flat until it is as nice as she can make it for herself and Coral, who is nearly two now and having trouble with her back teeth and her cough. As she talks she realises how long it is since she last talked to anyone, yet somehow it is not a relief. It is like it is all being drained out of her leaving her empty. She talks on and on, prompted only by Di's drawing silence and the greyish bruised face fixed on hers. Di absorbs it all without comment. It is like she is empty and needs to take it all from Wanda until she is full, so Wanda carries on. She tells Di about seeing her at the DHSS, about why she was there, because her money has been cut and she can't manage any more. She sat there all day and couldn't get a straight answer out of anyone except that it's probably a computer error. She has to go back next week but she just doesn't know how she'll manage. Di shakes her head. It's no use, she says. Not once they start messing you about on computer. It's the perfect excuse. You get less one week and you go back to complain and you get less again the week after. They never get it sorted. I know.

Wanda feels the emptiness of absolute despair. She stares down at the woven rug. But I don't know what to do, she says. You'll have to get a job, Di says. A part-time one where they won't declare you so you won't have to crack on. They pay you less but if it's a bar, like, you get tips. Wanda stares at her. But, she says, I can't get a childminder. Not on money I'll get. Who'll look after Coral?

I will, says Di. Wanda does not know what to say. She knows absolutely that she does not want Di looking after Coral.

I've got five of my own, says Di. One more won't make any difference.

It's very kind of you, Wanda says, but Di waves her hand. Any time, she says. You know where I live — two floors down, number seventy-six. I'm always in. Wanda begins to say she can't possibly, but Di waves her hand again. You need a job, she says. You'll never get any money out of them now. You get a job and don't crack on. Play them at their own game. Bastards. She eases herself to the edge of the sofa. I'll have to be going, she says. Why don't you bring Coral down sometime to have a look at us. She rises unsteadily to her feet. Are you alright, Wanda says. O I'm alright, says Di. Right as rain. Tough as old boots. Don't worry about me. She edges her way along the corridor. At the door she pauses. It were a bit of luck me finding you here tonight, she says. All other bastards were either out or deaf. You come down any time. Don't forget. Wanda says she won't forget, then Di is out of the door and Wanda closes it and leans against it. She feels drained. There is a dull headache behind her eyes.

In the lounge she collects the mugs and rinses them in the kitchen sink. Then she goes back into the lounge. She is trying to make sense of what has happened. She has just told everything about herself to a complete stranger who has told her nothing back. Except that she should get a job. And that she will look after Coral. She must know Wanda cannot give her anything for it. What made her offer?

Wanda goes over to the big window and looks across and down at the windows in the other part of the block. On the same level as her a man crosses and re-crosses his front room in his shirtsleeves. Below him Wanda can see the wrinkled stockings of an old woman who is watching telly. Ninety-five, eighty-five, there are children in seventy-five but the sixes and the fours are round the other side. Di's number is seventy-six. Wanda thinks of the man she saw playing and laughing with the children outside the DHSS, the same man who must have stamped all over Di to get her in such a mess. She cannot get the different pieces of him to fit together in her mind. It can't be a nice place to take Coral, Wanda thinks. She shouldn't take her there. But she must get a job, she thinks, or that won't be good for Coral either.

Wanda watches an enormous cloud descending slowly to earth, blue-black in the centre but the edges are livid with light. She can't get over the way she told so much to Di, someone she knows nothing about. She told her everything, except about Sim. She will never tell anyone about Sim. He is her own most precious secret. She hugs it to herself at nights, fitting the different pieces of him together into a complete picture; the long slow look in his eyes, the gentleness in his fingers the night they spent together on the banks of the canal with the round, yellow moon. It is a complete, beautiful picture in her mind.

Below Wanda tiny people move in and out of houses across the estate. She can make out Mr and Mrs Whitcombe inching their way arm-in-arm towards their flat. Every Thursday they go to an old-people's club on the far side of the estate and return arm-in-arm. They never go out alone.

The enormous cloud is almost touching the tops of the tower blocks. If it descends any further Wanda will be able to see its other side, brilliant and massy with light. When she was little she used to think heaven was on the other side of the clouds, that they were a dirty grey on the earth side, but purest white and golden on the other side, in heaven. If she could just swing herself high enough she could launch herself into the clouds and be swallowed by a pea-green sky. Then she could find out what the other magical mysterious country was really like and never come back, but always the swing returns, pitching her towards the hard, dry earth. Up and up she goes, higher and higher, then down with a lurch of her stomach, down, down, down, then up so fast she wants to laugh and cry at the same time, her feet flying up so high she thinks they must almost be in heaven this time, then down again as her mother calls, down, slowing down till she comes to a full stop.

Down and down descends the cloud, like judgement day. Wanda waits for the revelation of light and glory, but as she waits the spattering of rain increases so that the whole window is patterned with silver tracks. And it gathers force, tumbling down out of the boiling clouds and bouncing off the garage roofs and balconies, pounding harder and harder until it gathers into a great lake on the flat roof of Dunkirk Terrace below.

*

Valerie stares slowly at the mess around the room. Spread fold upon fold across the floor like some dark blue vegetable growth is the chiffon dress ordered years ago from *Vogue*. On the window sill is a photo of her mother wearing it. It is the only photo her mother will have in the flat. It is at least ten years old. On it her mother is radiant, dazzling, her hair tinted and lacquered, sequins shining. She is clutching the bottle of champagne she won for singing 'The Old Mill By the Stream' in a holiday camp competition.

Not long ago Valerie took pictures of her mother. She remembers running in from school, stopping suddenly as she notices the flat. It looks as if everything in it has been smashed up. Her mother is sprawled across the bed. All her face is bruised and there is a thin trickle of blood from her nose. Her nightdress is screwed up around her waist.

What's the matter, says Valerie, what's happened.

Her mother mumbles something about falling over.

Valerie feels sick. She leans against the wall. She is going to be sick. Then suddenly she feels hard and cold. She pushes herself away from the wall and goes into her own bedroom. In a drawer she finds her camera. She holds the camera close to her mother's face. Her mother moans and rolls to the other side of the bed. Click goes the camera, and click again as her mother tries to clamber off the bed, and click again as she crawls across the floor in the tangled bedding, and again as she tries to pull her nightdress down, click . . . click . . . click.

But on this picture her mother is beautiful. It brings back memories for Valerie of nights in smoky nightclubs, when the babysitter has let them down again. She has to sit in the dressing room and be quiet as her mother dresses and makes up, transforming herself from Jean Crowther into Stella Marcel. Valerie zips up the dark blue chiffon for her mother then peeps out from the dressing room door across the red tablecloths, the gold and red panelled walls, the chandeliers and mirrors, to where her mother is singing on the stage in a deep throaty voice like Edith Piaf. Valerie does not see the stains on the tablecloths, the pools of spilled drink on the floor. In her sleepy, smoke-filled eyes her mother is like an angel, singing in the beautiful floaty dress and standing above everyone in a kind of golden cage.

*

When Coral wakes up she is breathless and clammy. She has been threshing around like a great fish, all the bedclothes are in a tangled heap on the floor. There is the pounding of the football on the bedroom wall again. Slowly she gets up and hauls the bedclothes back across the bed. Then she pulls on a long T-shirt and goes into the kitchen.

Outside the lads are pulling down the clothes-lines which are wound around concrete posts for the washing. Coral does not hang her washing out any more since it was cut to shreds one day. She hand-washes at the kitchen sink and drapes her things over the chairs or bath. Mrs Whitcombe leaves her line out sometimes though, if her arthritis is bad and she can't get it down. They have got Mrs Whitcombe's line. One of the lads is rubbing it up and down the concrete post. His face is very red. You fucking bastard, he screams because it will not break. Then his friend flicks open a knife. Slash, slash goes the knife, cutting up the line into smaller and smaller pieces.

Coral puts the kettle on the stove. She is almost out of tea and there are only crackers in the fridge. On the table there is the stack of envelopes and the typewriter. If she can type three hundred before the week is out she will have fifteen pounds to buy some food. Then she will have to go out.

When Larry left, Coral didn't want to go out. She stayed a long time in the darkened bedroom. When she got hungry she ignored the hunger, but eventually she had to get up. Everything was strange, unrecognisable. Then she got hungry again. Larry had left no money but there was a little in a jar which Coral saved from time to time, always spending it before the jar was full. When she counted she found there was nearly four pounds. If she did some typing before the end of the week she would have some money. But for now she could at least go to the shop.

The thought of the shop makes Coral feel bad. Don't be stupid she tells herself facing the door. But she is sweating slightly. Her hands shake as she pulls back the catch.

Down the steps she goes. Outside she feels horribly exposed. The sky arches like a massive blue lens focused on Coral. Her breath is ragged and uneven. She has to go past all the gang playing football. As they call out at her she keeps her eyes downcast. She will look at no one.

Inside the shop her heart begins pounding unevenly. The shop assistant is talking about her sister's baby; another girl, and she wanted a boy this time. She barely looks up as Coral approaches.

Can I help you, she says.

Coral feels that her face is very hot, almost bursting. She can hardly see.

A loaf please, she whispers. The shop assistant stares at her. What kind, she says. Coral does not know what kind. Larry likes white, thick-sliced, but he isn't there. She moves her lips a little. But she cannot hear what is being said to her. She must get out of the shop. Turning she stumbles to the door. Outside she doubles over, clinging to the wall.

*

Val shuts the windows and the curtains in her mother's flat. She

76

will leave the flat as she found it, though she does not know why she bothers, her mother will not notice anything. She is ready to go, she wants to be going. Outside the old grey cat presses against her legs as she locks up but she will not go back inside for his food. She walks away, choosing a different path off the estate to avoid Kelly and the bikers.

You can only run your own life, they say to her at the meeting. Work on your own sickness.

She would run her own life well enough, she thinks, if it wasn't for her mother. She is not the one who is sick.

But other thoughts sneak into her mind as she trudges through the wet brown leaves.

Why does she have so many migraines?

Why does she never seem to get anything done?

Why, when it looks like she might be about to get something done, does she have a panic attack?

Why is she taking Geography and Economics A-levels when she was always good at art and music?

No, she will stand by that decision. That was a rational choice. Was it?

It was the sensible thing to do. She does not want to end up in the gutter like her mother. She does not want to be airy-fairy like Ros. Ros can afford to be airy-fairy. She wants to set up a greetings-card business of her own, and her father will give her the money. She paints cards with designs on them for third-world charities, and local landscapes, watercolours of the moors with the multi-coloured heather and butterflies and faintly in the distance the roofs of council estates.

Valerie paints landscapes too. Great towering abstracts of crumbling rock with windows in them, made up of all the materials she can find for free. It is almost the best bit, hunting for materials on the croft or common, or by the road.

Ros wants her to paint about her life.

I am, she says.

But Ros wants her to paint about her life realistically, so that people will know what it is like to live on a council estate and be unemployed.

Why don't you paint so that people will know what it is, she complains. At least give them a clue in the title.

But Valerie calls her work *Voiceless*.

It is council-estate life, she says, from the inside.

Ros is cross. You can't turn yourself into an abstraction, she says. Valerie is cross too. It seems to her it is Ros who wants to turn her into an abstraction, making her look at life from the outside. She continues to paint dark gloomy abstracts which Ros doesn't like.

The art teacher doesn't like them either.

I don't think it really comes off, she says looking at one after another.

It's really got to be that little bit *special* to work as an abstract.

I just don't think they really *work*.

Even now, waiting to cross the road in the dripping cold Valerie can feel the words burning into her.

She stops painting abstracts and goes back to painting the flowers in the bowl on the desk, or the model at the front of the class-room. And eventually she drops art.

Of course with music there is never enough money to continue her lessons which she starts and finishes time and time again, or to buy her an instrument of her own. To do her A-level she has to learn an instrument. So that is that.

Before choosing her options Valerie is seized by the desire to have a solid grounding in her life. She chooses Geography and Economics.

It's typically working-class, says Ros. If it's not dull and boring it can't possibly be worthwhile.

At least it will get me a job, Valerie says. She doesn't have a father who will subsidise her every move.

It all makes perfect sense. Except that she hasn't passed any of the exams. She would have been thrown out last term if her mother hadn't gone round again to see the head. She had gone there, to Valerie's school, dressed up to the nines. As long as you can look the part, she says, and put on the voice, you'll be alright. And it had worked. She had spun the Head some line about trouble at home and Valerie had been allowed to stay. But she still can't do the work. So maybe it wasn't such a practical idea after all.

Valerie gazes up at the dripping eaves of her flat as she lets herself in. It all boils down to money, she thinks. She stands still, taken by this idea. All her options, every choice she has ever made comes down to money in the end, some less obviously than others, but all the same in the end. She opens the door and goes inside.

There are stairs up to the flat then a long corridor. There is the bathroom first then further along the room where Valerie lives. There is a table with two chairs, a bed and a sofa. Now Ros has gone Valerie can sleep in the bed. There is a bookcase and a lamp. A door leads into the tiny kitchen. Valerie sits down on the bed. All the things she looks at belong to Ros: the rug on the wall, the lamp and a flowered chair. There is almost no trace of Valerie – a neat pile of books on the table, shoes tucked beneath the bed, a coat hanging behind the door. Now Ros is not there the flat is tidy, as if no one lives there at all.

Ros's letter lies on the table unanswered. It is a bright chatty letter about discotheques and nightclubs and parties. She wishes

Valerie was there and wonders if she has found a job yet to help pay for the flat.

Valerie goes to the kitchen and plugs in the kettle. She takes the tea bags and dried milk out of her bag. There is a card from the meeting pinned to the cupboard door. JUST FOR TODAY it reads; Just for today I will have a programme. It will save me from two pests, hurry and indecision. Valerie pours hot water onto a tea bag. But suppose there is nothing to do, she thinks, nothing to decide. Perhaps they haven't thought of that at the meeting. There is Ros's letter of course. Or her essay. The effects of the deflation of the pound on the national deficit. She walks towards the window. Nothing to do, she thinks, nothing to decide.

There is an art in doing nothing she has found. If you do it properly you don't even notice the passing of time. There is a sequence of days but no progression. There is only the suspended moment.

Valerie sits down at the table. Time is money, she thinks, money is time. Without one there can't possibly be the other.

She wonders what her mother is doing.

The last time she saw her mother, over a week ago now, the police were with her. It was the middle of the night. The neighbours had called them; there was a terrific row going on in the square. Her mother had turned the record-player up full volume and was dancing in the old chiffon dress. She had opened a large tin of baked beans and poured them over the upturned faces of her neighbours.

The police have to break down the front door, then the lounge door. When they finally get in she throws her record collection at them.

When Valerie arrives her mother is slumped in a chair, the old dress falling off her shoulders, grey hair hanging round her face. A policewoman had made her a cup of coffee.

The police take their notes and leave, except for one. His massive frame fills the doorway. He looks at the mess in the room and shakes his head. Then he settles himself in a chair.

Now then, he says, what's all this carry-on.

Valerie stares at the floor.

The policeman says it is not right smart of her mother, making a public nuisance of herself and falling out with her neighbours. Folk have to learn to live together and get on. Her mother is going to have to get her act together or there'll be real trouble one day. And he might not be around to pick up the pieces. He will overlook it this time, but he doesn't want to hear of it happening again. He wags his finger in the air.

All her life Valerie will see him wagging his finger in the air.

Her mother sags forwards in her chair, her head hanging almost to her knees. The policeman turns to Valerie. It is her turn now.

Valerie holds her breath. The policeman clears his throat. He is waiting for her to look at him. Valerie stares at the carpet. She wonders why he cannot feel her hatred radiating towards him. She is willing him to go but he is unmoved, sitting squarely in the chair as if by divine right.

Can't you keep an eye on her love, he says.

Of all the unhelpful things ever said to Valerie this is the worst. But he expects an answer. He is not going to leave unless she answers. Valerie nods sharply, once.

That's better, he says. He rises to leave. So think on now, he says, and let's have no more fuss.

As his footsteps retreat down the landing Valerie turns on her mother. She, hauls her upright in the chair and slaps her face hard, several times. She pours the hot coffee down her mother's throat and it runs down her chin and chest. She vomits suddenly, down her nose and mouth, but Valerie doesn't care. She makes more coffee. Finally her mother is more sober. She leans back in the chair heaving. Valerie collapses on the sofa. She feels the calm of absolute exhaustion. She stares upwards at the wisps of dust on the ceiling and is dully surprised to hear her mother speak:

Sometimes – you know – I think – she says, and is silent again. If I could just die – quiet like – not do myself in, but just – pass on – you know – she stops again. Then everything'd be alright – for you, I mean.

She does not look at Valerie. She strokes the greying strands of hair back from her face.

But I can't seem to do that, she says.

Valerie stares at her mother. She looks ridiculous, in the evening-gown, with no teeth and the thin trickle of blood from the side of her mouth where Valerie has hit her. There is nothing to say. Valerie lies back and stares again at the wisps of dust on the ceiling, floating in the breeze from the window.

She has screamed at her mother that she wishes she was dead. She has wished for it intensely in private. But now she knows, as she stares upwards at the waving strands, that she does not want her to die at all. Valerie lies on her back on the sofa knowing this truth for the first time. She does not want her mother to die.

*

After the ambulance takes Coral's mother away Coral is sent to her aunt's. Her aunt is kind to Coral in a rough, harassed way, but she lives in a tiny terraced house with four children all fighting for the scraps of her attention. Coral does not feel like fighting. She moves from the window of one room to another watching for her mother. If she watches hard from every window, and does not tread on any of the red squares on the carpet, her mother will come to take her home.

Coral sips her tea. It is bitter because there is no sugar.

Soon Coral must go to school. It is a different school, nearer her aunt's. Coral pays no attention at school. In the playground she stays alone. If she stands in a certain spot and cranes her neck, she can just see the tower block where she used to live. She presses her face against the railings.

Coral washes her cup. She wipes everything down in the kitchen. She is wiping away the traces of her life. It is funny, she thinks, how you can live and leave no trace.

Coral knows she should start typing. Once she gets started she will be alright. She sits in front of the typewriter and stares at the platen.

A long time ago Coral is clinging to her mother's skirt. Her mother takes tablets, shaking them from the container to her hand and sipping water slowly. She hardly sees or hears Coral. It is like she is in some faraway place of her own. Coral wants to be there with her. She follows her around and will not go to play. She tugs and clutches at her mother's skirt:

Mam, mam, please mam –

Just a little while Coral, not yet, not now –

But mam, mam –

Please Coral, just a minute, please –

Coral follows her mother into the bathroom, though she knows her mother hates being followed in there.

mam, mam, mam –

Coral's mother presses her fingertips onto the wallpaper and rests her face on the cool wall. Her lips are moving soundlessly – go away go away go away go away . . .

*

Valerie sleeps. She is in a dark room. She has left company in another part of the house because she has remembered the baby.

It is her baby but she does not want anyone to know. It is shut inside a wooden casket with a sliding lid. She is waiting for it to die. But all the time it claws upon her mind. So now she is coming to see if it is finally dead.

The casket is in a closet in the dark room, inside a cupboard in the closet. She opens one door after another. They close silently after her.

The wooden casket is heavy with the weight of the baby. As she slides the lid back she knows the baby is not dead. It has grown bigger. Its eyes are open wide, and china-blue. It has pink cheeks and fluffy golden hair. Valerie feels a suffocating horror. She slams the lid to, terrified that she will hear the baby cry.

Valerie's eyes are staring wide into the darkness. She feels herself shut in, suffocating. She fumbles for the lamp and stares about the floodlit room. Everything is strange, the ticking clock, the flowered chair.

These are Ros's things, Valerie tells herself. Ros was here, and left these things. The sense of unreality deepens.

On the mantelpiece there is a picture of Ros. She is laughing, pink cheeks whipped by the wind, golden hair flying. Above the mantelpiece is a mirror, the only one left in the flat. Ros has taken the others, but this one is riveted to the wall. Valerie has covered it with a shawl.

Slowly Valerie crosses the room, feeling each step before she takes it. The room winks and jumps before her eyes. When she closes her eyes there is a feeling like falling down a shaft, so she keeps them open, looking only at the red shawl across the mirror.

When she reaches the mantelpiece she is very afraid. Next to her is the picture of Ros, before her the covered mirror. Her legs are trembling as she draws the cover back.

She sees the white haggard face and roughly hanging hair. Behind her are the objects in the room. Relieved she rests her forehead on the glass.

Stupid, she tells herself. What did she expect to see? A pink face with golden hair? Or nothing at all, a blank space?

Valerie lets the shawl fall back. Her mouth is very dry. She crosses to the kitchen. Her breathing is easier now, her heart pumping blood more steadily. She reaches the kitchen and hangs on to the edge of the sink. She watches the cool water running into the glass and sips it slowly.

Why is her head full of shit, she thinks.

She carries the glass back to the bed, passing Ros's picture. Ros's head is not full of shit. It is clean and innocent like the rest of her, like a baby. Valerie settles herself in bed.

When Ros was here the flat was full of mirrors, artistically positioned to reflect one another. Ros would light scented candles, greenapple, cedarwood, patchouli, and strum lightly on her guitar, meditating on the reflections. Valerie could never stand this for long. She would retreat with her books to a corner of the room. But whenever she looks up Ros is there, multiple images reflected luminously from all angles of the room.

Valerie slides further into the sheets. She is very cold. Soon she will be warm, she thinks. After a while she switches off the lamp and lies still, staring into darkness.

*

Wanda does not love Coral, ononono. It is a secret she cannot whisper, even to herself. But she feels it in the no-place where her love should be, which is hard as stone. The beautiful princess has a stone for a heart. She has cut it out and hidden it at the bottom of a well. Wanda remembers this story whilst she is lying in the hospital bed. Coral is in a cot by her side, just a bumpy disturbance of bedclothes with one wrinkled foot showing. There is a square of light on Wanda's bedcover from the window behind. As the day passes, it moves down from Wanda's pillow to her hands and then her knees and feet. Leaf shadows play in the square of light making patterns which Wanda watches all day long. Sometimes she puts her hands into the square of light and sees her own flesh taking on the restless shadow play. The people of the hospital come and go, ward orderlies, cleaners, visitors. They do not disturb her. Sometimes people stand around her bed but she does not like this. She cannot hear what they say. All she can hear is the clanking of the tea trolley, the whirr of cleaning machines, the rustle of uniforms and the wailing of babies. None of this makes her feel like she has to respond, but the people round her bed bother her. What they have to say is too hot, white-hot, and too near. She wants them to go away, then she can rest her head again on the pillow of light. They want to know if she remembers being sick, if she understands why her hand is bandaged and why she can't breastfeed Coral any more. Wanda remembers her hand swelling up purple, with the skin all shiny and tight, and sweating till she thought all the water must have drained out of her body. More than this she remembers lights flickering and burning straight into her face, people passing in and out of view, their faces changing suddenly, becoming very long, then large, then yellow, almost orange. All that has finished now. Things are back to their ordinary colour and shape. All that is left is the golden square of light with its changing patterns. When a doctor tells her that she has had a bad case of blood poisoning, but she has had a big transfusion and will be alright now, just fine, she hears the television playing at the end of the ward, and small branches tapping on the windowpane outside.

The doctor seems relieved when she doesn't ask any questions. She does not seem to want to know anything at all. She gets up when she is told to, and washes, and picks up Coral when she is told to and washes her, or feeds her from one of the bottles they have in the hospital, or changes her with the towelling nappies they supply, but unless she is told to she doesn't move, or look at Coral. Sometimes when Coral cries a nurse tells her to pick her up, but she always puts her down again when the nurse has gone. She has had an illness in which everything changed the way it looked and now she wants to know why, when she looks at them, things stay the same. She doesn't want to look at things that do not move or change when she knows there are other ways of looking. So she looks at the pattern of leaves moving over her hands, or, if it is a dull day, at the vague wispy shadows on the white ceiling, or at the curtains round the beds which have squares and oblongs on them in different colours, and if you stare at them, first one shape stands out and then another.

The doctors are worried. They talk to the social worker and the midwife. They say that something must be done. What about her parents, they say.

They won't come, says the social worker.

Well she must have some other family, the doctor says.

So one day Mary comes, dragging a big bag and a smaller bag, and carrying Peter, who is two. I brought you some things, she says.

She puts Peter down, and he shuffles to the other end of the ward where there are some toys and another little boy has come visiting. Mary props the big bag on the bed and unzips it. She pulls things out of it. Wanda's jeans and trainers, some knickers and her favourite sweatshirt, which is grey-green, like her eyes. Wanda looks at the things on the bed and the peaceful feeling which is golden like the square of light becomes like a solid grey lump.

Mary talks all the time, about Bob's promotion, and Kirsty starting school, and potty-training Peter, and the new one on the way. She does not look at Wanda or Coral but keeps pulling things out of the bag; Wanda's favourite picture from her bedroom, a small pan and a hairbrush. When she pulls out the hairbrush she stops talking. For the first time she looks at Wanda quickly, and then away. She turns the hairbrush over in her hands. On Friday nights when Wanda couldn't sleep for all the clips which seemed to be stuck straight into her scalp she would wait for Mary to get in. Mary would take them out gently and brush her hair and tell her stories of everything that happened in the pub or disco, what everyone wore and said and did, and how they all trapped off. It made Wanda feel very grown-up, and the world outside her bedroom seemed very exciting, full of shady nightclubs, and whispered plots in ladies' rooms. Mary lets her try on her lipstick and perfume, then Wanda has to get back to bed. In the morning Mary quickly pins her hair back up again before her mother sees. Her mother is always cross because Wanda's hair is not as curly as she likes it to be.

Mary holds the hairbrush and looks at Wanda. Her eyes are full of tears. Wanda looks away. She is not going to cry. She only cried once in the hospital, after the anaesthetic wore off, when she unwrapped Coral and saw for the first time the mottled wrinkly skin, scaling in the folds, and pink and puckered over her left eye and cheek. She cried then like she would never stop, but not any more, not now. But Mary always did cry easily. Her face crumples up like she is trying to stop, then she says why did you do it Wanda, and she is really crying now, loud sobbing noises fill the ward. Mary always did cry loudly. Wanda remembers whole weeks of nights when she could not get to sleep for Mary sobbing in the next bed; especially when their mam wouldn't let her go out with Steve any more and so she ended up with Bob. The worse she feels the more noise she has to make. She is making a lot of noise now and everyone in the ward is looking their way.

Why did you do it, she says again. Mam's gone mad, she'll never get over it. They just stay in all time and won't answer door. They won't see anyone . . . her voice trails off into sobs. Wanda does not know what to say so she says nothing. The square of light illuminates the things Mary has brought for her on the bed. The hospital smell, of antiseptic, anaesthetic and old tea is very strong. At the bottom of the bag Mary brought is Wanda's old sleeping bag. Wanda looks at this and at the other things on the bed. In the silence Mary's sobs die down. She blows her nose.

Where is it anyhow? she says. She gets up and goes to the other side of the bed. What's up with her skin? she says. After a moment she leans over the cot and picks Coral up. She is wide-awake but quiet, her arms and legs making quick, jerky movements. She snuffles and makes little noises but doesn't cry. Mary holds her and sits down with her on the side of the bed.

What are you going to call her, she says, but Wanda doesn't know. Mary rocks Coral to and fro and begins to croon. Suddenly Wanda knows that she does not want Mary to go. She wants them to be like the other families that come and go on the ward, surrounding the beds with flowers and cards, passing the baby from one pair of arms to another, taking photographs. And when the time comes for the mother to leave the hospital she never leaves alone. There is family there to bring her clothes, carry the baby and the suitcase and the flowers and drive her away, back to her home. Wanda and Mary could be a family, with Wanda's baby. Wanda always loved Mary, though Mary was never pretty. Wanda was always the pretty one. Their mother used to say she was glad she had one pretty daughter and one sensible one, to help out. Mary used to cry because she would never be pretty. It always made her face look all mottled and blotchy like it is now. She even looks a bit like Coral with her skin all blotchy. They could be a family. As she watches Mary rocking Coral she wants to reach out and hold the three of them together. She puts out a hand and just touches the edge of Coral's wrapping which lies on Mary's sleeve. Mary does not look up but she knows that Wanda's hand is there. The three of them stay together for a moment, just touching, like one family. Then Mary says where are you going, after I mean, and Wanda knows they are not like a family at all.

I'd say you could come to us, Mary goes on, not looking at Wanda, but you know what Bob's like . . .

Wanda knows what Bob is like. She understands that she cannot go to Bob's house, not even to visit. Then Mary gives Coral back to Wanda and Wanda puts her back in the cot.

At the other end of the ward Peter begins to cry. Mary hurries to pick him up. She comes back with Peter red-faced and roaring under one arm. I nearly forgot, she says, and hoists the smaller bag onto the bed. Wanda looks inside. There is a sterilising unit with two bottles, some towelling nappies and a plastic potty. Some baby clothes of Peter's are stuffed down one side. I couldn't bring much, Mary says, because of the new baby. Wanda looks at Mary and tries to smile. There is nothing left to say. Mary shifts Peter on her hip to stop him kicking her. Wanda thinks Mary is going to kiss her but Mary doesn't move. Then when Wanda looks back into the bag Mary drops a kiss awkwardly onto her head. Take care of yourself, she says, then she goes away, walking quickly down the ward, past one bed and then another, clutching Peter and Peter's bag, her brown curls bobbing as she walks, heels clicking on the polished floor, click,

click, clicking down the ward, along the corridor, out of Wanda's life.

Wanda sinks back on the pillows. She does not know what to do or think. It is like she has worn herself out in the effort to become someone else. She has become someone completely different but she does not know who. It is like she is floating in empty space.

*

Coral pours water into the teapot and swills it round a bit. As she pours her drink she feels suddenly that Larry is there. She feels him all around her in the little room. She looks up half expecting to see him there.

*

The nurses try to interest her in babycare manuals and magazines. On the covers there are beautiful women with perfect shiny nails and curtains of hair falling round their smiling babies. Wanda pushes them away. She is not them; they are not like her. She lapses back into silence and is not even interested in the square of light. Then Joyce comes on the ward. Joyce is a big woman with dark hair and loose, yellowing flesh. She has had her seventh child, a boy called Darren. She wouldn't have come into hospital at all but she had to have a caesarian this time. She perches on the edge of Wanda's bed and tells her all this and doesn't seem to notice when Wanda doesn't respond. I were same age as you when I had my eldest, she says. She looks about forty-five, but her eldest is only eighteen. She shuffles and stoops around the ward though she has been told to stay in bed, wearing a pink towelling robe with so many threads trailing it looks like it is going to unravel itself. Her bed is always surrounded by visitors, mainly kids. She is always glad when they have gone.

Stop picking your nose Martinique, she says. Chantal get your feet off that bed. I only come in here for a break, she says when they have gone, sitting on the edge of Wanda's bed and lighting up. She wants to know all about Wanda's hand. That'll have been saline drip, she says, and now you can't feed your own baby. That's terrible. Wanda does not think it is so terrible. She remembers trying to breastfeed Coral, sweating silently – as the bullet-hard gums clamp down on Wanda's swollen nipples. But Joyce thinks it is terrible and tells everyone so. She sits on Wanda's bed and tells her about all the other terrible things that happen in hospitals. When they opened Joyce up for the caesarian the surgeon left some swabs inside. Now every time he passes through the ward she calls out after him, don't forget, if there's anything else you want keeping safe, chequebook, glasses, *Radio Times*, owt like that, just open me up and bung it in. Any time.

She will not let Wanda sit in bed on her own. Come over here love, she says. Bring littl'un. She carries Coral round the ward like she is her own. In fact she carries everyone's babies round as if they are her own, picking them up absently and wandering off.

Don't you worry about her skin, she says to Wanda. I bet you any money it'll clear up. She'll be a right cracker one day, won't you love. In fact what you can see of her skin's right pretty now. Sort of coral-coloured you might say. It does not look coral-coloured to Wanda, but the word stays with her and it is the word that comes to mind when the social worker drives her to the registrar.

Joyce tells Wanda she ought to try to get out. It's getting worse in here, she says. Joyce has been in hospital twenty-seven times, counting all the births, and she should know.

Government cuts, she says, staff can't cope. They'll have you taking your own appendix out next, lining you up in corridors, heart bypasses to left, brain tumours on right. And if you make a mess they'll have you done for wilful bleeding. All staff here, she says, are students, doing full-time jobs for no pay. And none of them'll have a job when they've finished. Just like my old dad. Had to do everyone's job when he were fourteen and an apprentice, then when he finished his apprenticeship they sacked him so they wouldn't have to pay out full money. It's no different today. That's what they call progress. I feel right sorry for them though, she says, looking at the nurses.

It does not stop her heckling them though, over the food.

What's this, she says, picking up a limp piece of greenish stuff off her plate.

Lettuce, says the nurse.

Come off it, Joyce says, even caterpillar knows better. It's just walked off plate in disgust. Eh girls, we're not having salad without caterpillar are we? Only bit of protein we get.

In the second week there is a strike and the salad is off. Everyone gets packet soup with bread rolls. Joyce looks at the tiny splash of soup at the bottom of her plate. Eh nurse, she says, come back, me plate's wet. One woman's bread is mouldy on the underside. When the nurse asks if they want white- or brown-bread rolls Joyce gets everyone to say green. At the same time she runs round helping the nurses though she is not well herself; distributing nappies and washing the dirty ones in the bath because the laundry staff are on strike, brewing up and taking the food trolley round. Eat it all up girls, she says with a wink at Wanda. Any trouble and we'll have to have seconds.

All the time on the television the Prime Minister says that the NHS has never had it so good; no other government has done so much for it. But here in the hospital the nurses themselves are falling ill, they are running round so much, and all the patients who are feeling a bit better have to pitch in. No one helps so much as Joyce. We'll be sorry to see you go, the nurses say.

Wanda is sorry to see Joyce go. It is Joyce who gets her talking and eating again so that the doctors think she is fit to leave. And it is Joyce who makes her want to leave, to start her new life. It won't get any better here, she says. The only way you'll be leaving is feet first if you don't look sharp. Then there is an outbreak of salmonella and all the patients are mixed up on the wards. When two die on Wanda's ward and are left in their beds all day and night she decides Joyce is right and she had better get going, though she doesn't know where.

It is Joyce also who gets her to accept Coral, just by accepting her herself. It is like you cannot do it all alone, other people have to accept your baby too. One day Wanda looks at Coral and feels not love but pity, so much pity she is bursting with it, for the baby who has nothing on her side, not even her own body. She picks Coral up and looks at her and is amazed by how many movements she makes. Her arms and legs continually kick and flail like she is trying hard to grow into her body and manage it properly, though without success. Wanda holds Coral very close. Poor baby, she whispers, poor, poor baby. She decides then and there she is ready to leave. So one day she is driven away by the social worker, first to the registrar and then to the hostel. Now when she remembers the hospital it is mainly Joyce she remembers, and the red-faced nurses rushing round and the sequence of light moving downwards from her pillow. But Coral's skin hasn't cleared up yet like Joyce said. It is still all blotchy and puckered.

Wanda turns the pages of the magazine she is reading. It is full of beautiful women. She is cutting out the pictures so she can stick them onto the walls of her bedroom and kitchen. Coral is trying to climb up Wanda's skirt. She cries when she slides down again and dribbles into it, posseting slightly. Then she crawls away, spilling her orange juice over the oilcloth. She crawls all the way round the table, trying to reach Wanda from the other side. She tries to pull herself upwards by clutching at the edge of the table and knocks Wanda's cup onto the floor. It smashes and a dark pool of tea spreads outwards.

All day long Wanda follows Coral round cleaning up after her, feeding her at one end and wiping up the mess at the other. It would be so much easier if she loved her, just a little bit, because to do so much work for someone you cannot love is a terrible thing. It is like a punishment that goes on for ever. Wanda picks Coral up and tries to look at the magazine, but Coral pulls at her hair and the flesh of her face, and digs her fingers into Wanda's eyes. Wanda puts Coral down. Coral tries to climb up again, onto Wanda's knee.

You can't love someone unless you can see some beauty in them, Wanda knows this now. She needs some beauty to love so she cuts out pictures of beautiful women, sneaking the magazines out of doctors' surgeries and dentists' waiting rooms and removing the pictures that appeal to her most. She has found one now, a picture of a coffee-coloured woman with shining black hair in a bun at the back of her neck. She is wearing a silky black strapless evening-gown and standing by a black baby grand. Behind her are French windows with white silky curtains blowing in the breeze and round her neck is a single pearl. Moonlight sculpts soft hollows in her turned face. It is an advert for chocolate. Wanda is cutting it out for the space above the kitchen sink, so she can look at it when she washes up. Maybe Coral will look like that one day, she thinks.

Coral clutches and tugs at Wanda's skirt, burying her face in it and crying and jerking herself up and down. Wanda cuts out the picture, rounding the corners to the shape of an arch. Coral's cries get louder and louder and Wanda begins to hum. As she gets up to pin the picture to the wall Coral is still clutching her skirt. Her upturned face is ugly with tears. You cannot love someone unless you think they are pretty, no matter what anyone else thinks. And Wanda does not love Coral, ononono. She cannot tell anyone but she feels the absence of her love pressing in on her all the time, invisibly, like the air. She feels it whenever she looks at Coral, with a cold clear glinting look like crystal. It is a secret she cannot whisper, even to herself, but she feels it all the time, in the no-place where her love should be, which is hard as stone.

*

The morning is bleak with a soaking drizzle but Valerie decides she will go out. She will go to look for a job.

As she walks towards the 'Bridge the rain seeps effortlessly through her duffel coat and the T-shirt underneath. Valerie trudges on, head downwards, past the pub on the corner, the junk shop. As she approaches Estelle's she crosses the road.

Estelle's is the posh shop, wedged in between Factory Seconds and the bookie's. All the clothes in the window are the same shade, changing weekly, and there are no prices to be seen. Valerie's mother used to shop at Estelle's. When the jobs were fewer and further between she asked for credit, but eventually she was told she was no longer welcome there. After that she was always hanging round the shop, reporting back to Valerie on the new colours and designs.

Ninety-five pounds that green blouse, she says. She has just asked the woman who bought it. She must think we've all fell off a flitting, that woman.

Valerie is bored by all this, but her mother hangs round the shop every day. It's all from Oxfam she tells the customers as they enter and leave. She peers through the window as they try things on and taps on the glass. You look like a match, she tells a thin woman in a yellow suit and a red cloche hat.

Estelle calls the police regularly but her mother always returns.

In the hot weather the door of the shop is propped open. Valerie's mother leans against it in her nightie, sheepskin jacket and headscarf. Ask her what she paid for it love, she calls to the fat woman in the spotted purple.

Suddenly Estelle herself is at the door, quivering like a thin blonde insect. She seizes the sheepskin jacket and propels Valerie's mother backwards.

Get out of my shop you evil-smelling bitch, she says.

Valerie's mother is delighted. She has always known Estelle was really just a common tart. She hawks and spits at Estelle's feet. Estelle turns white. You bitch, she sputters.

Valerie's mother crows in delight. Right in front of the eyes of Estelle and her customers she hitches up her nightie and cocks a leg at the drain pipe. A thin spatter of urine trickles down.

So that is why Valerie always avoids Estelle's on her way to the 'Bridge. At the job centre half the boards are empty. Experienced machinists are required, metalworkers, typists. There are two bar jobs, but Valerie hates pubs. And someone is needed to stack shelves at a local supermarket. Valerie takes the number of this card. She will call now, on her way home.

The manager, Mr Harrop, is at the back of the store.

I've come about the job, Valerie says.

He looks at her, first one way, then another. Anyone would

think she wanted to be a stripper. I'll let you know, he says, turning away.

Valerie is ashamed. As she hurries down the steps she wonders why she doesn't feel angry rather than ashamed. The manager should be ashamed. But then he is not the loser.

As time went on and there were fewer jobs her mother got more bitter. Nobody wants you, past forty, she says. This is always true in the nightclub business, but now her mother, who is gaining weight, finds it is also true of office work. The agency sends her to one interview after another. She waits outside a string of offices with younger, slimmer women and her twenty years' experience seem to count for nothing.

She used to get regular work at the Comfy Club. The manager, Jim, is very fat and nearly bald. But he has a lot to say about the way Valerie's mother looks.

Can't you fix your hair, he says, and Valerie's mother, not knowing quite what he means, tries different rinses and heated rollers.

Putting it on a bit aren't we, he says, pinching and prodding at her arms, her buttocks. Her mother smokes more and hardly eats, saving the calories for the drinks she is supposed to accept from the customers.

You'll have to do something about those teeth, he often says. Her mother's teeth are discoloured from the smoke. She spends a lot getting them cleaned and filled.

You might as well have them out, says Mabel. Mabel works the club on the nights when Valerie's mother isn't there. They're not worth the trouble, she says. I got rid of mine years ago. It cost me a bit but it was worth it. Now I just leave them in soak overnight and there's no fuss. It all comes off, see? she flashes a gleaming set.

Mabel is a heavy smoker, but her teeth look fine. She is past fifty but Jim has kept her on. They say she knows too much about Jim to be given the push.

Valerie's mother gets it into her head she has to have her teeth out, though the dentist says they are strong enough. They are costing her too much, she says, and she is conscious of them all the time, at interviews, or singing in the club. She is sure she will get more work with better teeth.

One night two are broken accidentally when a fight breaks out in the club. The next week she has them all out.

She is sick for a week. She doesn't like the new teeth and they give her ulcers. Then she gets an abscess. For over a week she shuts herself into her bedroom and horrible groaning noises can be heard through the door.

It is typical of her that she doesn't notify the club. One night she turns up, thinner than before but heavily made-up. Someone called Melanie is advertised outside. She looks about sixteen, singing on the stage in a tasselled leotard. Valerie's mother pushes her way through the crowd.

Jim doesn't want to know. He hardly listens, his eyes fixed on Melanie and her swaying tassels. He can't find a spot for her, even one night a week.

That's business love, he says. He turns to the punter at his side and jerks a thumb at Melanie.

Look at the arse on that, he says.

Valerie's mother makes such a scene she is thrown out of the club onto the road outside. From this time on jobs are harder to find. And sometimes she misses interviews, or fails to turn up for the job she gets.

*

At Marks & Spencer's the shop assistants are very well trained.

They will not speak to customers except to be polite. And Laurie is sure there are more store detectives here than anywhere else. She wanders thoughtfully up and down the rows of tinned asparagus, pheasant soup, red dragon pie. In the mirrors her face is round and glowing in spite of the fluorescent light. She is looking for Marje, the only shop assistant there who will talk for minutes at a time. Laurie turns a corner past the pickled cucumber and there is Marje, unpacking toilet rolls. She smiles tremulously at Laurie. Marje is a stout woman, nearly fifty with a tragic home life. Not many people listen to her at all.

Laurie fingers the stock casually as Marje tells her about her terrible week. She has a twenty-year-old son called Robert. Robert used to be a healthy, active teenager, a member of many clubs. His father died when he was eleven but he seemed to take it very well. Marje learned to drive to make sure he didn't miss out on anything. Then, when he was about seventeen he suddenly lost interest in his clubs, in going out at all. He stays in the house and when Marje tries to persuade him to go out he retreats still further into his own room. He will not come down even to eat. If Marje doesn't take him food he doesn't eat at all. Soon he stops washing and will only get dressed if Marje screams at him. She consults doctors, psychiatrists. Give it time, they say, or, humour him a little. So with the last of her savings Marje buys him a personal stereo and a small TV. She drags an armchair down from the attic and puts a kettle in his room. If he won't go out, she reasons, at least he can have some kind of life in there. She tells herself it is only a phase but three years later he is still in his room. She has to take breakfast to him on a tray and make him get up before she goes to work. She switches the telly on for him. He used to seem interested in certain programmes but now when she gets home the channel is unchanged. It is as if his life is shrinking steadily, to the size of the house, his room, the

100

armchair in his room. Soon she thinks it will disappear altogether, though there is nothing physically wrong with him, the doctors say. But when she puts her arms round him he doesn't move at all. And last night when she got home she smelled a funny smell in his room. She went towards him in growing fear as she realised what it was. He had dirtied himself in the chair without bothering to get up.

Marje's grief is like an aura of heavy dampness all around her. Her chins wobble as she stacks the shelves. She is not popular at work because of this aura of oppressive gloom, and because she is forgetful, and snappy with the customers. Because all day long she worries about what might happen while she is away from home. If there was a fire, she says, he would just sit there and burn. Standing close to Marje Laurie feels her grief as a kind of heaviness in her own chest, behind her eyes. With one part of her mind she feels Marje's grief acutely. With another part she is noticing the enormous range and variety of paper you can wipe your bum on these days. There are rolls with different scents, deodorising or impregnated with germicidal lotions. There is recycled paper and toilet tissues moistened with camomile. There is every variety of colour and texture. Toilet paper to suit your *individual* needs, the caption reads. Laurie hears her grandmother's voice. When I was a girl we had nowt but squares of newspaper on a string in an outside privy. She would have been horrified at the price. Two weeks' pay in them days, she would have said. Laurie picks up a pack of avocado-coloured-alpine-scented-extra-long-extra-soft rolls and puts them on the shelf. Really she wants Marje to move up a section to the frozen pies. The problem with shopping this way is that her food supply is erratic. She has spent whole days on Horlicks and mayonnaise. If Laurie has an ambition it is to be able to supply herself regularly with all the shopping she needs without paying, thus bypassing certain crucial aspects of the consumer economy, but she does not seem to get any closer to this goal. She slips some new blue flush into her bag and tries to think of comforting things to say to Marje. She remembers how close she herself has been to Robert's state and for a moment considers recommending a life of crime, but checks herself. She can never do this. She can never offer a single soul the benefit of her experience. Sometimes she wishes she could confide in her shop assistant friends, offering them something in exchange for all their confidences, but she knows this is impossible. The relationship is one way only. She is its eyes and ears.

Deftly Laurie steals Marje around a corner to where the rows of bread begin. Here again there is the same bewildering variety, crusty cobs, sesame buns, croissants. As always Laurie feels slightly stunned, paralysed by so much choice. As Marje talks about the family and friends who no longer visit, and the manager who says that her attitude is poor, and if it doesn't change, though they have been very tolerant so far, they will be forced to review her position, Laurie stares at long French loaves, garlic bread and granary cobs, unable to make a choice. She even feels nervous at the possibility of making the wrong choice. At last she drops a packet of soda bread inside her bag.

Then, whilst tentatively fingering a pack of pikelets, she catches sight of Fat Anj in the next aisle and almost drops the packet she is holding. Fat Anj is walking with the same absorbed air as always, smiling and humming to herself. Laurie often sees her round the estate or in the Cozy Caffy and now here, in Marks & Spencer's. She is always humming and smiling, wearing the same dark skirt with tassels round the hem, her thick brown hair loose around her shoulders. All day long she walks, over moorland, through town centres and round the estate, always coming back to the estate though she doesn't seem to live there, or anywhere else for that matter. She will never talk about herself, she slides away if the conversation gets personal. Even when she does talk you can sense the restless energy pressing her on somewhere else. This much Laurie has gathered from Brenda who waits on in the Cozy Caffy. She is sharp enough to talk to, Brenda says. Nothing short of a shilling if you don't ask her anything personal. Laurie is fascinated by Fat Anj and the way she seems oblivious to the world around her. Though homeless, it is like she makes her own space around her by humming and smiling. Seeing her here, in Marks & Spencer's, it suddenly strikes Laurie that they could be playing the same game, Fat Anj and Laurie, cheating the system together. She must get food somehow, and you can't claim social without a fixed address. They could be partners, she thinks, but how could she ever bring the subject up? Besides she can never seem to talk to Fat Anj herself. It is always the same. Outside her role as thief she can't talk to anyone.

Laurie and Marje are moving on slowly. Marje has got herself another trolley and is stacking vegetables, eggs and cakes. She talks about the holiday she wants to take with Robert, they haven't had a holiday for years. Laurie thinks this is a good idea. She drops quail eggs, small cherry tomatoes and baby hearts of lettuce into her bag. Then she thinks she might have pushed her luck far enough. Any more and her bag will bulge visibly. She is preparing to leave when she sees the cake. Rich rum and butter cake it is called. Laurie can taste the moist alcoholic sweetness. It is this, the experience of sensuality she misses when she is not working, almost as much as her illicit triumphs. She cannot resist the cake, though it is tricky manoeuvring it into her bag whilst

Marje unpacks the swiss rolls. If you look closely at her bag you can just see the box. Laurie holds the bag awkwardly behind her leg. She will have to leave.

I'll have to go, she says to Marje. But take care of yourself. And try not to worry. You never know what might happen. You didn't know all this was going to happen to Robert, she goes on, and you don't know when it might stop. Life's just not predictable really, she says, though she remembers a time when she had no means of support and things seemed predictable enough. Anyway I'll have to be going, she says. Give my love to Robert. Marje smiles a watery smile and Laurie heads towards the door.

This is always the most frightening part. If anyone stops her it will be at the door. Laurie's mouth is dry, her stomach trembles. No matter how many times she does this she never gets over the fear.

Laurie sees the door in front of her. There is a man entering. He holds the door open for her. She prepares to smile. Then she feels the hand on her arm. Excuse me, says a woman's voice.

Laurie's stomach lurches. She stares into an unsmiling face. She must run, she thinks, she must hit out hard and run. But she cannot move.

Is this your glove, the woman says. Laurie stares at the glove. It is multi-coloured, fingerless. Shelagh made it. I think you dropped it just now, the woman says. Suddenly she is smiling, pleased with herself, and is gone.

Laurie can hardly get herself through the door. She feels like she has turned to water, like she will never be safe again. She is not safe until she is out of reach of the store, round one corner, then another. At last she is out of the precinct. Laurie leans against a wall letting the hard, rough surface support her as her knees give way. No one can say, she thinks, that she does not earn her living.

*

Valerie arrives home and lets herself in. As she climbs the stairs she wonders what to do with the rest of the day. She could write to Ros but she has nothing to say. Tomorrow is her birthday. She does not know what she will do then either. She has one pound thirty-four.

Perhaps something will turn up, she says to herself with irony. They are always saying this to her at the meeting. No one can predict the future, they say. They say this to her when she says that all she can see in the future is her mother living like a bag lady in the doorways of shop stores in town.

Perhaps she should go to a meeting, she thinks. It might make her feel better. But there is the fare, and money for tea and biscuits, voluntary, but you feel bad if you don't put any in. Even salvation has its price she thinks, going into the kitchen. Of course they disagree with this at the meeting. Most people are as happy as they make up their minds to be – it is written on the card pinned to the cupboard. It might even be true. But then most people don't think of themselves and their money as being the same thing. They think that if their money situation changes they will be the same people on different money. Valerie knows differently. She fills the kettle.

Valeries knows that money is something inside you, not outside, in a pocket or a bank. It is something inside. That's why if she and Ros have a pound each Valerie thinks she has money and Ros thinks she is broke. It is part of the barrier between you and the next person, part of what makes you yourself. The more money you have the more of a barrier there is, but when the money goes the barriers break down and anything could happen. You could be anyone at all.

Valerie pours hot water on her tea bag and thinks of her mother. At the meeting they are always saying that her mother is not to blame. She is not in control. As she pours the tea Valerie understands this for the first time. Her mother is someone who has no barriers left.

Valerie carries her tea to the table and looks without enthusiasm at her books. There is her essay to be done; the effects of the deflation of the pound on the national deficit. She picks up her books listlessly and turns them over. They are full of the latest words of the consumer economy, which have no meaning for Valerie. They are full of information on the working classes, where they live, how they live and most of all what they buy. In the class-room Valerie sits and listens to the teacher going on about the habits of the working classes, their employment and unemployment, where they shop and what they spend. Valerie sits at the back of the class and listens to herself being discussed as if she wasn't there. It is an unreal feeling, like she doesn't exist at all.

Valerie sits holding her book and looking out of the window. At the meeting they say everyone has a rock bottom. When they reach it they come back up. It has nothing to do with money, they say. But one of the first signs of coming back up is that your money begins to sort itself out. When you are sick your money is out of control like your behaviour and the rest of your life. Or perhaps it is just that the way money controls you is finally obvious, the rest of the time you manage to hide it.

Valerie shifts restlessly in her seat. This is not getting her anywhere. She cannot put it in her essay. She must think about her essay. She grips her book tightly and stares at it, feeling the familiar nervousness. She wonders if her mother will remember her birthday . . .

On her birthday there is a card from Ros with a letter, and one from her aunt in Sheffield with a ten-pound note inside. There is nothing from her mother. But something has turned up after all. She can go out now and do some shopping.

In the end the rain is so bad she shops in the mini-market downstairs. She buys milk, sugar, bread, a tin of soup and a vanilla slice. Then she sits in the flat with her hands cupped around a mug of tea, breaking her vanilla slice up into smaller and smaller pieces. She feels worse and worse inside. The rain pelts against the windows. I will go out, she thinks.

Soon she is at her mother's, but she has forgotten her key. She rattles the door. Mam, she calls. She bangs at the door with the flat of her hand. Eh, says Alice Clegg behind her. Valerie turns. In the next doorway is Alice Clegg. She is enormously fat. Behind her is Sonia, her neighbour, who is very thin. Alice Clegg and Sonia have terrible fights. They say some of Sonia's children look like Alice Clegg's husband. All one side of Sonia's face is pulled downwards from the time Alice Clegg smashed a bottle into it, but now apparently they are the best of friends. Alice Clegg stands protectively in front of Sonia. Her face has a hungry eager look that Valerie recognises. She stays near her mother's door and waits for what is to come.

In spite of the rain Alice comes a little way down the path. Eh, she says again. There were a right to-do here the other night. She waits expectantly, but now Valerie feels stiff and cold. She makes no response.

Sounded like someone were being murdered.

Valerie still says nothing.

I said to Steve, we can't have this carry-on, you'd best get police. But before we could get them she were out in square. With a knife.

Both Alice and Sonia wait for the impact of this but Valerie registers nothing. She feels bad but she will give nothing away. Alice is put out by this. She looks back to Sonia and then at Valerie again.

I said to Sonia, get kids inside Sonia love, we'll all be murdered in our beds, didn't I Sonia. Sonia nods. They both look at Valerie. Valerie feels bad, very bad. Is that all, she manages to say. All? says Alice Clegg in horror, Sonia chiming in this time like an echo. In't it enough? I tell you she's not safe. She shouldn't be allowed out on streets. Something'll have to be done, she says.

Where have I heard that before, Valerie thinks. She feels very tired.

Can you tell me where she is now, she says.

Eee I don't know, says Alice Clegg in surprise, as if this is hardly relevant. I know police come and took knife off her, that's all. No one's seen her since. Don't want to neither. Sonia were fair shook up weren't you Sonia love? She doesn't know how she'll cope if she comes back, do you? She turns to Sonia, who looks upset. Something'll have to be done. No one's safe with her around. We could all be murdered in our beds.

What do they want from her, Valerie thinks. Do they want her to beg forgiveness, promise it'll never happen again? Her face is rigid. Without a word she turns and walks away. Behind her Alice Clegg moves right out onto the path in the rain.

Don't bother bringing her back here, she cries shrilly. We don't want her do we Sonia?

No, comes Sonia's voice faintly.

Hard-faced bitch, says Alice Clegg as Valerie turns the corner.

At the end of the path leading off the estate is a pack of dogs worrying at something on the ground. They look up as Valerie approaches, lips curling back from their teeth. The leader limps towards Valerie snarling, sniffing at her jeans and coat. He barks suddenly, once, then they are all around her, barking furiously. The smell of them is powerful in the rain. Valerie hears a snarling rush, teeth knock against her leg. Her heart pounds unevenly. She hates dogs. They can sense her hatred of them.

She makes it to the road. They surround her all the time, barking savagely, eyes rolled back, but they do not attack. No one will help her she knows. Her eyes are blurred so she can hardly see but she steps out into the road. A car skids past honking furiously and the dogs fall back. She makes it to the other side.

All the dogs on the estate are the same, half-owned, vicious. They have houses where they go for food but if the police come no one owns them. They prowl around the estate, hungry, watchful, striking from time to time in packs, barking and howling well into the night. To live on the estate you have to somehow befriend the dogs or own fiercer ones yourself like Jed, or live in hiding.

*

Think of the jobs you could get, says her mother.

It'll open up a whole new world for you.

You won't have to be like me and your dad, flogging your guts out for nowt.

The world's your oyster now, love.

I'm right proud Laurie, her mother says.

Laurie remembers these words as she struggles to find the right words for her essays, or to describe to her mother what it is really like, the experience of being a very small speck of sand on a very large beach, of being trapped in a transitional space between the world she cannot return to and the world she cannot enter. In tutorials she struggles to find the right words to express her thoughts. She cannot work out why she always feels so stupid when she was always the brightest in her class at school. Then she realises that inside her head she is always carrying a hostile audience. When she tries to translate herself into terms her tutor can accept she hears always the jeering laughter of the people from her street:

Ooo what a toff.

Give us a taste of that plum you got in your gob.

When she tries to talk in the old way, their way, she sees always the resigned, dismissive faces of her tutors. In her first essay she conscientiously copies the language of the literary critics on her reading list and is told that she is 'complicating the issue with opaque terminology'.

She tells her mother it is not like she thinks, but whatever she says her mother thinks she has found the brave new world.

I'm doing it for you Laurie, she says when Laurie tells her how tired she looks after a shift at the laundry. So you'll have what I never had, nor your dad neither. Not that that idle shiftless sod, she says of Laurie's father who has been out of work for six years now, ever missed owt, but you're more like me. Except that you'll get on. Months before she gets her A-level results, before she even begins her A-levels, when it is finally decided she is staying on, her mother tells everyone on the street that her daughter is going to university. Laurie remembers this whenever she thinks of giving up, which is almost every week.

You don't know you're born, says her mother proudly, referring to the hours Laurie works. Though in fact Laurie puts in a lot of hours trying to adapt her language into a suitable mould.

She is impressed by the eloquence of her personal tutor. It is as if he takes her stumbling thoughts and turns them effortlessly into something exceptional and exact. She tries to imitate his style and in the course of this translation something happens which she does not expect. She becomes obsessed.

You've got it bad, says Shelagh, watching Laurie pour herself feverishly into her work. Laurie does not reply. Her desire to be recognised by him, for her tutor to be the one to lift the thick veil of invisibility surrounding her and make her feel real is so intense and consuming she is losing contact with the world around her. She reads well into the night, hoping to overturn all previous critical preconceptions and offer new insights into established texts. Before each tutorial she rehearses what she is going to say. In practice she says very little. When he asks her a question she cannot speak. When he passes by her and looks at her work she cannot think.

You know what it is, says Shelagh. You're taken in by him. All his posh speeches, that suave manner, typical middle-class crap and you're taken in by it. It's nothing to him and you think it's marvellous. It's natural to him like swearing is to me, only I don't get any brownie points for it. But he's bowled you over with it, that's what it is.

Laurie doesn't know what it is, but she does know she wants it to stop. She sits in the library, her books spread out in front of her, wholly unable to concentrate. She stands outside his room, unable to enter, unable to stay away. It is like being paralysed. If he asked to roll his car over her she is very much afraid she would simply lie down in the middle of the road.

Fiona Smythe is in the same tutorial. And she likes him, Laurie can tell. But she is not smitten in the same way as Laurie. Whilst Laurie stares down hard at her books, hoping no one will notice the state she is in, and rehearsing over and over the words she is about to say, any minute, Fiona leans over the desk towards him, gazing levelly into his eyes. Laurie is eaten alive with jealousy. What makes her so confident, she says. Money, says Shelagh. She went to a better school than him. This is true of course. Fiona went to the same school as Princess Anne whereas her tutor went only to a minor public school and then to Cambridge.

Laurie wants the suffering to end. She can do no work, get no sleep. She has all the classic symptoms, described in nearly every set text on her course. She is in danger of failing the whole degree.

Shelagh devises different plans for getting to meet him. Why not ask him to the pub, she says, or no, she says, seeing Laurie's horrified face, wait a minute, I know, you could ask to interview him for the student magazine. Laurie protests, it is a lousy idea. But Shelagh makes her get out a pen and notepad and work out what she will say. Dear Dr Woodhouse, Laurie begins, please could you help me as –

– You haven't had an orgasm for ages, Shelagh finishes for her then rolls with laughter on the bed.

Fiona Smythe gets the best marks in their group, though she never seems to do any work.

Do let me borrow your notes, she says to Laurie, or, Could I just look at your essay?

He'll know if you're copying it, says Laurie.

Don't worry, says Fiona, he won't recognise it by the time I've finished.

Fiona gets an A for her efforts, and Laurie gets a B.

It stinks, that's what, says Shelagh. I told you it all boils down to sex in the end. But Laurie thinks it has something to do with the kind of language you use. When she dreams at night it is always the same dream. She is writing an essay when her tutor comes to see how she is doing. He stands behind her and the words will no longer come. She cannot control the pen which slides and scrawls all over the page. As she struggles she is terribly aware of his gaze. A kind of panic seizes her. Turning she grips his jacket.

Help me, she says, help me. But the face grinning down at her is carved and wooden.

At least, Laurie thinks, no one knows what she is going through. In the tutorial she avoids his gaze. She prides herself on her discretion. Then one time Fiona sits down opposite her in the foyer and lights a cigarette. Now look, she says. I'm going to tell you something because I don't want you to hear it from anyone else. She takes a long drag on the cigarette. Last night I asked Peter to the pub, to join a few of us for drinks. Then afterwards I asked everyone back to my place, only the others couldn't come. So Peter and I went back. Together.

Laurie feels herself sinking, slowly. Terrible implications register. Why is Fiona telling her this?

I'm only telling you, says Fiona, so you won't hear it from anyone else, and so you won't build it up into something it's not. It's not anything really. Nothing to write home about, if you see what I mean. She takes another pull on the cigarette and looks at Laurie as if waiting for an answer.

After a long pause Laurie says, are you going to see him again? It is not what she means to say. It is pulled from her in a whisper.

O yes, I expect so, Fiona says. After all one can hardly ditch one's tutor, can one? She looks at Laurie kindly. Well anyway I must be going. But don't let it get you down. It isn't worth it. I mean it. Okay? She stubs her cigarette out and is gone, in a flurry of silk scarves and expensive perfume.

For a long moment Laurie stares after her. She feels her face burning. Consciousness of Fiona's good intentions is almost the worst of her miseries. Then she feels that she has to get out of the foyer. Pressing her hands down on the leather seat she presses herself upwards. Carefully she gathers her books together, from time to time pushing away a wisp of hair which keeps falling into her eyes. All her movements seem to take a longer and longer time. She slips her bag over her shoulders and folds her arms across her books, pressing them against her breasts. She is very afraid she will meet someone she doesn't want to see. She doesn't want to see anyone. Slowly she leaves the foyer, staring at the floor. Slowly she crosses the campus, watching the wind chase cloud shadows over the grass. She passes the library, and the physics department. By the time she reaches her flat her steps are dragging so much she is hardly moving at all. She hopes Shelagh is not in. She does not want to talk. She does not want to speak at all, about anything. The flat is empty. She places her books down gently on the table and sinks down beside them, letting her head sag slowly forwards until it touches the smooth, cool surface. Her lips are pressed together like they will never open again.

*

All these memories pass through Wanda's mind as she stands in front of Di's door. Call in anytime, Di said, but Wanda cannot make herself knock. She has pushed the trolley down two flights of stairs and through six sets of swing-doors, but now she wants to turn back. There is a lot of noise coming from inside the flat. It seems like a lot of people are there. Wanda cannot go in. She presses the handle of the trolley down and begins to turn it away from the door.

But she has to start work. She needs to ask Di if she will babysit for Coral, just till she gets herself sorted out, because even if she gets the job she has seen, what she earns will not pay for a babysitter. And she has to go back at the end of the week to see if they will take her on. The DHSS are sending her even less money than before, just like Di said. She went in to try to sort it out the week after Di came to her flat. She had to walk the four miles with Coral and a big bag of things to keep Coral amused, fed, and changed because she knew she would be there all day. It was a hot bright day with no air. The heat infuses itself through the windows, burning the side of Wanda's face and her hair as morning wears into afternoon. She has not been seen yet. Or rather she has been seen once by a clerk who said she would have to be seen by someone else, and would she please re-join the queue and fill in the form, and then she was seen by a woman who said she had filled in the wrong form, and would she please take the right form back with her and fill it in and then someone would see to her soon.

Gradually the office has emptied and now there are only two people left besides Wanda. It is very quiet. Coral is finally asleep, her head heavy and sweating against Wanda's shoulder. Two fingers rest in her mouth pulling her lower lip down. From time to time she remembers in her sleep and sucks them softly.

Wanda knows that if Coral sleeps now she will be awake all night but she doesn't want to have to cope with her again, getting bored and fretful, sick of the toys Wanda has brought and the book she has read to her twice. She has been changed three times, the dirty nappies have been wrapped in the polythene bags Wanda brought. She has eaten eight custard creams and drunk a bottle of orange juice. She has pulled her toy train apart. When Wanda put it back together Coral pulled it apart again. She has thrown her doll to the other side of the room and will not let Wanda bring it back.

Earlier, when the office was full of people and kids she made friends with a little boy called Steven who was only three, though his mother looked about fifty. The little boy has gone now. His father came and took him home and Coral roared when he left until everyone looked at Wanda as though it was her fault. The mother is still here, sitting hunched and massive on the bench to one side of Wanda. She has a mottled, greyish-pink face and dull, dead eyes. She sits leaning forward slightly as if defying anyone to try to make her move. In front of them a lad is sprawled the full length of the bench, his mousy hair spread out like a fan, one hand trailing on the floor. His breathing is ragged and uneven, loud in the empty room. Besides this there is only Coral's softer breathing and sucking, the slow ticking of the clock and the tap-tap-tap of a fly buzzing drunkenly into panes of glass.

Wanda looks at the clock, it is well past three. She got there at twenty-past nine that morning and already there was a big queue. When she got there everything she had to say was clear and sharp in her mind but as the hours pass she can feel it all slipping away from her, dissolving in the heavy, soupy atmosphere. Now it is almost time for the offices to close. She knows she will not get to see anyone now, and the thought makes her sit stiffly in her seat, fighting the trembling in her stomach. She knows she should be furious, she should make a scene, she shouldn't let them get away with it. What she wants most of all, however, is to leave, to get out of the hot, thick atmosphere and go somewhere she can breathe, and not have to look at the riveted-down benches, the grey-green flaking paint. She wants to leave though she hasn't got anywhere at all, and it is only this thought that keeps her there, sitting stiffly on the bench. She won't give up now, though she has already lost. She will sit it out. At least it couldn't be said that she hadn't tried.

For she had tried, when the woman sent her away to fill in a second form. She had tried to speak up for herself, to tell the woman she had been waiting all morning and had just filled one form in.

Well if you just fill this one in, the woman says, I'll try to make sure you're seen to immediately.

Wanda feels an urge to screw the paper up. I suppose this is the right one then, she says.

That's right, the woman says. If you just fill it in someone'll see you when you've finished.

That's what you said last time, Wanda says. She feels cold and hot with rage, but the woman just says again that if she fills in the form someone will see to her after.

As well as her rage, Wanda begins to feel for the woman sitting facing her on the other side of the shatter-proof glass, repeating the same message over and over again. She begins to feel what it must be like to sit there every day, hour after hour, facing the anger of people you do not know, when it is not your fault really. People like Wanda never get to see the people whose fault it is.

Wanda does not want to feel this at all. She grips the edge of the counter, trying to hold on to her rage, but still she feels it slipping away into a kind of helplessness. Well I'd better be seen to this time, she says. The woman sighs. She does not look at Wanda, or at anything. Her glance slips away sideways, to the counter, her hands, the fire instructions on the wall.

If you fill in the form, she says, you will be seen.

Wanda returns to the bench. Her face is bursting hot. She is furious with herself now, but what can she do? She sits down and looks at the form. It is a different colour, but the questions are nearly the same. She sees herself going up to the counter again, and someone saying again that she has filled in the wrong form. She will bang on the shatter-proof glass and scream. Why can't she stay angry when she needs to? She always begins to feel for the person she should be angry with. If you want to get anywhere, she thinks, you shouldn't feel for anyone at all.

Wanda looks up from the form and the sun pours liquid heat onto her face. She reminds herself that it is not just her, no one has had any luck today. Earlier a scrawny woman sat down next to Wanda. There'd be sparks flying when it came to her turn, she said. She was going to give it to them straight. It looks like if anyone gets anywhere with them she will. Then when it is her turn she sees the same woman Wanda saw. To each question she replies in low tones that no one can hear, even when the other woman is shouting at her and banging her fist on the counter. Eventually she turns to face everyone on the benches and says — She says I can't have any money or owt, but I am entitled to a National-Health wig.

There is complete silence. Then people begin to laugh. Soon everyone is laughing loudly and Wanda smiles too. Even the woman behind the counter looks like she does not know whether to laugh or be cross, and soon she disappears through the door at the back. Someone else returns to deal with the scrawny woman who eventually leaves with a white and furious face. Wanda thinks it is all crazy. Maybe the world only makes any kind of sense when you have money.

Now it is nearly half-past three and Wanda can hear footsteps approaching the door at the back. She knows someone is going to tell her to go, and that she will just leave. That is the way it always is. You go to the offices mad as hell, determined to fight it out, then after they make you wait all day all you can think about is going home; not even money any more, or how you're going to live, but home.

There is the clerk. The office is closing now, she says.

Wanda's stomach lurches, she can't help it. She knew it was going to happen, but it doesn't make her feel any better. Jesus

VALUE VILLAGE 2010
1810 STORE ST
VICTORIA   BC

CARD NUMBER
5892971305260894311
ACCOUNT TYPE
CHEQUING
DATE/TIME
01/04/07   16:28
S980109270-332-078

PURCHASE

$44.07

APPROVED - THANK YOU
407737

04-07-2001 IUCL8240

Christ, says the lad in front, hauling himself up from the bench. Now look here, says the woman sitting next to Wanda, but Wanda is already half-way out of the door.

No point arguing, she tells herself as she bumps the trolley down the steps. They all know it stinks so there is no argument. The trembling is worse in the pit of her stomach. And she is tired, tired to death, she can hardly walk. It's always the same, days like this, you get all worked up, stomach churning, then you don't get to see anyone and it's like being kicked. You can hardly walk, but you have to walk, all the way home.

Wanda crosses the street and turns the corner into a little square. She sits down on a bench beneath the war memorial and sags forwards over the trolley handle. She feels very old.

There is a breeze now, cooling the sweat on Wanda's face and whipping drifts of paper round and round the square. Round and round the square they go, looking like the shreds of a wedding gown left by some demented bride. Wanda leans backwards on the bench watching the swirling drifts of paper. It is very quiet. No one is around at all. It is peaceful. Peace and quiet; two commodities well out of Wanda's price range. She likes it here. She does not want to leave. She has the thought that she could stay here in the square for ever and no one would ever know, or trouble her again.

It does not stay quiet long. First a tramp shuffles into the square. He ignores Wanda and begins to rummage through the bin. Then a businessman with a briefcase crosses the square. He ignores them both but their eyes follow him. Wanda can see the tramp looking like he is thinking of asking for money but the businessman walks past like he hasn't seen the tramp at all. If someone asks him later if there was anyone in the square he will probably say no. He walks through the square like he is someone. He walks like he has never been treated like shit in his life. He is used to being seen, not like Wanda and the tramp. It reminds Wanda of the time a famous actor and actress came to town to film a crowd scene. It seemed like everyone was in the town centre that day, pushing past one another to the cordoned-off area, straining and straining to see like they can't see enough. Wanda can hardly get through the crowds with the trolley. She can't see anything, and no one sees Wanda at all. It seems like being seen has nothing to do with the way you look, just how important you are. It is the same in the DHSS. You watch the clerks closely, trying to work out what they're thinking and how to get through to them, and they hardly look at you at all.

In the trolley Coral stirs and whimpers and then stays quiet. The thing is, Wanda thinks, with all this invisibility she feels like she is losing sight of herself. She does not know how people would see her if they could. Sometimes she thinks they really can't see her at all, and if she walked into a shop and out again, with a record maybe, or some perfume, no one would see her, because she really is invisible. It is a strange thought, like she is not quite real.

There is a light spattering of rain. She should leave the square now, or she will not get home before dark. Still she sits there, almost dreaming, sagging forwards once again over the trolley. When Coral wakes up, she thinks, she will go. But not yet, not just yet. It is peaceful and quiet in the square. She feels like she could be anyone, anywhere. At home she can only be Wanda.

Then Coral wakes up properly and rubs her eyes and cries. It is time for them to go. Coral will be quiet if she is being pushed in the trolley. With an effort like waking from a dream Wanda rises to her feet and slowly, slowly crosses the square, pushing the trolley before her on its back two wheels, pressing harder with her right arm to stop it veering to the right, dragging her feet behind her. It is four miles home.

The streets of the town are busy, the first shops shutting down, people with money doing last-minute shopping, others hurrying home from work, to a home with lights and people and food. Wanda thinks about someone being home for her, telling her to put her feet up and making her a cup of tea. But she will go home to a lightless flat, a single packet of custard creams and two apples, some tea but no milk.

The streets of the town are noisy. Traffic is piling up and music blares from the doorways of emptying shops. Girls just wanna have fu-un, goes one song, and in the next doorway, I'm yours, you're mine, automatically sunshine. Everywhere people are getting in Wanda's way, pushing and hustling. Sometimes it seems like they get in her way on purpose, wandering straight in front of the trolley then stopping to look in a shop window or cross a street. Sometimes she feels like ramming the trolley into their legs, most of the time she is too tired.

Kiss me honey honey kiss me, comes a voice from a shop doorway and we'll find a world of our own that only two can share. The music jangles on and on from every doorway, kiss me, don't leave me, let's be together, like there is nothing else on earth to think about. Brightly lit posters of models advertise perfume, compact-disc players, American Express. Buy now pay later say the adverts in all the furniture stores, massive discounts. On a newspaper billboard there is a woman with How To Win Millions stamped across her chest, and on the other side Send In Your Coupons Now printed across her bum.

Wanda never knew people could get in her way so much until she had a trolley, holding her up like she isn't held up enough. Not that she has any reason to rush. She wonders where everyone else is rushing off to. Wanda herself seems to be going slower and slower. It is almost like she has stopped and the rest of the world is rushing past on a speeded-up film. All the tunes go round and round in Wanda's head like a soundtrack. It reminds her of the film they made in the town centre with scenes of the market square and town hall. They might have shot a scene in the square where Wanda has just been sitting. Maybe if they had seen her they would have made up a story about her, a young woman in an unhappy marriage, sitting a while in the square to think about her lost love. Maybe something about her caught the eye of the producer and he said to the cameramen, follow that kid, she's got something, I don't know what but I like it. Maybe we can use her. So the cameramen follow her all the way home, capturing the way she walks and dresses and talks to Coral from time to time. Don't lose her, the producer says, but let her think she's alone.

Thinking about this gives Wanda enough energy to get more than half-way home. Then to get her the rest of the way she starts thinking about the kind of stories they might make up about her. She could be someone with a terminal illness who hasn't told her husband or children yet, or someone who is deaf and dumb, though very beautiful, on her way home to parents who have decided to have her put away. It crosses her mind to wonder why the stories are all so tragic but she doesn't think about this for long. She carries on thinking about herself in the eye of the lens and the image being made of her, for without being seen she will not have the energy to move.

But now Wanda stands in front of Di's door and thinks about turning back, though there is no one else she can ask. K.T.'s parents have moved her down south, to mix with a better class of person and she doesn't know where Joyce lives. She either asks Di or she doesn't work. Only three weeks ago she decided she could never leave Coral at Di's, but here she is. But she cannot make herself knock at the door. So she is about to turn away, she is pressing the handle of the trolley down, when the door opens and a man she doesn't know is standing there. He stares at Wanda. Come to see Di, he says and Wanda nods. Di, he calls over his shoulder, someone to see you, and he holds the door back so she can push the trolley through.

The flat is like Wanda's, a long hallway, but with two bedrooms leading off, and a front room at the end. Wanda wonders where they keep all the kids. She pushes her way into the lounge and stops. It is full of people and smoke. Wanda can hardly see. Then Di says, it's Wanda, come on in, and she sees Di sitting at a table with four other women. There are cards on the table. Di waves Wanda over. We're just reading the cards, she says, sit down. A woman called Elsie with no teeth is reading the cards. On the other side of the table there is a very fat woman and a very thin one. Opposite Di is an elderly woman with a plump face and watery eyes. Di says she is called Ellen. This is Alice Clegg and Sonia, she says, waving at the fat woman and the thin one with her cigarette. And Elsie Mather, otherwise known as Gypsy Rose Lee. Pull up a chair. Gareth – another cup of tea.

Aw mam, Gareth says, but he gets up off the sofa where he is sitting with a great number of children watching a video. Wanda sits down, feeling at the back of her neck the other women looking at her and Coral and at one another. She unfastens the straps on Coral's trolley and sits her on her knee. Coral makes a grab for the cards and Wanda gives her the keys from her bag to play with.

Elsie is reading Ellen's cards. Your Alf's thinking of you all the time, she says. Ellen's eyes get more watery. She presses a hand to her breast.

He's not in pain any more is he, she says. Di winks at Wanda. He's out of his suffering now, Elsie says. And the pain in his bowels has gone.

Gareth brings Wanda a cup of tea. Coral makes a grab for that too so Wanda sets her down on the floor.

He says you're to keep your feet warm this winter, Elsie says.

O that's Alf, says Ellen. He always did worry about me keeping warm.

Next it is Di's turn. Wanda is hardly listening. She is thinking about what she has come to say to Di, that she thinks she has found a job. Ever since the day at the DHSS offices she has been looking hard. The gas bill came and she couldn't pay it, then the electric bill came and she couldn't pay that either, but she went down to see them and they said she could pay a bit at a time. The way things are she can't even pay that, but she doesn't say so. She goes on looking for a job. She goes for a clerical job but is passed over for someone with experience. Then she sees a bar job advertised but the pub is too far away, she will have to get a taxi back and that would take all her money. Then she goes for a job as a cleaner and one as a shop assistant but both times someone gets there just before her. She calls in at the local store on the off-chance and asks to see the manager, Mr Harrop. We want someone with experience, he says. Wanda wonders how much experience you need to work a till and says yes, she has experience. But he takes her to the back of the shop and sits her down at one of the new computerised tills and she can't work it at all. I'm not used to this kind, she says. Her face is bursting hot and she leaves the store as fast as she can. She will not go back in there for a while.

Then when she is walking past a local club she sees a sign in the window, bar staff wanted smart persons only need apply, and she stands outside the door a bit because she is not very smart and because the Comfy Club has a bad reputation. Then she goes in, leaving Coral outside, and asks to see the manager. The manager comes in wiping his hands on a towel. She is not his idea of smart she can tell. He looks at her critically and Wanda sees herself through his eyes. She is wearing a loose black T-shirt and a wrap-around Indian skirt – the same clothes she wore when she went into the hospital with Coral. As he looks at her she sees her own shabbiness in detail. I've got some other people to see, he says. Come back Friday. If job's still going you can have it then. Three nights a week, five pounds a night, not subject to negotiation, no questions asked.

Wanda understands. The pay is unusually low, it will cost her three pounds for a babysitter. He probably made it up there and then, but he will not say anything about employing her, and she won't need money for fares.

Wanda leaves the club quickly so she doesn't have to see herself any more through the manager's eyes. She tries to work out the money. She could do with working two nights a week rather than three because she is not allowed to earn fifteen pounds and still claim, and the DHSS don't take babysitting into consideration. She will actually be breaking the law, but the manager said it wasn't subject to negotiation. And she has to have more money. Each night she can't get to sleep for thinking about money, then she gets to sleep but wakes up again, with the dreadful sickness in her stomach. Something has to be done. That's why she is here now, to ask Di to babysit like she said she would, when only three weeks ago she decided she would never bring Coral here. But here she is in the crowded smoky room with the mugs of tea and cards, feeling strange. Elsie is reading Di's cards. And here is Kev, sauntering in from the kitchen, whistling and patting his pockets which are heavy with change.

It's hot in here, he says. I think I'll take my shirt off for a bit.

Eh up, says Di to the others. How much pleasure can the mortal frame stand.

Sometimes they are like that, Di and Kev, a kind of team, putting on a show for everyone else. Other times it starts off jokey and then gets serious. Kev circles round Di, lashing out suddenly and smashing her face into the kitchen cupboard.

Why don't you try a bit harder, she says, wiping the blood from her face. I hardly felt that one. And he hits her again, much harder. Her face flattens against the cupboard door.

That's right, she says. Show all your mates what a big man you are.

It's like they can't stop circling round each other in a frenzy of hatred. Sometimes Kev knocks Di to the floor and kneels on her and tells her where he is going to hit her next, and how hard, and when, and she spits in his face, but no one interferes. It is like they are locked into their circle of hatred. But right now they are friendly enough, Kev dropping his shirt over the heads of the kids and them fighting it off again, then coming over to the table and pulling Di's head back by her hair, and pressing the cards back in Elsie's hands to have a look.

Seen any tall dark handsome men lately, he says to Di.

If I have I wouldn't tell you, Di says pushing him away.

Then he looks at Wanda like he hasn't noticed her before and says well well well, what've we got here.

Keep your hands off, says Di. Elsie, read Wanda's cards.

I haven't got any money, Wanda says, but Di says it doesn't matter, Elsie will throw one in extra for free. Elsie looks at Wanda sourly but hands her the cards. Wanda is conscious of Coral all the time she is shuffling the cards, but she is alright, crawling through the legs of the other kids who are watching the video. Someone else arrives to see Kev and he goes back into the kitchen.

Elsie lays out the cards and examines them screwing up her

eyes against the smoke from her own cigarette. She taps the eight of diamonds with her finger. Now then, she says. There's an opportunity coming to you, bringing money with it and an older man. And there's another man here, she says, standing in shadows.

That's mugger, Di says, come to take it all off you again.

Alice and Sonia laugh but Elsie ignores them. This one's going to play a great role in your life, she says. And there's children with him, two boys.

Sooner you than me, says Alice Clegg.

Well, says Di to Wanda, what do you think of that. Wanda says she thinks the first bit is right. She tells Di about the job she has seen. O you don't want to work there, says Alice Clegg. It's dead rough. And it won't pay. Jim's mean as hell.

He won't declare her though, says Di with a wink at Wanda. Wanda doesn't like this. Now everyone will know she is claiming while she is at work.

Did you ever sort that business with the DHSS out, says Di lighting up. Wanda shakes her head. Didn't you go and see them, Di says.

Yes I did, Wanda says, but it didn't get sorted.

What did I tell you, says Di. Once they start mucking around with computers there's no end to it. They've cut all her money every week for no reason, she tells the others.

O I wouldn't put up with that, says Alice Clegg, would you Sonia? No, Sonia says. I'd get down there and sort it out, says Alice Clegg. What did they say to you?

Though she doesn't want to Wanda finds herself telling everyone about the day at the DHSS. As she talks, without meaning to, she makes her voice sound like their voices, and chooses the words they would use. When she finishes they are all agreed that they wouldn't put up with it, not for a moment. Wanda tries to tell them how it is but Di cuts her short. Anyway you won't need them, she says, if you get this job. So. Who's looking after Coral?

Wanda says, all her words stumbling out, that she thought Di might, like she said, just for a bit, till she gets herself sorted. Di raises both hands in the air. I said that? she says. No problem. Bring her down any time.

Wanda feels her face go hot with relief as she thanks Di. At the same time she is anxious to leave so she hurries round the floor after Coral and picks her up. Coral protests loudly.

The front doorbell goes again and before anyone can answer someone is walking up the hall. Sharon, says Di to the others. Come to borrow something.

Hiya Di, says Sharon. Can you spare a cup of sugar.

Wanda is looking for her keys but out of the corner of her eye she sees Sharon, a big girl with blonde streaks in dark hair. She sits down at the table without being asked. By now Di is dealing the cards for a game of rummy. Stay and have a game, she says to Sharon, but Sharon says she can't stay long, she has left Paula outside. Actually she has come to ask a favour. Well that's new, says Di.

Will you have Paula for me tonight, Sharon says. Only Tony's asked me to pub.

O I don't know, says Di. What do I get out of it? She seems serious. Wanda stops stuffing Coral's cardigan into her bag and listens.

I'll do all your cleaning, says Sharon, and look after all your kids for a month.

O well then, says Di. It's a deal, and everyone laughs. Wanda straps Coral into her trolley. She will not have to pay.

Kev comes in, whistling again and counting more money, in notes this time. What's for tea, he says to Di, but before she can answer a fight breaks out between two of the kids and orange juice is spilled on the floor. Di leaps up and Wanda begins to push her way out of the room. Di pauses in the middle of belting both kids. Eh, she says. What are you wearing when you go for the job? Wanda says she doesn't have anything to wear. Well we'd best get you something, Di says.

I haven't any money, says Wanda.

You won't have if you don't get job, Di says, so you'd best look smart. I tell you what, we'll go to flea market tomorrow and pick up a few bargains.

Wanda is not sure she likes this idea but she wants to be going so she says alright and pushes the trolley down the hall, hoping Di will forget.

See you tomorrow then, says Di.

Sometimes Wanda has a dream she likes very much. She dreams she is floating upwards, pressing her way through layers of air and bursting through each layer like it is a kind of skin. Through each layer the air is clearer and she can move more freely, and she goes on, higher and higher, until she comes to a place where she can float freely and breathe in the stillness.

This dream is not like that. In this dream she is in the lift and Coral is with her in the trolley. The lift is out of control. It is plummeting downwards so fast Wanda can hardly breathe or see. It passes all the floors, and the ground, and still it plunges down. Wanda presses all the buttons but there is no end to the falling of the lift. Then suddenly it stops but the doors stay shut. Wanda remembers there is a button she can press to open the doors but when she turns to press it Di is there. She has been there all the time. Let's get out Di, Wanda says. Long shadows flicker in the hollows of Di's face.

Not just yet, she says.

*

Coral puts an envelope into the typewriter and adjusts the platen. But someone is knocking at the door. When she opens the door Larry is there. Can I come in, he says. He walks past Coral into the lounge. He sits in the chair in which he always sat. He is wearing a suit. How are you, he says. Coral says nothing at all.

After a pause Larry begins to talk. His new job is going well. He has been given a car and a wide area of union work. He has applied for a mortgage. As he talks, as always, he begins to confide in her. He is worried about the exams he has taken, lately he has had a lot of headaches. In particular he worries about his mortgage.

After a while Larry stops talking. Then again he asks Coral how she is. Coral wants to say something but she cannot think of anything to say. Everything she thinks of seems out of place. She does not want him to leave. After a moment she says, I'm alright.

Larry says he will have to be going. He gets up and goes towards the door. Don't go, Coral says. Larry turns politely as if expecting her to say something but still Coral can find nothing to say. Larry opens the door and pauses. Then he says well, goodbye then, and smiles a little. Coral smiles back and grips the door. She carries on smiling as he walks away.

When he is gone Coral's hand begins to tremble violently against the door. She lets it fall and rubs it against her T-shirt. Then she holds her head tentatively in her hands. Of course she remembers what she wanted to say – why did he leave – but it is no use now. Not knowing what else to do she wanders into the lounge. She sits in the chair Larry has just left. It is still warm.

*

Laurie goes upstairs on the bus but even the top deck is full. She sits next to a fat woman in a tweed coat. All the pleasure of the morning is gone.

The fat woman sucks mints. Her thigh presses against Laurie's own. Laurie feels the dampness of her coat. They are so close, the two of them, but they do not speak. As the bus jolts and lurches they sway and press against one another, but their eyes stare straight ahead.

Desolation wells from the corners of Laurie's soul. She has failed in the job she set herself. At the first problem she gave in to panic. She feels again the touch of the woman's hand on her arm.

She feels that everything has been taken away from her. If she can't do this job what can she do? She stares down the long vacuum of her days. She feels very cold.

Laurie sneaks surreptitious glances at the woman next to her. She wants to bury her face in the tweed coat and follow her home. The woman does not seem to notice Laurie. Imperceptibly Laurie leans a little closer to her and the woman hutches sideways.

Then the woman gets off and Laurie is alone. She stares at a window too mottled to see through. She does not want to go home.

Outside Laurie's flats dogs tear and worry at something on the ground. They snarl as she edges past. Inside she can already hear quarrelling from the top flat next to hers.

The man is shouting.

You do nothing all day.

You're here all day and you do nowt.

There is a series of crashes and thuds. The woman is crying.

Laurie lets herself in. She unloads her bags on the kitchen table. She will not think of the woman's face bloodying and crumpling against the wall. She will think about the food in her bags, the lettuce, quail eggs, tomatoes, soda bread and the wonderful cake. She will make herself something to eat.

Scrambled eggs. Laurie doesn't know if you are supposed to scramble quail eggs but she is going to try. She cracks the eggs into a pan. Then she discovers she has no milk or butter.

Laurie kicks the fridge door to. She smacks the pan off the cooker and throws the tomatoes across the room. Then she sits at the table and lets her head drop into her hands.

She sees the cake.

Laurie rips open the cardboard box and the cellophane wrapper inside. She breaks into the cake with her hands, stuffing it piece after piece into her mouth. It sticks to her teeth and to the roof of her mouth. She swallows hard and the cloying sweetness makes her heave. Piece by piece she crams the whole cake down.

Now she feels sick. She wanders out of the kitchen, along the corridor, into the front room, then back into the corridor.

I can never go out again, she thinks.

As soon as she thinks this the fear returns, coursing through her like water that has been only temporarily dammed.

I must lie down, she thinks.

Laurie lies down on the bed in her anorak and boots, legs bent, feet tucked in. She pulls the quilt around her because the room is cold. From her window she can see the long slope of the hill. Above the hill clouds billow in changing formations like smoke. It is like the sky is floating apart and piecing itself together again. What is she anyway, Laurie thinks, but a collection of incoherent fragments: memories, dreams, fears, desires. As she lies in stillness, watching the sky, she feels the force holding these fragments together dissolving. She feels a sense of spaciousness, of boundaries breaking down. She feels like she has no substance and will float in separate pieces to the ceiling. Only the cake in her stomach is heavy.

Fragments of memory drift in and out of Laurie's mind, floating apart, piecing themselves together again. She can no longer tell them from her dreams. In spite of the noise from the neighbours, the sporadic barking of a dog, she has the sensation of falling into silence, like the silences between words. What will happen to her here? she thinks.

When Laurie wakes up it is dark and there is a terrific row going on in the square. As she lies numb and stiff with cold the memory of her failure returns. She can never go out again.

Laurie gets out of bed and is interrupted by a volley of sneezes. Her eyes stream and her feet are stiff and crippled. As she shuffles towards the door she feels her bowels loosening. Dear Christ, she thinks, she will be dead before her next giro. The noise outside increases. Now there are pins and needles in her legs. Multiple sclerosis, thinks Laurie. There is a dragging pain in her stomach. Cancer, Laurie thinks. In the bathroom she discovers a discharge. She puts a hand on the wall to steady herself. One thing she cannot be dying of is a sexually transmitted disease.

It is always the same, each time she decides to give up 'lifting. The fear returns, and sickness. It is as though, with nothing else to occupy it, her mind becomes obsessed with her body and its capacity for dysfunction. It is like, when her social outlets are stripped away fear remains, lying always beneath the social surface, waiting. She can no longer ignore vulnerability, power-lessness. She is living an illness.

There is a terrible row outside. All the dogs are barking. Laurie limps to the window. The square is dark but there are lighted windows all round, people peering from behind curtains, or propping their elbows on balconies. It is Alice and Sonia.

Sonia makes high yelping sounds like the surrounding dogs. She scurries to the farthest side of the square where the railings are. Alice Clegg lumbers over. It looks like Sonia is trying to squeeze herself through the gap where there is a bent rail.

You're fucking dead you, says Alice. She picks Sonia up by the hair and pounds her head against the railings. Sonia's arms flail helplessly. Her face is streaming blood. Instead of a scream there is a rattling noise in her throat.

A man comes out of the doorway of Alice Clegg's house in his shirtsleeves.

Come on Al, he says. Alice half turns, holding Sonia like a rag.

Stay out of this you, she says. The man shrugs and hesitates on the steps.

Alice throws back her head, eyes screwed tightly against the glare of the lamp. She draws her foot back, leaning forwards. Then she throws her weight backwards, driving her foot into Sonia's belly. You fucking dog, she says.

Laurie's fingers and forehead are pressed against the glass of the window but her eyes are shut. When there is silence she opens them again. The square darkens as the watching lights disappear. She hears a scuffling noise on the far side of the square but she can no longer see Sonia. All is quiet. Even the dogs have gone. Laurie is alone in the darkened flat. Slowly she limps back to her bedroom.

The objects in her room are ghostly in the small light. As she moves around searching for an extra pair of socks, the fingerless gloves, old memories return, fragmented, hideous. It is as though all the foolish and terrible things she has ever done are waiting in the shadow of her room. At a moment when she is unresisting they will move forwards silently to the foot of her bed.

Laurie does not know why all her memories are so bad. There must be other things in her past she can remember, times when she was not screwing up, but it is always the same old ghosts that return, moulding her past into painful and humiliating forms. She has come to accept this shameful version of her history as truth, as a condition of her life, though one she tries to push aside and do without. She knows it is also a condition of powerlessness, this absorption of shame and guilt, for without a past she cannot possibly have a future.

*

Where id Cowal? Wanda says. Where iddoo babee? Where oo id? Tum to momsums.

Wanda goes into the lounge but Coral is not there. She goes into the kitchen, but Coral is not there. Don't be fwighted, Wanda says. She looks in all the cupboards. Tum on Towal, tum on out. She goes into the bedroom but she has already looked in there. She presses a hand to her forehead and tries to think. Coral was with her before, she remembers that; then there is only the fizziness in her head, like a television screen off-channel. Now the pills are wearing off she remembers Coral should be there but she doesn't know where she can be.

Stupid cow, say the voices in her head. Losing your own daughter.

Mustn't call people names, Wanda thinks, not nice.

Cowal, she calls under the bed. Co-wal. I tan see you. Tum on babee, pweese . . .

Faintly, unmistakably, the fear is returning. As she crouches looking at the empty space under the bed she feels the familiar knocking sensation in her head and stomach. She pushes the hair back from her face. Cowal? she says. Silly tart, say the voices in her head. Coral isn't there, she's gone. You lost her.

No, Wanda says.

Can't even look after your own kid, they say. That's what they all think. That's what everyone thinks. But she has managed so far. And Coral is nearly four.

Naughty Cowal, Wanda says. Not nice to hide. She sits up and rests her head on the bed. She feels worse now. She could take a tablet. But she wants to find Coral first. Silently now she goes through all the rooms again. The telly is on in the lounge. We can change the way you wash your face for life, it says. Wanda pushes back the curtains and looks on the balcony. It is empty.

She can hear them all talking now.

Doesn't deserve to have a baby.

They have them then they think state'll keep them.

They don't know they're born.

Wanda stands still and presses both hands to her head.

She can't think where else to look. But she must try to think, and to talk properly.

Cowal, she says in a little voice. Mummee get cwoss.

Far below Wanda's window miniature cars and people crawl around the road. Everything that happens down there in the outside world is a long way off. In here there is only Wanda and Coral, except that Coral is not there.

Wanda goes into the kitchen for her tablets. She has to stop her stomach churning. She picks them up and puts them down again. She has to find Coral. Down the hall she goes, babbling on, in and out of doors, the bedroom, the bathroom, pink splashes in the bathroom, no that was Di, the cupboard at the end of the hall. She keeps her eyes half-closed as she goes because she is half-afraid of what she might see, but the cupboard is empty. Back into the lounge she goes. Fluoride is present in nature, the telly says, and an essential element in caring for beautiful teeth. Think, Wanda says to herself. She must try to think. There are voices like flapping wings inside her head. Back down the hall she goes, stumbling into a door-frame. Hurted arm, she says whimpering. Cowal mummy hurted arm. Tum on Cowal baby. Baby baby. Bylo baby. Baby bunting. Bylo baby bunting boo . . .

Coral used to be at Di's when she was not with Wanda. Jim started wanting her to do extra nights. By the time she got back it was so late Di used to say it wasn't worth waking Coral up, Wanda could call for her in the morning. Then when she called for her the next morning she usually ended up staying there all day. She didn't know why. A kind of tiredness would come over her and she could never summon up the energy to leave, to go back to the emptiness of her own flat, no matter how noisy or smoky it got at Di's. Day after day passed like this, like a kind of dream. She even started to smoke so Di's friends wouldn't think her standoffish, though she could never afford to buy her own.

Di didn't forget about the clothes. Just as Wanda was getting Coral ready there was a knock on the door and it was Di with two of the kids.

Gareth and Gavin's out playing she says, walking in just as if Wanda has asked her. Baby's asleep, but I'll have to bring these two.

They hardly fit in the lift with the two trolleys. Wanda holds her breath so she can't smell the muddy urine they are standing in, but Di talks all the time, about how they have been trying to get a move but the council don't think they're overcrowded yet. Though when I asked woman she didn't seem that keen on swapping places. You won't bloody try it will you, I said. But all they'll say is if we had another child or an adult dependant we'd definitely get a house. Kev were with me like, so I said to him on your back Kev, we'd best get at it right away. Di waits for Wanda's response so Wanda says What did she say then and Di says Nowt, she just rang bell for next poor bleeder.

Wanda is glad to get out of the lift so she can breathe. The trolley wheels make muddy tracks across the floor as they leave. It is a hot dull day. Di talks all the time as they go. She tells Wanda that the last council official suggested that she and Kevin should sleep in the lounge with Gaynor the baby, then there'd be two boys to each bedroom and there'd be room enough, and Kev said there'd be room enough in cupboard if they all stood up. Then she tells Wanda about giving all the kids first names beginning with 'g', Gareth, Gavin, Gael, Gordon and Gaynor, because their surname is Gee, so they can all say their initials are gee-gee. Then she tells Wanda that the job she should really go for is a kissogram girl. It's all rage now, she says; not many hours, good pay. Di has a friend who does it part-time. She has to dress up as a traffic warden or a policewoman and pretend to book fellow she's been ordered for. Then she starts taking her clothes off, and his as well, but only the top half. Then she rubs shaving cream into his chest and he rubs some into hers. And they won't declare you either, Di says, but Wanda doesn't fancy it much.

By this time they are at the market. Wanda looks at all the dearer stalls. She sees a white Edwardian-type blouse with a high neck and a forties-style dress in green and cream with padded shoulders. She cannot afford either of these.

They're no use to Jim, Di says waving her over to the 50p stalls. She rummages through a heap of clothes. Now here you are, he'll like this. She holds up a red T-shirt with a cross-over neckline. Wanda supposes it will do. I haven't got anything to go with it, she says, but Di soon finds a short frilly skirt, white with red hearts. Perfect, she says. Wanda thinks of the outfit she has recently seen in a magazine, a gold silky loose-fitting jacket and wide baggy trousers to match. She won't find anything like that here. Di is holding up a gold lurex tube-dress. Any three items for a pound, she says holding it up against Wanda. It looks like it will hardly cover her at all. No way, says Wanda, but Di is not discouraged. Eventually she finds a white, skin-tight top with a lace-up front. It'll go great with the skirt, she says. Two outfits for a pound. Wanda does not have the heart to say no. She is losing interest in the whole business since she cannot afford the clothes she wants. Di seems to know what she is doing. On the next stall she sees some stretchy pants with a pattern like snakeskin in grey and white. You could get away with these with your figure, she says. You'll need something other than the skirt. The pants are three pounds which Wanda cannot afford but Di beats them down to two. Then they look for shoes since Wanda only has trainers and pumps. They cannot find white or black so they settle for some high-heeled strippy sandals in navy blue for a pound. Four outfits, as good as, for under a fiver, says Di. But Wanda is depressed. She is cleaned out for the week and doesn't know how she will manage. Di dismisses this with a wave of her hand. It'll be worth it because you'll get the job, she says. Anyway, I can always lend you a fiver until your wages are through.

O no, Wanda says, but Di says what's a fiver between friends.

It is always like this with Di. When Wanda needs anything she can supply it and Wanda is never in a position to refuse. When Wanda says she could do with a coat to go with all this new stuff Di says she can borrow hers, and she lends Wanda a white gaberdine which is a bit short on Di but a fashionable length on Wanda, so Di says she might as well keep it for now, while she's working. If Wanda needs a babysitter for Coral, or a fiver to get her through the week, or some Calpol because Coral is ill, Di is always there; and if Wanda is at Di's at dinnertime Di will always make her some toast or chips, so sometimes Wanda stays because she has nothing in at home.

Wanda does not know why Di gives her so much. Sometimes she wonders if Di will ever want paying back, but she pushes this thought away because she cannot afford it. Anyway there is nowhere else to go.

Today Di treats Wanda to a cup of tea and a toasted teacake, and an orange juice for Coral. Wanda cannot help wondering where Di gets all her money from. She tries to ask what Kev does for a living but Di just says O this and that, and then starts on about how you can't do anything today that's legal and decent, it doesn't pay. At very least you end up claiming and working on side, she says, or you go under. You can't tell me you know anyone who isn't working some kind of a fiddle, says Di. We're in era of criminal enterprise now you know.

All the time she is with Di Wanda is never sure that she likes her that much. She does not know why she sees so much of her except that there is nowhere else to go. She likes Di's deadpan humour and the fact that she has always got something to say. She is never boring. Thick as pig shit, me, Di says. I never got anywhere at school. But she is not stupid. And she is not afraid, of anyone or anything. But Wanda doesn't like the way Di knows everything about everyone and is always running them down. When she thinks about it Di tells her very little about herself, but she knows all about Wanda. She darts out a question like a lizard darts out its tongue and before you know it you have told her what she wants to know. She knows all about Wanda's home and family, and school and Gary Buckley, the boy Wanda didn't want to marry. But she doesn't know about Sim yet. Wanda keeps a tight hold on her memories of Sim.

After the tea and toast Di says she will fix Wanda's hair back at the flat. She always has some peroxide in and a home perm. Wanda decides to go along with it all. She is getting into the idea of a new image. By the time Di has finished Wanda has spent the whole day there without meaning to. It is always the same.

Kev is no better, when you try to talk to him about money. One time when he comes into the front room with the usual wad of notes Wanda says Been selling your body again Kev?

No, says Di. He tried that once and we went broke. Bailiffs round and lot.

Just keeping up spirit of free enterprise, Kev says to Wanda. Like the good lady says. He pats the television as he walks past. The Prime Minister is on giving a speech. It's all monetarist policies now, says Kev. Survival of the fittest.

So Wanda never does get to know what Kev does for a living. All she knows is that they are never short of money and have all the latest gadgets in their flat, but because Kev has no official income they can't get a mortgage.

Wanda knows that a lot of people don't like Di, though there are always plenty of callers at the flat. She is not allowed in the Cozy Caffy. Brenda always stands in the doorway like a guardian angel if they approach, arms folded across her breasts, and Di always calls it the salmonella shop loudly as they pass. Then one time they are in the butcher's down the road and Di complains about the mince he sold her last time, which was already off, but the butcher says there weren't any other complaints. It were good enough for everyone else, he says. When she can't get her money back Di starts to lift the trays of meat from the window and spit in each one.

Eh, what d'you think you're doing? says the butcher. Get out of my shop. I'll call police. When Di won't stop he calls his daughter, Ros, Ros, call police. Wanda begins to manoeuvre herself out of the shop but Di says don't worry, I'm going. I wouldn't shop here again if you paid me, and they leave with the butcher shouting after them down the road, Just show your face in here again, I'll have police on you.

Wanda is sorry she went into the shop with Di but Di seems strangely satisfied and content, the same way she seems after fighting Kev. That'll show him, she says. Who does bastard think he is, but Wanda isn't listening. She is thinking about the butcher's daughter, who is fair-haired and pretty, and dresses the way Wanda would like to dress. She was wearing an off-the-shoulder sweatshirt and a silk scarf in her hair, a short print skirt and leggings. Wanda would like to look like that, casual but kind of artistic, but it would never do for Jim, who likes his staff to tart themselves up a bit for the punters.

*

Well this is it kid, Shelagh says.

It is the end of their degree. The exams are finally over.

'In what ways do Dickens's narrative strategies undermine the "ideology of solitariness" permeating his later novels?'

'Would you say that movement in *Henry V* is contrapuntal or diachronic? Give reasons for your answer.'

Laurie chews one pen after another. In the end she ignores all the questions and writes down anything she can remember about the texts.

And now it is over, the whole three years. Laurie and Shelagh wander despondently round the campus in the dull June days.

Each is haunted by the potential of what has just passed. But at least Laurie has completed her degree in spite of the problems of her second year.

You know what I think, Shelagh says. I think all this crush-on-a-tutor crap is a kind of pitfall dug especially for the working-class student by the intelligentsia of the country.

Shelagh voices many opinions as they trudge around the half-empty buildings. She is witty, insightful, articulate. It is a terrible waste since there are no more tutorials. But it is like they cannot stop viewing themselves through an academic lens. Behind each conversation their tutors watch silently.

It is time to apply for jobs. Fiona Smythe already has a job as Director of Arts for a South London area.

How does she do it, Shelagh wants to know. A job like that, no experience, nor nothing? Was it the money? Connections? Did she sleep with the entire Board? And if so, she concludes bitterly, why the hell did she need a degree?

Every day Laurie reads through the job ads in the papers. She is frightened by the interesting ones with good pay. She knows she is worth more than the others offer. Shelagh has been turned down at two interviews. As the end of term approaches they are unable to stay away from the campus. They cannot make the transition to a larger, more expensive world.

Soon the university will close altogether, in preparation for a new stream of students unknown to Shelagh and Laurie. Already their own faces are erased from the minds of their tutors. And the lease on the flat is running out.

Then one day Shelagh lets herself in and stands in the doorway of the flat. I'm getting married, she says. Laurie stutters her congratulations.

Shelagh is getting married to Mark, a medical student she has been dating for just over a term. He comes from a family of consultants who have secured a place for him in Canada. For various reasons it is better for him to be married before he leaves. So they will have to marry quickly. Next month.

Shelagh says Mark is crazy about her. She wants Laurie to be her bridesmaid. She talks a lot about Laurie coming to visit them in Canada. Soon all their conversations are weighted with silence.

The wedding is set for the day before the lease on the flat runs out. Shelagh is dressed brightly in purple silk with an orange shawl. She kisses all the guests. When it is Laurie's turn she kisses Laurie, for the first time in their friendship, and smiles brightly. Write soon, she says. Then she is whisked away by the other guests to the car.

Laurie goes home alone and sits for the last time in the dim red glow of the electric fire. They used to sit together in front of the fire with the lights turned off when the money was low. Heat before light, Shelagh used to say. Of course they never caught up with the reading.

The heat from the fire scorches the flesh of Laurie's face. She picks confetti from her clothes piece by piece. She does not know what she will do now. I will go home, she thinks.

Her mother is anxious when Laurie turns up. What's wrong, she says. Laurie reassures her that everything is fine. She just needs a rest after the exams, before getting a job.

Most of the kids Laurie knows have jobs, or are on training schemes. Molly Dobson is doing well for herself with a modelling agency. This is bad news for Laurie, since her mother was always anxious to impress a sense of Laurie's superiority onto Molly's mother.

Laurie is helpful at home. She brings her father cups of tea as he sits in front of the telly. She does the shopping and always has tea ready when her mother gets in from the laundry. At first she looks for jobs every day. At the job centre they want machinists, fitters, shorthand typists. She lacks experience for some jobs and is over-qualified for others. Sometimes she is sent to an interview. Before she goes she is confident of what she will say, how she will act. But in front of the interviewer it is like she is a different person. She begins to fade, to falter and stumble. She cannot understand it. How will she ever 'get on', to use her mother's favourite phrase, if she doesn't know from one minute to the next what kind of person she is going to be?

Soon Laurie begins to lie about the job applications.

O yes, she says, they were very interested.

They're putting me on a shortlist, she says.

Soon however her mother stops asking.

Secretly Laurie takes to writing. She notes down her failures and disappointments, her mother's sullen anger and the way she acts like she should never have expected anything better. Also she writes down the lies she tells about her interviews and applications. She feels that she must keep track of herself somehow, with all the different faces she presents. One day she writes a short story.

Rejection, she writes, is the one thing that gets harder the more practice you get. It is brilliant, she thinks. She is a great writer. The next day she reads it again. It is shit, she thinks. She cannot write at all. But at least whilst she is writing she feels like she is making a space for herself.

Then one day her mother finds all the scraps of paper stuffed into a file. When Laurie gets in she is sitting in a chair with all the pieces in her lap.

So this is what you do, she says, instead of looking for a proper job. There are tears in her eyes. Laurie can think of nothing to say. The next day she packs her bag and leaves. It does not seem necessary to leave a note.

*

The night she started the job Wanda sat in front of the mirror in her bedroom. She brushed on the powder blue eye-shadow and pale orange lipstick she borrowed from Di. It does not really go with the top she is wearing, which is red, but it will have to do.

Wanda sits in front of a reflection she hardly recognises. Her hair is bright and shaggy with the perm and the peroxide. As she looks at herself she feels like she does not want to go on with all this. It does not look like Wanda in the mirror, not the Wanda she has always wanted to be. The red top is cut deeper at the neck than she thought. She tries it first with a bra and then without. She thinks of the outfits she would have liked to wear, pale green jersey, clinging, classic, or a short black evening-dress. She wonders if she has got too much make-up on or not enough.

The flat is unnaturally quiet without Coral who is already at Di's. Wanda feels like she cannot leave the dressing table, she sits and stares at the strange reflection. A kind of weariness settles all round her like dust.

But Jim is impressed, she can tell.

You've smartened yourself up a bit, he says as she takes off Di's coat. Wanda is shown round the bar and how to use the till and told to smile a lot at customers. That is it. She has been taken on.

At first she cannot remember anything, it is terrible. She can't mix a cocktail, she makes mistakes with the customers' change and jams the till. The first night she spills beer down her skirt and drops an entire tray of glasses. She runs all the way home that night. She is sure she will be sacked, but Mabel says sacked? you should be so lucky. No one ever gets sacked from here. They have to bolt doors to keep them in.

The first two weeks she does not get a single tip. She tries not to mind about this – at least she can begin to pay off the bills – but she is only paid till eleven and it is never much before one when she leaves. Then she has to cross the estate in total darkness. She has never noticed before how few lamp-posts there are. The council will not pay for lights when the rates are low. But the estate is full of dark alleys and corners, or walls and bushes anyone could hide behind. Muggers' paradise, Di calls it.

Wanda hurries past the low-rise flats and maisonettes and her heels ring loudly on the concrete. She tries not to run because it would be like admitting her fear. She hugs the white mac more closely around her and walks as quickly as she can in her heels. She does not want to go home with anyone at the club.

I'll see you home love, says one punter after another. Come round back with me. Wanda always shakes her head, remembering to smile. Usually she looks so scared when the punters talk to her that Jim has to tell her to stop gawping and get on with it. She can never think of anything to say back to them like Mabel.

O aye, and what will you do if you get me there, says Mabel, run off home?

Not me lass, I could show you a thing or two.

Well I never, I'd have thought a man of your age'd have forgotten how.

Mabel is short and plump. Her red hair is grey at the roots, but she has a way with the punters. Wanda begins to try to copy her. When an old man asks her if she has a boyfriend Wanda says no, I've been saving myself for you. She goes red as she says it but the old man is delighted. He asks her what she is drinking and

Wanda says half a lager, but Mabel says she were drinking half a lager, but seeing as it's you, Jack, she'll have a triple gin. And Jack says Eh, I'm not made of money, but he passes Wanda a one-pound coin. Wanda is thrilled, it is her first tip. She presses it into the pocket of her snakeskin pants.

From then on things get better. Wanda feels like she is making a whole new personality for herself which she can wear at work like a wig. She begins to get the knack of serving drinks and the tips start coming in. She begins to look forward to going to work. She pays off her bills and buys Coral some clothes and then gets herself a strapless blue dress with thigh-high slits that Jim likes a lot. Eh, he says, looking down the front of the dress. You don't get many of them to the pound. Wanda laughs and slips past. The new personality that is Wanda at work never minds these comments. She weaves in and out of the tables wiping up rings of spilled drinks and dodging as many of the pats and pinches as she can. She feels that at work there is someone to be, but at home she is no one at all. Though sometimes when she is collecting glasses at the end she catches sight of herself in one of the long mirrors that are all over the place in the club and doesn't know herself at all. Still Jim is happy. He likes her best in the tight blue dress or the snakeskin pants. And the better she gets at her job the more he likes her. So it is good to be liked and to be in company in the warm smoky club. In the dim lighting you can't see the stains on the carpet, the spilled drink and overflowing ashtrays. You can only see the faces at the bar, and the brighter lights of the stage, and the gold cage where the singers sing. Sometimes Mabel sings, usually on a Thursday, or when the booked act doesn't turn up. She sings 'Tie a Yellow Ribbon', in a thin, tinny voice. Other nights she works the bar with Wanda and Jean sings.

Jean is billed as Stella Marcel. She has a good voice, deep and powerful, and she wears a beautiful dress. It is dark blue chiffon with a sequinned top. Sometimes Wanda imagines herself in Jean's dress. She would look better in it than Jean, who is past forty and doesn't have the figure. She thinks of herself on stage in that dress, the chiffon flowing round her ankles and the sequinned top hanging to her hips like it is supposed to, not stopping under the bust like it does with Jean. She imagines herself singing in a high, angelic voice. Actually her voice is sharp and reedy, scraping over the tunes like a knife on metal. But she couldn't do much worse than Jean, who starts off well, but then gets more and more drunk, till Jim makes frantic gestures to Bill the bouncer and George the piano-player to get her off stage. One night she sings 'The First Time Ever I Saw Your Face'. She misses her beat and all the high notes, then she gets out of the cage and staggers round the stage, nearly falling off. Her passionate finish goes on even after George has stopped playing the piano and walked off. Shit, says Jim behind the bar. She'll have to go.

Wanda feels sorry for Jean because Jim is always criticising her and because the other staff roll their eyes whenever she appears.

It's Lady Muck, says Mabel, still in same dress.

Sometimes she doesn't turn up and Wanda can tell Jim hopes she has gone for good. He is always saying he will look for someone else. He'll be lucky, with what he pays, says Mabel. Then one night Jean gets into a row with a punter who spills drink down her dress. A fight breaks out and Jean is socked in the jaw. She does not come in for a few nights. Then Wanda is off two nights and when she goes back there is a young girl, younger than Wanda, in the cage, wearing a tasselled leotard. Though she is very young she has a full round bust almost bursting out of the leotard. Her face is round too. She has red cheeks and light blue eyes with sticky mascara. Her brown hair is blonde at the ends and piled floppily on top of her head. A badge on her bust says Melanie. She can hardly sing at all.

There were a right scene here last night, Mabel says. Jean came in, just walked in like she hadn't been off for a whole week without letting anyone know. She takes one look at Madame Fifi up there and you should have heard her, screaming like a fishwife. Jim had to get Bill to throw her out.

Wanda is sorry for Jean. I thought you said he'd never get anyone on the money he pays, she says. But Mabel says that Melanie is only sixteen, and on some kind of Youth Opportunities scheme in the daytime, so she needs all the extra cash she can get. Either that or she's star-struck, poor cow, Mabel says. Wanda does not like Melanie, who wiggles her bum and makes breathy noises in time to the music, but Jim is clearly taken. He leans over the bar to get a better look and forgets to serve the customers.

If his tongue hangs out much further he'll be able to lick carpet clean instead of paying someone to hoover, Mabel says.

Wanda doesn't like this either, but this surprises her. She should be pleased to get Jim off her back. He is always squeezing past her in the narrowest places of the bar. Ooops pardon me, he says. That's not a gun in my pocket, I'm just pleased to see you. If he wants to get past he doesn't say so, he just puts his hands round her waist and shifts her sideways. He reaches round her to serve the customers or to get to the till and every night he offers her a lift home, the long way. But Wanda's new personality can handle this so it doesn't matter. She can be as rude as she likes back and Jim thinks it's wonderful.

Get your hands off, Jim, she says, I've just washed, or, Put me down, you don't know where I've been.

No, says Jim, putting one arm up in front of her as she tries to get past, but I know where I'd like to take you. Wanda tries to get past him the other way but he puts his other arm up. Where's that then Jim? she says. Sunset Retirement Homes? Chapel of Rest?

O no, says Jim, I weren't thinking of resting. Wanda ducks neatly under his arm. You'd best take another of them pills, she says. It's not good for your blood pressure, all this lusting and carrying-on. And Jim laughs and tells her she is a caution and a cracker. But now he seems to have lost interest, just when Wanda was beginning to think she could tap him for a rise. And when Jim comes up from the cellar and says to Wanda and Mabel that he is thinking of getting them leotards too, and Wanda says she'll wear a leotard when Jim walks stark naked through the precinct, Jim laughs, but he is not amused. Then he turns up with T-shirts printed specially for the club which have Whatever You Want You Get at Jim's Comfy Club printed across the bust and says he is thinking of having wet T-shirt competitions on Friday nights. Mabel puts hers on but Wanda walks off saying when hell freezes over, and Jim isn't pleased at all.

*

Valerie is home. She feels hard and cold inside, examining the bruise on her leg. She no longer wants to know about her mother. I will do my essay, she thinks.

Valerie holds her book tightly. She stares hard at the pages, willing her eyes to focus. She is trembling in her legs and arms.

Valerie gets up and prowls around the flat. She clutches the material of her T-shirt and rubs her hands against her legs. She walks from the window to the kitchen door and back again.

Valerie lies crouched upon the bed. There are griping pains in her stomach and she is bathed in sweat. Her hands are clenched and sticky, her mouth is very dry. She wants a drink of water but she cannot get up. If she gets up the room will fold around her.

Valerie rocks backwards and forwards on the bed. She grips the bed tightly and it judders beneath her. If she shuts her eyes she feels the familiar sensation like falling down a pit.

Her lips are very dry. She moves them soundlessly.

Yea though I walk . . .

She cannot remember it.

Yea . . .

Walk through the . . .

She rocks backwards and forwards trying to remember the words.

Yea though I (forwards)

walk through the (backwards)

valley of the (forwards)

shadow of death (backwards)

I will fear no evil

She slows her rocking down.

Yea

though I *walk*

through the *valley*

She adjusts her breathing to the words.

Better. She is feeling better. Soon she can uncurl herself, just a bit, and open her eyes.

Yea though I *walk* through the *valley* of the *shadow* of *death* I will *fear* no *evil*

At last she stops rocking. She stares around the room. Ros's laughing face is on the mantelpiece, there is the flowered chair.

She wants a drink. She wants to go to the toilet. But she will have to get up.

Yea though I walk, she breathes, through the valley of the shadow of death . . .

Always when she is like this it is the old words that come to her. Only the old words have meaning.

Slowly Valerie unfolds herself into a sitting position. Her legs are numb and stiff. She stares at the kitchen door and thinks of water.

Slowly, slowly she steps away from the bed, clinging to the flowered chair. Yea though I walk, she whispers, through the valley. She hangs on to the kitchen door, then grips the sink. The glass knocks against the tap as she runs the water. The water is cold, metallic. She feels it running, spilling down her chin and chest.

Now she must go to the toilet, clinging all the way on to the rail of the stairs.

There is no sound in the toilet except for the faint gurgling of the cistern. Then there is the sound of Valerie's urine spilling into the bowl, unnaturally loud. It is the sound of fear. It is the loneliest sound in the world.

Back in the kitchen Valerie runs another drink then sits on the stool staring out of the window.

Alcoholism is a family sickness they tell her at the meeting.

I'm not the one who's sick, she says. There is riotous laughter. But why, why is she sick.

It is dark now but the clock has stopped. Valerie does not know the time. She gazes at the rain spouting from the eaves and gutters, dripping from the big bins in the shop yard, soaking all the litter. There is a lamp outside, illuminating fine sprays of rain and the broken glass glittering around the yard. There is the shadow of a cat.

It is not like the real world, she thinks. It is like she lives in a nightmare thrown up by the real world.

Valerie goes slowly back to bed. She does not know the time so she might as well go back to bed.

Valerie is running like a cat in the shadow of tall bins in alleyways, past backyard gates. She knows that behind one of these gates is her mother's yard, her mother is brewing tea in a lighted kitchen. But all the gates are tall, and some are topped by broken glass.

Valerie crouches and springs right over a tall wooden gate. But the yard is long, full of broken glass and litter, and there is no light in the house. But as Valerie turns away a light is switched on her, sweeping an illuminated track up the yard. There is a hammering on the gate behind . . .

Valerie pulls herself awake but the hammering does not stop. She lies a while staring into darkness, listening to the knocking of her heart, the pounding on the door. She does not want to move.

Eventually she hauls herself out of bed. It is intensely cold. All her limbs are heavy as she stumbles down the stairs.

It is the police.

Of course.

Her mother has had an accident.

She is in the hospital.

They can take her there now if she likes.

Valerie blinks stupidly. She says, what time is it.

The policemen look at each other. Half-past five, one says.

Valerie nods. It is very cold. One of them is speaking again. If you'd like to get ready, he says, and come with us.

Yes, says Valerie. She doesn't move. Then suddenly she recovers and turns back up the stairs. She pulls on jeans over her T-shirt, then her duffel coat and shoes, and hurries down again. The milk bottles are frozen on the step. Valerie walks with the two policemen to the car. Their breath comes out in clouds. Valerie sits in the back, the two policemen in the front. Even through her jeans the leather is cold. The radio hisses and crackles. The headlamps sweep an illuminated track up the road.

*

One day when she is pushing Coral round the precinct Wanda sees a dress and it seems to her like she has always wanted it. It is short and black and close-fitting, strapless but with a fine gauze material up to the throat and down the sleeves. It is very expensive. Wanda has to walk past it four times before making her mind up. She cannot bear the thought of anyone else wearing it, she sees herself in it, it is hers. If she wears it at the club, she thinks, she could get herself that rise. So one day she buys the dress using the money from the next gas and electric bills, and because she cannot wear it with the blue sandals she buys shiny black court shoes and black earrings to go with it, and a new pink lipstick. That night she brushes her hair out straight and long, and puts on the dress and the shoes and the lipstick. She looks at herself in the mirror turning this way and that. This is more like the Wanda she always wanted to be.

She causes quite a stir at the bar.

You come into money or what, says Mabel, and Jim says I didn't know I were paying you that much, no wonder I'm broke. Wanda doesn't answer. She is not her old barmaid self tonight, not in this dress. She smiles graciously at all the customers and is discreet in response to the many comments. She is very conscious of herself as she walks across the floor, trying to get used to the new self she sees in the mirrors, the Wanda she always knew she could be, stylish and radiant.

Jim is very impressed. He follows her around all night and hardly looks at Melanie. By eck Wanda, he says, I didn't know you could look like that. Wanda takes a chance.

I could look like this more often if you paid me more, she says. Jim leans back on his bar-stool and smiles.

You're asking me for a rise, he says. Wanda lowers her eyes and looks humble. I know it's ungrateful, after the way you've showered me with money all these months, she says, but yes. Jim laughs and slaps his knee. Then he looks at her again and says he is always open to negotiation, but at that moment he is called to the phone. Later he disappears and it is not mentioned again.

But the next night he is there watching her again, and towards the end of the evening he takes her to one side and stands very close to her by the cellar door.

I suppose a young girl like you, he says, could always do with some cash.

Well I could, Wanda says, your wages being what they are; and Jim says, I'm a reasonable man, then he puts the palm of his hand against her cheek. Wanda says nothing. She is not sure what is being offered now. Jim lowers his voice.

So why don't we get together and talk about it eh, just you and me. Wanda still says nothing and Jim leans even closer. Wednesday nights, he says, the wife stays with her sister after bingo.

Wanda remembers her pub-girl personality. Why Jim, she says, batting her eyelashes. What are you suggesting. Jim looks innocent. Just a bit of extra money, he says. Like you said. Fifty pound maybe. For a moment Wanda says nothing, then she says fifty quid? I wouldn't even show you my knickers for that. As she dodges away she says I wanted a rise, not a disease, and Jim roars laughing. But he doesn't give up. He squeezes past her when she is serving a customer and touches her bum. Think it over, he says. Wanda ignores him completely.

But the next night he takes her arm as she is going to the toilet. Look, he says. I'm a reasonable man, like I said. I'm willing to pay for a good time. We could call it an even hundred if you like. Wanda pushes past him into the toilet. She looks at her red face in the mirror. She should be angry. She wouldn't want Jim if he was the last man on earth, but she is confused. She feels like she has some kind of power; at the same time she feels that she is being moved more and more onto Jim's ground. She doesn't know how she should play the game, or whose game it is, or how far she can go. She doesn't know what Jim's next move will be, or how far he will go.

There does not seem to be any limit to how far Jim will go. Wait till you see what I've got for you, he says, pressing up against her at the bar. Ten inches of throbbing red meat. He puts his arm round her as he reaches into the till. Fifty quid's nowt, he says, that's just for starters. You could have that just for sitting on my face.

Wanda is repelled, yet fascinated. Other people can hear him, she is sure. She cannot quite believe in this mysterious power and the lengths to which it will make him go. She says nothing, does nothing in response to him. It is like he has paralysed her.

One night as she is getting ready to leave Jim stands in front of her. Look, he says. I've laid my cards on table. What more do you want. Wanda tries to leave but he stops her. Two hundred pounds, he says. That's my last offer. What do you say? He leans forward waiting for an answer. He is not joking. For the first time Wanda sees there is nothing she can do. If she does not do what Jim wants it will be difficult for her to stay at the club. She has not seen so clearly before how all the cards are in his hands. For a moment she stares at his red, shining face then Mabel calls out, come on Wanda, haven't you got a home to go to? and

Wanda says I'll have to be going Jim, and hurries out. In the cloakroom Mabel takes her arm and steers her into the toilet. What's going on with you and Jim, she says. Wanda decides to tell her. Mabel is scandalised. Two hundred pounds, she says, he only ever gave me fifty. Wanda is surprised now. You mean you, she says, and Jim – ?

Of course, Mabel says. Of course me and Jim. What do you think? She says it with half a laugh, but she is not amused. Wanda does not know what to think. She splashes some water on her face and looks at Mabel in the mirror. So, what do you think I should do, she says. Mabel shrugs and re-applies her lipstick. It's up to you, she says. Do you think I should do it then, Wanda says. Mabel raises her eyebrows and pats her hair into place. You'd be a fool not to, she says.

The next night Wanda goes to the club as usual, but she has not been looking forward to it. She does not know how much longer she can put Jim off. All night she feels his gaze following her around the bar. She wonders when he will speak, and what he will say when he does. But he is quiet that night. Half-way through the evening he disappears into the back room to do some paperwork. The club is nearly empty. In one of the quiet periods Wanda goes up to Mabel. I don't think I can, she says. Mabel lifts one eyebrow. I don't see why not, she says. Wanda looks across at Jim who is talking into the phone. The folds of his face wobble and shine as he talks. Mabel looks too and says, well he's not Clint Eastwood, but you can always shut your eyes. There is a half smile on her face. Close your eyes and open your legs and see what God'll bring you, she says, then she turns to a customer and says, what's your pleasure Alf, or shouldn't I ask.

Wanda collects some glasses, thinking hard. She could really use two hundred pounds, with the next bills coming and all her money gone. She could buy some new things for Coral. They could go on holiday. Then she thinks of Jim and a kind of cold sick fear descends upon her.

Later Mabel is smoking a cigarette by the bar. Wanda stands beside her and Mabel says, made your mind up yet? Wanda shakes her head. I don't think I can, she says. Mabel rolls her eyes. Suit yourself, she says. But what have you got to lose? Two hundred pounds for half-an-hour's work. Where else are you going to get a deal like that eh? Local job centre? She pats her hair and clears some glasses off the bar. Then a few minutes later she says, and another thing, you'll get your job security here. He's not going to sack you afterwards is he? Wanda is not too sure of this, but Mabel seems very sure, confident of her place in the club. Walking past the other way she says, half an hour that's all. Thirty minutes of pushing and shunting and it's all over and done with. And he's not kinky. You've no need to worry about that. Mabel seems anxious to prove a point. Wanda is almost convinced. Then she thinks of Jim pushing and shunting and grunting all over her and she knows she cannot do it.

That night Jim stops her again as she is about to leave. I've had enough of this, he says. He is not smiling. I've offered you two hundred pounds and that's my last offer. So you either let me know one way or another or it's all off. I mean off.

Wanda feels like she is being threatened, but she doesn't know exactly what with. That's the way it is with people in power. They know what they mean and you have to guess. She feels like she has to say something so she says, I'll let you know, Jim, then she grabs her coat and hurries out of the club. This is it, she thinks. She can't go in again unless she decides to take Jim up on his offer, but still when she thinks of the two of them together her skin crawls.

You must be off your head, says Di. Two hundred pounds. Jesus. Where else are you going to get an offer like that. Two hundred pounds for half an hour. Christ. Talk about looking a gift horse in the mouth.

Christ, says Fat Anj. I wish he'd ask me.

No one tells her she shouldn't do it, or gives her one good reason why not. They all think she is mad. Wanda begins to think she is mad as well, especially when the gas and electric bills come and she has no money, and the day seems to drag on for ever when there is nowhere to go in the evening. Still she can't make herself go back into the club and accept Jim's offer. She tells herself she is having a few days off.

Wanda pushes Coral round the stalls on the market, then she shops in the precinct. She tries to find a way out of it all that won't hurt her but she can't. More than anything she hates the thought of being out of work again. Already she feels the slide into apathy and dullness, trudging round shops she can't go in, looking at goods she can't buy. There is nowhere else so convenient for her to work. They don't declare her, she doesn't need a taxi home. She doesn't understand why she can't go ahead and get on with it like Mabel. As she walks round and round the market all the different arguments go round and round inside her head, but they all boil down to this: Wanda should be able to do it if Mabel can. Mabel doesn't think any the less of herself for it, neither should Wanda. When she thinks like this she almost decides she will do it, she will go and see Jim right away. Then the next minute she pictures herself lying still and pale and crumpled beneath the grunting, sweating Jim and she feels cold and sick again. She knows she can never do it. But she doesn't understand why.

Laurie is waiting for her giro. It is raining.

Gusts of rain rattle the window, droplets of water leak through the frame.

Laurie sits staring into the mirror.

There are the usual noises from the surrounding flats, the scraping of chairs, the clatter of crockery, a low murmur of voices. No one is shouting. In the mirror Laurie's face is flat and grey, split by the disjointed crack down the middle. She looks like a boy, with the short hair she cuts herself. Beneath the anorak she always wears, the jeans and jumpers and T-shirts, it is hardly possible to tell she is a woman. She does not look like a man, but a boy. It is like someone has pushed her back in time and left her there, unable to make the transition into woman-hood.

In front of the mirror Laurie twists and turns. Whose eyes is she looking through?

Now that she sees no one from one day to the next, her reflection has become important. Sometimes she presses her face and fingertips right up to the glass looking, and finding something different each time. She is forgetting how to look at herself. She misses the gaze of other people telling her what to see. All those different pairs of eyes, being stripped away from Laurie's own. What will it leave, this stripping-away? Something that is uniquely, essentially Laurie? or nothing at all, a blank space in the mirror.

It is like living in a make-believe world.

In a world of her own.

Living on cloud nine.

She is like the rats she once saw in Mark's laboratory, running round and round a sealed-off circuit with no hope of ever getting into the real world outside.

Laurie looks past the mirror, out of the window. There is Sharon, pushing Paula in the trolley. It is unusual for them to be out so early. In spite of the weather Sharon wears a short skirt and stiletto heels. Her legs are bare.

What kind of make-believe world must Sharon be living in to dress like that, on a day like this, Laurie thinks.

Once Sharon begged Laurie to babysit, she came crying to her flat.

She had no money.

Paula wouldn't sleep through.

She never had a night out.

Laurie felt sorry for her. She seemed so young, at twenty, to be left with a toddler. At least if she sits in Sharon's flat, Laurie thinks, she could look at a different set of walls.

Sharon's walls are covered with posters. Marilyn Monroe is there, James Dean and Humphrey Bogart. Near the door there is a large black-and-white poster of Vivien Leigh, wrapped in Clark Gable's arms. There are other pictures of models and rock groups, wearing shiny black leather and dark glasses. Pages of make-up tips, diet and dancercise instructions are cut out of glossy magazines and tacked to the wall.

Sharon is going to a disco.

Where's me eye-liner, she says, stumbling from one mirror to another. She can't see a thing without her glasses. She is wearing a gold lurex top beneath a black leather jacket, and pink and gold make-up. I'll be back before midnight, she says.

She kicks at Paula's toys and swears. Paula sits silently on the couch.

She'll be a good girl for you, Sharon says, honest. Won't you cherub? Paula does not respond. Sharon cannot find her handbag, comb and then her purse. She sprays herself liberally with perfume. It's imitation Chanel, she says. She hugs and kisses Paula. Mummy'll be back soon, she says. Mummy miss her baby.

Then she is gone, in a cloud of glitter-dust and perfume, promising to be back around eleven.

Paula erupts, hurling her toys and the cheeseplant across the room, swinging on the cupboard door until it breaks. Laurie runs after her saying,

wait a minute Paula,

please be careful,

think of the people below.

When she picks her up Paula drums her feet vigorously into Laurie's legs and smacks her in the eye. She roars when Laurie tries to read to her. Soon Laurie is very tired.

Sharon does not come back by twelve. She is not back by one. At half-past two Laurie hears singing on the landing and shrieks of laughter. Sharon is trying to get her key into the lock. Laurie flings open the door. There is Sharon, propped up against a man old enough to be (possibly) her grandfather. His shirt is open and the hairs on his chest are grey. Together they stagger past Laurie into the lounge. Paula is quiet now. She is sitting on the settee sucking her fingers. When she sees her mother she emits an ear-splitting yell. Ba-bee, Sharon says. She lunges forwards attempting to pick Paula up and the three of them collapse on the settee.

Laurie sees that conversation will be difficult. She grabs her things and goes into the hall, past the poster of Vivien Leigh and Clark Gable, onto the landing which smells of beer and piss, up to her own flat. Inside she can still hear music from the record-player and Paula's far-away bawl.

163

Laurie watches Sharon turn the corner, her thick legs mottled in the freezing rain. No, she thinks, she is not the only one living a fantasy.

That's what Shelagh used to say about Laurie's obsession with her tutor. You're living a fantasy. I suppose you know nothing could ever come of it?

Laurie did know, but it only seemed to make things worse. Sometimes even now the pain recurs quite vividly. She remembers what Shelagh said about it all being a trap for the working-class student. She said that at the height of her paranoia but she never really followed the thought through. And in all her talk she never really answered the question why, when Laurie searches for a description of her obsession, the emotion it seems to resemble most is fear.

Laurie walks from one side of the kitchen to another. At least Sharon can go out, she thinks, which is more than can be said for Laurie, until her giro comes.

Laurie sits at the table. She tries to work out her money for the fortnight. This week she will get thirty pounds. A fortune, says her grandmother's voice. We'd have worked all year for that.

It's different now gran, Laurie says. That is the strange thing about money. Money values go up and up, but the fact remains you never have enough. This week Laurie will have thirty pounds, but she needs fifty. Some things never change. That's what Alex says in his leaflets about the economy. He says that if the income of the masses in this country was ever to meet their needs, the present system would collapse.

At last Laurie hears the steps ascending, past Sharon's flat, towards her own. As the letterbox flips open she hurries into the hall. It is the giro. Laurie clutches it tightly. At last she can go out. Smoky curtains of rain blow across the estate, but she must go out. It will cost her a fortune on the bus but she cannot bear the thought of staying in. Laurie tugs up the zip on her anorak. She is going out. She is going to leave the stained and leaky flat.

It is funny how the bus ride itself becomes important when you have nowhere in particular to go. Laurie catches the first bus that turns up. It is going to the city centre. As usual she sits upstairs. These days it is mainly habit which creates for her a sense of self.

The bus is nearly full. There are shoppers and people like Laurie, converging like birds towards the heated buildings of the city centre, saving on their own bills.

At the next stop the inspector gets on. He glances up and down the bus.

Now then ladies, he says, let's be having you. He begins to collect the tickets.

Nice weather for ducks, he says to an elderly woman near the front. He presses the bell for a young woman leaving the bus. We're good to those we take to, he says, leaning forwards.

He has something to say to every woman on the bus. All the women are nodding and laughing, rows of fur hats, felt hats, knitted hats nodding up and down. But as he approaches Laurie she looks straight into his eyes. They are unfathomably cold. The puckered mouth is like a small pink slit and the light hazel eyes glint icily. He has nearly reached Laurie. She shrinks back in her seat and looks away as she holds out her ticket. He leans over her when he gives it back.

Off to see your boyfriend, he says. Laurie says nothing. Nice day for it, he says, laughing gustily. He passes on and does not seem to notice Laurie's silence. It does not matter to him at all. He is concerned only with the projection of his own image, she is invisible to him. So are all the women, just things that reflect back his image, the image he wants to have. It is only the women he is interested in. There are one or two men on the bus but he only looks at their tickets and says thank you. He must get a better reflection from the women.

He has reached the woman in the back seat now.

Cheer up, he says, it may never happen.

It is a relief when he gets off the bus.

Laurie thinks about looking into his eyes and seeing her own invisibility registering there. She wonders if her invisibility could ever be used to her advantage; if it could ever be anything other than a handicap.

When Laurie gets off the bus she decides to go to the library. It is a long time since she looked at books. When she left university she thought she would never want to look at another book. But now she can browse all day if she likes, without the pressure to learn. She can do her shopping in the late-night shops on the way home.

Laurie touches the books. She buries her face in them and smells them. She has sold all her own books for extra cash. She feels like they have been stolen from her. She feels like she ought to have money for books. Maybe she ought to try stealing them back, she thinks, and regain a great collection. It would be something to do in the flat on the long winter nights. She presses the book she is holding back into place. It's wrong to steal, she thinks.

When Laurie leaves the library her head is buzzing with ideas. She feels like she could go home and write a book of her own. She crosses the square and buys herself a bacon muffin. The rain and wind have died down now. She can always walk a few stops to make up for the money she has just spent.

The sky is a vivid pageant of black and red. Birds are descending in a thick cloud onto the roofs and gutters of the city centre. It is a sight Laurie loves to watch. As she walks she cranes her neck. She cannot stop thinking of Shelagh. They spent a lot of their time together in libraries. Shelagh says the university library is a monument to human ingenuity. Even after three years they cannot find the books they need. Shelagh will only base her essays around critics with unpronounceable names, like Schyzkj, who only wrote two books, but Laurie has a list full of critics with names like Williams, or Taylor. She wanders hopelessly into one section of the library then another. The librarian is unhelpful. He explains patiently what she already knows, that if the book is not on the shelves it will be in the Stack section below, and journals are in a section of their own. Shelagh pulls hideous faces at him behind his back. An architectural iniquity, she hisses, following Laurie around, extemporising itself along the parameters of its own despair. She picks up a book by someone called Williams, but not the one Laurie wants, and opens it. Of course when one says reading a book, she says, one is actually referring to a process of entification from the intrasubjective topography.

Laurie listens and laughs. Increasingly their conversations are this way; Shelagh talking, performing, projecting an image of herself, Laurie listening, applauding, reflecting back to Shelagh her own image.

It is a shock to realise this. Laurie pulls her anorak more closely around her against the night air. She has left the city centre behind, the streets are quiet now, and dark, the only sound the soft flapping of the sole of her boot against the pavement. She is thinking of Shelagh imitating the tutors and critics, reciting *Hamlet*, one way or another managing to acquire the language she began by despising. At first, like a clumsy comedienne, she only managed to grasp its more clichéd aspects, its pretensions. It was not all like that, of course it wasn't, but thinking about it Laurie sees it was inevitable that they should see it that way. But Shelagh managed to go further than Laurie with her language. Far enough, Laurie thinks, to make the transition right out of her own class. Laurie thinks of her lecturers and Shelagh and the bus inspector that morning, all of them using Laurie as a mirror, looking at her but seeing only themselves. And Laurie's language has also changed. She has lapsed more and more completely into silence.

Ahead of Laurie is the subway which will take her to the late-night shops. She hardly sees it. She is thinking of the changes that can happen to you once the way you speak and write and think has changed. She is wondering what will happen in her own life, in the silences she lives in. She enters the dark tunnel of the subway.

*

Wanda does not go into work that night nor the next. Then she is not due in for three days. After that there are other reasons why she can't go in. One night the window in her front door is put in. Wanda sits bolt upright in bed, heart hammering, sure she can hear a hand scrabbling at the inside lock. She shouts out and turns on the light but all she hears are footsteps pounding away on the landing and down the stairs. There is shattered glass all over the floor of the hall. Wanda sweeps it up. She does not know how to get the window fixed. She should report it to the council but that will mean leaving the flat with the open gap in the door where the window was. As she kneels sweeping up splinters of glass with the small dustpan and brush she has the feeling of being trapped, like an insect under glass. Before the voices in her head all start up again she thinks of Di. She will go to Di's and risk leaving the flat for a few minutes. Di will know what to do.

Wanda cannot get back to sleep. In the end she stuffs the gap in her door as well as she can with cardboard and sits on a chair waiting till morning. Nothing else happens that night. In the morning first thing Wanda goes to Di's, thinking Di will maybe sit in the flat whilst Wanda calls the council.

O you don't want council, Di says. They'll only put another glass panel in that'll be broken in no time and they'll make you wait a week for that. What you want, says Di, is one of them metal panels like we've got, and a new lock.

But how can I get them, Wanda says. I'm flat broke. Di waves her cigarette. Kev'll do them for you, she says. I'll tell him when he wakes up. Wanda begins to protest but Di cuts her short. You can pay us back when you're flush, she says.

Wanda feels the same mixture of relief and resentment she always feels when Di offers to do something for her. She knows she can't refuse. Are you sure he won't mind, she says. Of course he won't mind, Di says. Take a seat. But Wanda feels like she should get back in case something happens to the flat. When she looks for Coral, though, she finds her already in front of the video watching the cartoons. Let her stay, Di says, so Wanda goes back to her flat alone.

As she goes back up the stairs Wanda thinks she is tired of always having to say thank you to Di. She is tired of feeling in debt. But she reminds herself that it must be better than messing around with one of the loan sharks who collect around the estate. Even Kev wouldn't mess with them, Di says. Wanda should stay well away. So Wanda goes back to her flat and waits for Kev.

It is a long day, with nothing to do. Wanda is almost frightened by the silence inside, though there is plenty of noise coming from the outside world. She tidies up and cleans the bathroom. Then she watches the luminous colours of the sky and tries to identify the people down below. Pete and Mikey and the gang are playing football up against the wall of one of the low-rise flats. Wanda thinks about what it must be like to sit in all day with the pounding of the football on your walls and your windows rattling. Then she thinks about Jim and his offer, and of all the things she could do with two hundred pounds. Then she thinks about meeting the other man Elsie Mather saw in her cards. He will be a banker, or an accountant. He will have dark hair and be called Terry, or Mark. She will meet him one day when she is sitting on a bench in the precinct. He will have watched her a long time before coming to talk to her. He will be fascinated by her; it will not matter to him about Coral. He will be twenty-six or seven, Wanda will be twenty-one. He will never have met anyone like her before and he will see clearly that she should not be living where she is. In no time he will have asked her to live with him; he can arrange a cheap mortgage. Then he will take hold of her hand and ask her to marry him because he cannot live without her. After that everything moves very fast. The mortgage comes through quickly and Wanda moves in. Coral is four and a half, or five. Wanda is a bit worried that Terry will not marry her if she moves in with him, but things are getting worse at the flats. And there is no need to worry, the wedding is all arranged within a few weeks of her moving in. She is married in a 1920s-style wedding-gown, with a short frothy veil. Afterwards she does the whole house over in Habitat prints, curtains, wallpaper, rugs and furniture, like she has seen in magazines. It is a beautiful house, a three-bedroomed semi with a garden. After a while she has the two boys, Jonathan and Anthony, when Coral is seven, and ten. Terry will get promotion, he will work hard but Wanda will not be lonely, because Terry will be there in the evenings and Coral will help a bit with the boys.

Wanda can see it all clearly, like a moving picture in her mind. When she has finished she feels a kind of blankness inside. She moves around the flat slowly like she is part of her own dream. She has noticed this before, the power of fantasy to suck you in and leave you empty. And your fantasies get stronger when there is nowhere else to go.

Finally there is a knock on Wanda's door. Wanda pushes herself slowly to her feet. It is Kev, with all the gear. Cheer up, he says. It may never happen. As he works he whistles and sings, but to everything he says Wanda just answers yes or no. She feels very strange; in the grip of a powerful strangeness which will not go away. After a bit she goes down the stairs to collect Coral.

Di's door is open and Wanda walks into the lounge. There is Coral with the others, watching a video. Wanda sees the video. There is a black woman all tied up with no clothes on. A white man is pushing his cock into her face. Wanda grabs Coral and drags her out of the room. Di comes out of the kitchen. What's up, she says.

Have you seen what they're watching in there, says Wanda. Di looks round the door and rolls her eyes. Eh you lot, she says. I've told you before about messing with your dad's videos. Get it off.

Aw mam, Gareth says. It's nearly over now.

Wanda is half-way down the hall with Coral. Aren't you stopping for a cup of tea, says Di.

I don't think so, Wanda says.

Why not? says Di.

Wanda is very conscious of not wanting to offend Di, especially whilst Kev is doing her door. I don't really want Coral watching stuff like that, she says. Di looks back over her shoulder. It's off now, she says. Back to Scooby Doo. Come back

171

in and have a cup of tea. Then as Wanda still hesitates she says, I could do your hair for you if you like, the roots are showing.

For a moment Wanda doesn't move. Then she puts Coral down. She lets Di do her hair though it is permed and frizzy enough as it is. When it is still wet she goes back upstairs to see how Kev is getting on.

Kev has just finished. The new panel and lock are in. No one'll get in here now, he says. Wanda is pleased. She offers Kev a cup of tea and puts Coral in the bedroom with her toys. Wanda never knows what to say to Kev. She offers him money for the job, though she doesn't have any, and when he refuses says it must be nice to be rich. Then they sit in silence. When he has finished his cup of tea Wanda wants him to go, but Kev says let's have another cup. Wanda makes him another cup, thinking all the time about how being on the receiving end of things puts you at a disadvantage. The people who are giving hold all the cards. It seems like everyone but Wanda holds the cards. But she takes Kev the cup of tea and then sits looking out of the window at the people scuttling like beetles across the road. Then Kev leans forward and puts his hand on Wanda's arm and strokes it. When Wanda stares at him he says, I've always liked you, Wanda. Wanda can think of nothing to say at all. For a long moment she stares at him then there is a wail from the bedroom. Wanda has never been so glad to hear Coral cry. She jumps up almost knocking the chair over and runs into the bedroom. Kev is following behind. Wanda scoops Coral up and holds her like a shield. You'd best go now, she says, or I'll never get her to sleep. For a minute she thinks Kev is not going to go, then he turns and walks away. Wanda hears the click of the door as he leaves. Still holding Coral she sits down on the bed. This puts a different light on everything. She feels like she cannot go back to Di's. She can't leave Coral there any more. If she gets another job she will have to pay for a babysitter, and maybe a taxi home, the estate is so far from anywhere and cut off. She will never find a job that will pay for both these things and then not declare her to the social. Wanda rubs her forehead with her fingers, letting Coral slip off her knee. Backwards and forwards she rubs with her fingers but it doesn't seem to help. Whichever way she looks at things she is trapped.

No one's helpless, says the voice in her head. There's always a way out. If you've got it in you, you make it in the end.

You have to work for what you get, says another voice. You never get anywhere without work.

If you don't work you deserve everything you get, says another voice. The weakest must go to the wall.

Wanda gets up suddenly, determined to get rid of the voices. She will get Coral ready for bed. They will both have an early night. At least she can go out in the morning now that the door is fixed. She will go to the job centre. Perhaps something will turn up.

At the job centre there is a job for a cleaner but it would cost all her wages to have Coral minded. A shop assistant is wanted at the local supermarket where she went before. All the other jobs want training, qualifications, experience. Wanda turns away from the job centre. Beggars can't be choosers, says the voice in her head. Where there's a will there's a way. She thinks about Jim. You've got to have money to get started, says a voice. Money makes money, that's how the system works. She must do it, she thinks. She will go to see Jim right away. Then without her wanting it to, an image of Jim comes into her mind, and there is the cold sick fear. She does not know why she is so frightened. He makes her sick. Beggars can't be choosers, say the voices in her head.

That day Wanda doesn't have the energy to save money by walking all the way home. So she gets on a bus, the driver and all the passengers glaring at her because she can't get the trolley folded up at the last minute. She pays 30p, instead of the 80p it should be. This means that she has to sit and worry the whole way that inspectors will get on, or that the driver will notice when she gets off. She rests her forehead on the windowpane and watches the streets of the town slide past.

Behind her a woman in a headscarf sits down with a friend and starts talking. On and on she talks, about men in prison that should be hanged, and social-security scroungers and how decent people have to subsidise the ones that don't work. As she talks something strange happens to Wanda. She feels like the woman's voice is getting right inside her, entering every part of her body like there is no resistance. Through and through her skin it goes, like her flesh is open and there are no layers of protection around her; then through and through her bones, like she is not really there at all.

Then when she gets off the bus and reaches the estate, she sees Pete and the other lads at the entrance to the flats where she lives, looking like they have nothing to do. Somehow she will have to get past. As she pushes the trolley towards them she can feel them grinning though she keeps looking down.

Hey Wanda, says Pete, show us your tits. Wanda tries to push the trolley the other way but Pete stands in front of her again. Give us a feel, Mikey says. He stands next to Pete, making clutching movements with his hands. The others stand in front of the doors so she can't get through. Fuck off Pete, Wanda says, and Pete says language. Then Wanda rams the trolley into Pete's legs and he howls in pain. The others fall about laughing, but as she goes into the flats they follow.

There is a notice stuck to the door of the lift. Out of order, it says. Wanda groans aloud. She pushes the trolley through the swing-doors and Pete and Mikey and the others follow. Without looking at them Wanda begins to bump the trolley up the stairs but with each step she takes the others take one too. They all act together like they know what to do without saying. Wanda does not know what to do. She can only hope that they give up before the ninth floor. But at the back of her mind is the small hammering fear that they are not going to give up.

On the second floor Wanda nearly gives up, she is so tired. Then Pete says, come on you lot, give her a hand, and he seizes the front of the trolley. It's alright, Wanda says, I can manage, but Pete does not let go. As she goes up he lifts the trolley and begins to rock it from side to side. Coral doesn't like this and neither does Wanda. Stop it, Wanda says, let go.

It's Mikey, bumping into me, Pete says. Stop it Mikey, there's no room. Pete pushes Mikey and Mikey runs up the stairs to where Wanda is and grabs hold of her end of the trolley. Wanda holds on too, she will not let go. But more hands grab hold of it, heaving it over the stairwell. It is a straight drop, two floors down.

Stop it, Wanda screams, let go.

Rockabye baby, Pete yells, pushing the trolley, and Coral cries loudly.

Inside Wanda a voice is saying that they can't do it, they won't dare, but the rest of her is screaming. She hits out and tears at their hair. It is all she can do because the trolley is now out of her hands. Then a voice says Eh, what's going on. It is Kev. Put it down, says Kev. He has the kind of grin on his face he has when he is beating Di. Mikey begins to lower the trolley to the floor, then Pete shoves it hard, further over the edge. No, Wanda screams. Kev seizes the rail and propels himself feet first towards

Pete. Pete lets go of the trolley and Wanda grabs it. Fuck off Kev, he yells and bounds down the stairs.

After a struggle Wanda gets the trolley back onto the floor and tries to calm the screaming Coral. But she doesn't want to hang around in case any of them comes back. She half-expects Kev to come back up the stairs, offering to help her up. Then she will not be able to get rid of him. Though he has just helped her she does not like him much better than Pete and his gang. When it comes down to it he thinks the same way as them. She has come across it before, people looking at Coral and then getting ideas about Wanda and sex. She doesn't want to see either Kev or Pete again so she bounces the trolley roughly up the stairs. Then, between the fourth and fifth floors it suddenly hits her, what might have happened, and she begins to shake. Soon she is shaking so hard that her knees give way and she collapses on the fifth-floor landing. She wants to get inside her flat and lock the door but she cannot seem to get up again. She will be safe locked up in her flat. But sooner or later she will have to go out, and then what? Wanda tries to push this thought away. She screws her eyes up tightly and covers her ears, but she can still hear the voices hammering away inside her skull – You'll be trapped inside for ever – trapped – trapped – trapped – trapped – trapped –

*

Out of nowhere the man comes.

Got a light, he says.

Laurie is afraid. She shakes her head. The man seems to grow in confidence. He is blocking her view of the exit which is behind him. She must push him hard, she thinks, and run.

Suddenly he is pushing her hard, back into the wall.

What have you got then, he says. He pushes his hand into the pocket of her jeans.

No, Laurie says. She twists away from the wall but he comes after her, his hand still inside her jeans. Again she pulls away and again he follows. It is ridiculous, they are almost dancing. They are staring straight at one another in the half-light. Neither of them is certain what to do. Then there is a noise in another part of the subway. Laurie shouts for help and rushes at him, almost knocking him over. Then he has her. Gripping the bottom of her anorak and its hood he swings her round, yanking her off her feet.

No, says Laurie. No No No

He hauls her back down the passage, her feet scraping the floor, arms flailing.

Nnnh, says Laurie, Nnnh Nnnh Nnnh

She tries to grab the subway railing and her face bumps and scrapes along the wall. Lights flash and spin. Then suddenly the world inverts itself and Laurie is on her back, sprawling like an impaled insect. Somehow he is kneeling on her arms which are above her head. He leans forward over her body and tugs open the anorak zip. Laurie spits and kicks but she cannot reach him. She is suffocated by the weight of him pressing down. He searches her inside pockets. Then he digs his hand into the other pocket of her jeans and scrambles sideways, releasing her. Laurie curls into a ball, arms wrapped tightly round her head.

You must be joking, he says. Don't flatter yourself.

Laurie tilts her head fractionally out of its tucked-in position and peers upwards.

He has her purse.

A different kind of panic seizes Laurie. Slowly he flicks the purse open and withdraws all the money. Must be my lucky day, he says. He throws the purse well past Laurie down the passage. Fetch, he says.

Laurie does not move. Her breathing rasps in her chest. Ta-ta, he says. Then suddenly he is gone, disappearing as quickly as he came into the shadows.

Laurie scrambles towards her purse. It is empty.

She cannot go to the police.

Standing there, clutching the empty purse, Laurie knows she has to go to the police. She will have to try to get some money out of the DHSS, anything, just to tide her over. They will not listen unless she has been to the police. Laurie curses herself.

Why didn't she catch the bus?

Why hadn't she spent the money earlier?

Why did she have to walk down the subway?

A terrible sense of humiliation seeps slowly into her. She wipes her sleeve across her face. The sleeve is wet. Her nose is bleeding. The blood runs through the fingers of her hand and down her sleeve. She presses the other hand against the subway wall and moves unsteadily along the passage. As she moves she hears the blood dripping steadily onto the concrete.

She must look a sight.

She has to go to the police.

Finally, at the thought of this, Laurie begins to cry. She cannot stop herself. Tears roll down and mingle with the wetness on her sleeve. She stumbles out onto the open street where there are lights, and cars. She feels like everyone is looking at her.

*

Valerie sits in the consultant's office.

We will have to operate, he says.

The injuries from the car are not too serious, the real problem is the liver. Unless they operate she will die, and even if they do her chances aren't good.

Valerie stares at the smooth polished wood of his desk. She says nothing. She has always known this would happen. She has been waiting for it all her life.

Her mother was run over on the stretch of road between her flat and Valerie's. It seems she was crouched over at the time the car hit her. The driver may not have been aware that he hit someone. She suffered bruising and broken ribs, nothing too serious. But for some reason she did not get up again. She lay there for hours, on a night of unprecedented cold. Valerie thinks about her mother, lying in the road like a slug. She feels the urge to laugh.

They will need Valerie's permission for any treatment they give her mother. After the operation, if it's successful, they will need her consent to any further treatment. The consultant recommends institutionalised care, electrotherapy. He coughs sympathetically. But first they will need her permission to operate.

He expects Valerie to say something.

She says, so all you want to do is to cut up her liver and burn out her brain.

The consultant is less sympathetic now.

It's her only chance, he says.

Valerie thinks of her mother lying blind and shrivelled on the hospital bed, tubes running into her from all directions. It seems she will either die or live an invalid in an institution. How can I make that decision, she thinks. But she knows she will have to, because yesterday she was eighteen years old.

The consultant explains that they will need her permission as soon as possible. Valerie feels a terrible anger against her mother.

Without looking at the consultant she pushes back her chair and leaves his room.

She must get out of the hospital, she thinks. She rounds the corridor and pushes open the swing-doors. She is outside, in the very pale, intense light of early winter.

*

The police interrogate her about the man.

What did he look like?

Was he black?

How tall was he?

What was his voice like?

Laurie does not know. She sees him vividly and yet cannot see the details. White, she thinks, not very tall, a northern accent. More northern than here.

Where then, they want to know. How tall exactly?

She is sent into another room.

Were you sexually assaulted? the policewoman asks. She has a bright, hard stare like glass. Laurie thinks of him slowly flicking open her purse, fingering the money. It feels like an assault.

No, she says. She signs another piece of paper.

They want to know all about her.

How old is she?

What is her occupation?

How long has she lived at her present address?

Laurie watches them putting together a picture of her she does not recognise. They think she is unemployed and wants to claim extra from the social. She signs more papers. Her hands are shaking so she can hardly write. They examine her signature closely.

As Laurie sits in the grey stuffy room with the fluorescent lights, she begins to feel like she has always been there, like she will never leave. She feels like they will find something out about her on the computers, something she does not even know herself, and keep her there. As she stares at the yellowing 'wanted' posters, the fire regulations and peeling paint, she feels the ugliness of her life, the loss of beauty, like an amputation. She stares down at the floor.

They have not finished with her yet. They make her go over everything she has just said and ask her if it is true. They ask again if she has been sexually assaulted. Laurie nods and shakes her head. They make her speak up.

She is very tired. Her head feels bad, it is very hot. Her arms and legs are beginning to stiffen with bruises, there is a pain in her stomach. She is sure she is sick.

She wants to go home. They tell her how lucky she is, it could have been a lot worse. She was lucky she wasn't raped, wandering around subways like that after dark, all that money in her purse. She ought to be more careful. She can go now but she should be more careful next time, or she might not be so lucky.

Laurie does not feel very lucky. If he had raped her she might at least have had some money left to live on. She asks them how she is going to live through the next fortnight without any money. They can't answer that, it is not their department. She should have thought of that before she went hanging round subways in the dark with a fortnight's money in her purse.

Laurie leaves. She edges her way through the shadows on the streets, wincing sharply at every sound. At last she gets home. She pulls open the door at the entrance to her flats and she is inside, on the landing, with its familiar smells of cigarettes and beer and piss, the scrawled letters, MUFC, Kelly is a cunt, the broken glass. Someone has dropped a packet of chips and trodden them into the stairs.

Laurie lets herself in. She wants a bath. She runs the water though it is not very warm. She thinks of the ways it could have been, of outsmarting him, fighting back harder, hurting him, producing a knife, a gun, firing straight into the leering face.

The water is lukewarm. As she climbs in her skin goes to gooseflesh. She twists and turns in the water, trying to get comfortable. Her back hurts.

Tomorrow she must go to the DHSS. It will take all day. Even if they decide she is deserving they will only give her part of the money she has lost. That is the law.

She thinks of resisting the man to the point of death, of him producing a knife, hurting her much more than he actually did, of being discovered in a pool of blood. She remembers him hauling her through the subway. She wishes he had killed her.

Laurie stirs and shifts in the water, trying to get warm. She thinks about going to the doctor, asking for some tablets. I'm so nervous doctor I just can't sleep. The doctor writing the prescription. Laurie coming home, getting into bed. It would be just like going to sleep.

Laurie stares at the greenish water, the long bony toes protruding from it at the other end of the bath. There is a dragging pain in her stomach. She looks down, between her legs. There is the blood, in a thin pink curl like smoke.

*

One day the social worker comes. You may as well let me in, she says, through the door. I'm not going to give up that easily. It won't look good if you don't let me in. Either I'll be back or someone else from the department. You'll have to let us in sooner or later.

Wanda leans against the door with her eyes closed. She wants the voice to go away. But the social worker knocks again. If you don't let me in I shall have to take the matter further, she says. Wanda opens her eyes onto the devastation of her flat. What's the use of having a lock, she thinks, if you can't keep anyone out. Suddenly and savagely she undoes the locks. Thank you, says the social worker, and steps inside. Wanda follows the woman down the hall. They pick their way through shattered glass, litter, broken crockery and dirty washing. In the front room the social worker picks up one of the chairs that has been knocked over and sits on it. Coral is eating a piece of bread and jam on the floor. May I examine her, the social worker says. She examines Coral, turning her this way and that. The police are rather concerned about her, she says.

The police. Banging on the front door till they almost burst it off its hinges, then pushing it back so hard she is thrust into the wall.

They're a bit worried about your childminding arrangements.

Emptying the litter bins and all the drawers onto the floor, grinning over her underwear, lifting the mirror and dropping it so that it smashes into a thousand tiny pieces . . .

They suggested that Coral's case should be investigated.

And the officer in charge says, not wearing anything under that T-shirt are you love . . .

Wouldn't you say that your choice of a childminder is a little unusual?

Funny company you're keeping, the police say. Wanda will not answer any questions. She keeps her jaw tightly shut to stop it trembling.

How often do you leave Coral with Mr and Mrs Gee, the social worker says.

The police officer inspects Wanda's hands and arms, taking her hands in his and turning them over. Then he steps forwards.

Wanda has to step backwards. He steps forwards again and she steps backwards. They are almost dancing . . .

Did you know they are involved in peddling drugs.

If Wanda says anything she will make it worse. It will not come out right. That's the way it is with people in power, whatever you try to say comes out as what they want to hear. It is like they put a frame round you and in that frame everything you say seems wrong because it is out of place.

Why did you need to leave Coral with Mrs Gee?

Wanda does not want them to know she has been working. They seem to know already that she has been claiming. It is like there is a big pool of information about Wanda and everyone except Wanda has access to it.

I'd advise you to tell me now, or you'll only make things worse for yourself . . .

When the police officer has made her walk backwards all the way across the room he says, I don't think you're telling us everything you know. And if I find out you've been keeping something back it'll be worse for you. Understand?

The social worker is not pleased by Wanda's silence, but she cannot find anything wrong with Coral. Wanda takes Coral off the social worker's knee and sits holding her and staring at the floor. She can almost hear the social worker making notes in her head; uncooperative, probably something to hide.

There will have to be an investigation, she says, both the social services and the DHSS will have to be notified. She will try to ensure that payment of benefits does not cease during the period of the investigation for Coral's sake, but Wanda should expect a visit any day.

I'll be going now, she says. I'll see myself out.

Wanda sits very still. She is going to be investigated. But she doesn't know what that means. Someone will be following her around, asking questions, making reports. What else does it mean? When she thinks about it the social worker hasn't said very much, and what she has said is not very clear. What she has not said, however, comes over loud and clear. She does not think Wanda is a fit mother. She is going to arrange for Wanda to be assessed by people who think the same way. And what they think counts for a lot more than what Wanda thinks.

Wanda walks around the room rubbing her hands against the material of her skirt. Then she presses her fingers to her forehead. She can't look for work now, she thinks, she is being investigated. They might take her money off her. They might take her to court. She feels like she is clinging to a rock, with a bright light switched on her and people staring at her from all directions. They will take Coral off her, she thinks, because she can't cope. But they have made it so she can't cope . . .

Wanda walks up and down the front room, then down the hall, then into the kitchen, then the bedroom. They have made her feel like she is in the wrong. She can only see herself through their eyes. She cannot remember her own side of the story. She is in the wrong. It is the only place she can be.

Wanda shuts the bedroom door and presses her head against it. She moves her head from side to side and presses both hands to it as hard as she can. It feels like it is bursting. All the words in her head are chasing themselves round and round. Then from somewhere in the room there is a high strangled whine. Then it is coming from her; tearing itself up from her stomach and lungs over and over again; a dreadful noise, like the noise of an animal being murdered.

The next day there is no food in the house. Wanda wakes up early with the familiar thudding in her stomach and chest. The thought of there being no food in the house makes it worse. She has to go out. People will be watching her. Pete and his gang will be on the stairs. The investigator will be parked outside. But she will have to go out for some food. If she goes out very early she might not run into them. She can worry about getting back later. Slowly she dresses Coral and doesn't notice when Coral whines. By the time she is ready to go out the fear is unbearable. Her mouth is very dry, she is covered in a light cold sweat. She needs something to calm her down. I will go to the doctor's, she thinks.

It is hard to leave the flat. But it is only half-past seven and she does not meet anyone. She checks in the car park, but there is no one sitting silently behind the wheel of a car waiting for her.

By the time she gets to the doctor's all the voices are clamouring in her head like a flock of birds.

Can't even look after her own kid.

Might make her pull herself together.

They don't deserve to have children.

When she has got the tablets she unscrews the top right there in the street and takes one, then another, though it says to just take one on the label. Then after a bit there is a dull, deaf silence like cotton wool. As she walks along the street she feels like she is going slower and slower. Soon she has a feeling like she is trapped in glass. She is moving through panes of thick glass that give way as she walks but will not let her through. It is like being trapped in a massive lens. But she is not frightened, for the first time in weeks. She feels like she will never be frightened again.

So while she feels like this she does what she feels she has been meaning to do for a long time. She pushes her way slowly in the moving panes of glass, through the streets as they fill up with people and traffic, to the Comfy Club. She watches herself moving towards it. She seems far away.

There is no one there of course, except for the cleaner, but Wanda leaves a message: Tell Jim to come round if he still wants to do business – Wanda. She says it as clearly as she can with the thickness in her tongue, and watches whilst the cleaner writes it down with a stub of pencil and then leaves it on the bar for Jim to find. Then she makes her way home with a feeling like it is all over now, it has all just rolled away. Nothing frightens her, not even going home. She has made a decision and she is going to go through with it.

Later when the tablets wear off she is not so sure. She is nervous and jittery, but she keeps thinking about the two hundred pounds and about it only taking half an hour. Still she cannot settle. She sits down and gets up again, and then wanders from the window of one room to another. She looks down at the car park, at a long black car she is sure she has seen before. Maybe it is the investigator. She snaps at Coral for no reason, then hugs her. She tells herself it doesn't matter about the investigator in the car park, they can't object to her having visitors. But all the time she is frightened that they already know what she is going to do. They know everything about her. Even now they are reading the message she left Jim.

Wanda takes another tablet to stop herself thinking like this. Later she makes toast for Coral, though she cannot eat anything herself. When she finally gets Coral to sleep she puts on the black dress. She puts on lipstick and combs out her hair. She needs to look as good as she can tonight. Then she sits down by the table and watches the moon in the clouds.

From this angle she cannot see the roofs and chimneys of the town, just the cold white moon. She feels like it is attached to her by a long invisible string, disappearing behind a drift of clouds then coming out again. It will always come out again, no matter what happens to Wanda. Even when she is gone the moon will drift in and out of her windows. It is a strange thought, but comforting. She feels like nothing matters, not the investigator, not Wanda and Jim, for the moon will always be there, fat and buttery, or pale and thin like it is now, like it was when she was with Sim. Wanda feels almost calm as she watches the moon and sits by the little table, waiting for Jim.

*

Towards the end of their time together Larry got a job. It was a good job with the unions, and regular pay. Larry was pleased. Coral however was lonely and bored. She typed from time to time then prowled around the flat. She moved from the window of one room to another watching for Larry. Sometimes he had to work extra hours or weekends and then Coral fell into a kind of hopelessness. More and more often he would be late without telling Coral.

One Saturday Larry said he was going to a union meeting in Manchester. Coral wanted to know if he wasn't away often enough without going at weekends too. Larry said he had no freedom. Coral turned away from him and stirred the soup on the stove. Larry left without saying goodbye.

After he had gone Coral decided to make his favourite meal, pizza, for his return. Pulling on her shoes and coat she hurried out. She dragged out the shopping a little, hoping he might already be there when she got back, but the flat was still empty. Coral cheered herself up with the thought of the pizza as she unloaded her bags. She cooked it carefully, preparing the bread dough, frying onions, mushrooms, peppers, heating the tomatoes gently with basil.

Larry does not come back. Towards midnight Coral leaves the flat and wanders the streets crying. She does not know how to look. Several times she returns to the outside of the flats where they live, scouring the windows for a spot of light, but the windows stare back vacantly. He has had an accident, she thinks, but she cannot go to the police. They spend all their time trying to avoid the police.

Coral sits on the stone stairs leading up to the flat. They are cold and dank. They smell of urine and there are huge sprawling letters on the wall. There are cigarette stubs all over the stairs, smashed beer bottles and dented cans. Crisp and chip papers blown by the breeze from under the door chase each other round the bottom landing. Coral is getting numb and stiff but she cannot face the empty flat. In the end though she hauls herself up the stairs and lets herself in. She walks around a little then goes to bed.

In the stark white morning Coral awakens alone. She clambers out of bed and hurries into all the rooms of the flat but Larry isn't there. Coral sinks heavily into a chair.

Minutes later Larry lets himself in. Coral rushes to the door but in response to her frantic questions he is silent. She clutches at him and he pushes her away. He goes to the bedroom, pulls out his bag from the wardrobe and begins stuffing his things into it.

Coral screams at him, why, why, what is he doing, but Larry says nothing. She rushes at him and strikes out hard at his chest and face. Larry raises his fist. Coral sees the blow coming towards her, she will always see it this way. She hears a crunching sound as his fist smashes into her face. For a moment she is struggling for balance, then there is a sharp, terrible pain as the

base of her spine hits the corner of the open drawer. A low
moaning noise is pulled from Coral and everything goes black.
When she opens her eyes she is staring upwards and Larry is
staring down at her. Coral will always see his face. He is looking
at her as if she is nothing to do with him, as if he doesn't know
her at all.

Coral sits with her face in her hands. Already Larry's visit is
taking on the tinge of unreality. She no longer knows what is real
and what is not. None of it makes any sense.

*

Jim does not come that night. At two o'clock Wanda undresses
for bed. Anything could have happened, she thinks, taking
another tablet. Maybe he will come tomorrow.

The next night Wanda dresses up again and sits by the table in
the front room. She plays with the lipstick, turning it over and
over on the table. She is beginning to feel ridiculous. All dressed
up and nowhere to go, says the voice in her head.

Jim'll be here soon, she thinks. Maybe he will just be friendly,
and say something that will make everything alright, even when
they are in bed together. It will be just like being with a friend.

Then as the time ticks slowly by she thinks, maybe he didn't
get the note, it could have been lost, dropped onto the floor. Or
maybe he has lost interest. Maybe he is getting what he wants
from Melanie. Anything could have happened. She thinks of him
reading the note aloud to the other people in the club, and telling
them what kind of business she wants to do. She begins to think
he never fancied her at all, he was just playing some kind of joke
so he could laugh at her later.

Now he has not turned up she cannot stop thinking about the
money. She thinks of all the things she could buy with two

hundred pounds. She thinks of them with a kind of savage hunger. She thinks of him coming back every week and bringing her two hundred pounds each time. She tries to stop herself thinking about it but she can't. She sits by the table in the little room watching the moon get thinner and thinking about the two hundred pounds.

Then the next night Jim arrives. Wanda is not dressed up at all. She stares at him and puts her hand up to her hair. What's up with you, he says as he walks in. He sits down on her settee and takes off his jacket and shoes. Wait a minute, Jim, says Wanda, and hurries into the bedroom. She cannot face him like this. She kicks off her trainers and jeans and looks round for something to wear. The room is a mess, there is dirty washing all over the floor. The black dress is crumpled on the floor too, where Wanda left it last night. Wanda grabs the blue dress Jim always liked and pulls it on. She drags a comb through her hair and dabs on some powder-blue eye-shadow. Then she gathers up the dirty washing and dumps it in the bath. She slips on the blue sandals and picks Coral up, wrapping her in the duvet. All the time she is doing these things she is watching herself and the movements of her hands. It gives her something to think about other than Jim. She carries Coral through to the lounge and settles her down on the sofa. Jim is standing by the window.

That's better, he says. I was beginning to wonder why I bothered. He has loosened his tie, opened his shirt. Wanda will not look at him. She does not know what to do or say so she keeps herself partly turned away from him, fussing with the duvet cover. She is taken by surprise when he comes up behind her and squeezes her tightly.

Very nice, he says. Now how about taking it all off again.

Wanda pushes him away and walks unsteadily into the

bedroom. It is not going to be alright, she can tell. They are not going to be friends.

Behind her Jim sits down heavily on the bed. The sense of unreality deepens. Wanda wishes none of this was happening. It is like a dream she cannot wake out of. She wishes she had taken a tablet. Behind her Jim is waiting. She cannot get undressed in private. He wants his money's worth.

Then Wanda thinks she doesn't need a tablet. She can play it Jim's way if he likes, why not, since she can't play it hers. It is Jim's game. She can be exactly what he thinks she is.

Slowly, with her back still turned to Jim she begins to move in time to the music in her head, to the lights and cameras focused on her. She lifts her skirt up slowly, bending over to show Jim her knickers. She kicks off her sandals one at a time and unzips the dress. Jim laughs like a schoolboy as she throws each item his way. She throws the blue dress over her shoulder at him and then the knickers. It is all happening in her head just like a film. When she has finished she strikes a theatrical pose.

Jim's face is very red and shiny. He pats his knee. Wanda moves over towards him and sits down lightly. But Jim holds her hard and jiggles her up and down so that her breasts bounce and shake. Bylo baby bunting, he says. Then he laughs suddenly and his tongue sticks out. It is thick and red.

Finally in the bedroom Wanda hears a snuffling noise. Cowal? she says. It is not from under the bed, she has looked there before. She looks behind the curtain, but Coral is not there. Then she opens the wardrobe door and pushes back some clothes. There is Coral, crouched down behind Wanda's coat. Coral has no clothes on. She is very cold. There are bruises and bite marks all over her body. Wanda is very frightened as she lifts her out. I can't take her to nursery, she thinks. If the social worker comes she will not let her in. Coral whimpers and her head lolls to one side in a funny way. Wanda feels worse and worse inside. She doesn't know if she is more frightened because she has done this to Coral, or because she might have done serious damage, or because she doesn't remember doing it at all. All she remembers is Coral being bad when Wanda was trying to feed her. She has been refusing most of her food recently. Wanda has to spoon-feed her to make sure she gets some of it down. She buys in special food that she cannot afford, but today Coral smacked the bowl down onto the rug and screamed. Then Wanda held her down tightly, spoon-feeding her from another bowl, but Coral spits it out, spraying the food all over Wanda's face. After this Wanda remembers nothing.

Wanda holds Coral on her knee and croons softly to stop her whimpering. She strokes the hair above her ear which is sticky with blood. Then she carries her through to the bathroom and washes her gently, gently, but Coral still cries hard. Then she carries her into the bedroom and tucks her up in Wanda's bed and tries to get her head straight on the pillow. She strokes Coral's hair until she goes to sleep.

Later, in the lounge, her fear gets worse and worse. She thinks the social worker will come, and the police, demanding to be let in. They could have planted film and tape in the flat and have the whole thing on record. Perhaps they are watching it now. Wanda stares wide-eyed at the central-heating ventilator. Perhaps there is a camera in there and it is all on film. She stumbles over to the ventilator and presses her hand across it, fingers spread wide. Then she turns round, covering her mouth with her other hand because she thinks she is going to be sick. She will tear down a curtain from the window and hang it in front of the ventilator. She hurries over to the curtain but as she clutches it she sees the thermostat dial behind. It is in there, the camera is in there.

Wanda falls back, clutching at her face and hair. There is a shadow behind the long curtain. Someone is out there, on the balcony, filming everything for use as evidence against her. Her hands rub the material of her skirt up and down, then she drops on all fours. But it is no good. The cameras automatically adjust, focusing downwards. Wanda scuttles sideways to the door like a crab, but the door is shut. She is trapped in this room with all the cameras focusing their lenses on her. She puts a hand up to her face. No, she says. Her voice is high and shrill. Leave me alone, she says, get out. There is a rustle of the curtain but nothing moves. Still scuttling sideways Wanda presses herself into the space behind the settee. She crouches there, head tucked in, arms above her head. No, she whimpers. Go away. Go away go away go away go away . . .

*

Coral goes into the kitchen. She fills the kettle though she is almost out of tea.

Why does she tell herself such terrible stories?

When Larry left he walked from room to room methodically packing his things. Coral followed him around, not knowing what to do or say. She cannot bear to see him go, but all she can do is watch as the last things are packed away. There is a swelling sensation in her throat and she does not want to cry so she cannot speak. When Larry has fastened his suitcase he pauses for a moment with his back to her. Then he turns to face her but neither of them speak. Coral can hardly see his face. She does not want him to go without seeing his face properly. Larry reaches out and strokes her cheek, she will always see his hand reaching out.

I'll be in touch, he says, alright?

Coral nods blindly but she feels a desperate fear. She feels that her stomach is all twisted and she can hardly breathe. Then Larry turns and picks up his bags and walks past her without looking up. Coral grips the bedroom door and he goes up the hall. He opens the front door then pauses and half turns round.

Well goodbye then, he says. He walks out, closing the door. That is the last she ever sees of him.

*

The flower-beds are brilliant in the autumn light. All other colours fade in its intensity. The trees are nearly naked but there are a few leaves left, clinging golden to the tapering boughs. Everywhere is light and colour. Valerie flinches away. Her head is hurting. She crosses to the shade and turns a corner.

And there is Marcie, holding flowers.

Marcie, says Valerie.

Marcie holds her very tight and guides her to the steps. They sit down on the cold stone. Marcie's arm holding flowers is draped loosely round Valerie's neck. Valerie can smell the perfume of the flowers. She just wants to sit there in the light with her eyes closed, smelling the perfume of the flowers.

After a while Marcie says, how's your mother. Valerie tries to tell her. The story all comes tumbling out. She does not know if she is making sense. When she finishes there is silence, then she says, I just feel like I never had a mother, but now I'm expected to take responsibility for her.

Marcie says nothing for a minute, then she says, well, you do have a mother. Even if she'd only carried you for nine months it'd be something, but she wasn't always like she is now. And probably, you know, she did her best.

Valerie is shocked by this idea. It has never occurred to her before. But Marcie goes on, in a soft, hesitant voice.

It isn't easy, having kids. You start off with the best intentions in the world, but somehow they never quite work out. Every night you put them to bed and think, I'll be better to them tomorrow, but the next day comes and it's all just the same again. It all gets on top of you. It gets me the way the mother always gets the blame if something goes wrong when there's all these other things to think about – where you live, how much money you have, the school, what your husband's like if you have one. It's all out of your control somehow, before you know where you are. All the odds are stacked against you.

She is silent a minute and then says, your mother'll have done her best you know. She'll have set off like the rest of us, all high hopes and good intentions, maybe more than the rest of us because she were on her own, having to prove herself, and then it'd all get out of hand. She'd have to watch it all getting out of hand, crumbling away. It can't have been easy . . .

Valerie is thinking about the idea of her mother doing her best. It seems incredible, impossible, but somehow true. It may look like she maliciously planned to do her worst, but it was not like that. All the time she was doing her best . . .

Marcie is getting up. She says, I just wanted to take her these flowers. Are you coming? Valerie shakes her head. She hears the click of Marcie's heels retreating, then slowly she gets up.

She is going away from the hospital. She can't give them her decision just yet. She will go to her mother's, to pick up the things she needs for the hospital.

*

Laurie will never be so vulnerable again. Even now when she remembers that day she feels a weakening rush of shame and pain. But it will never happen again. She has constructed for herself a form of defence.

She is going shopping. Not just for food this time but for supplementary items, vitamin pills, agnus castus, oil of evening primrose, propolis tincture, pulsatilla. She is going to visit the health shop.

Some time ago Laurie's periods became irregular and then stopped. The doctor did not seem to think this was worth bothering about, but it worried Laurie, because the symptoms of her period would intensify for weeks though nothing happened. It was like living in suspension. At the library she read about the supplements she could take, but they were all expensive.

Laurie packs empty cartons and bottles into her bag. She looks at herself in the new mirror with the chrome frame. Her face is small and pointy. There are three spots on her chin. She sticks her chin out examining them. It is nearly time for her period.

Laurie is like a child, looking forward to the acquisitions of the day. She hums to herself as she pulls on the anorak, the fingerless gloves. Just give me money, she hums, that's what I want. She skips down the stairs two at a time.

Phyllis is not in the health shop today. There is a new shop assistant. Her face pinkens as more and more people pile in. Laurie asks to see the agnus castus tablets, and the oil of evening primrose. She pretends to examine the labels. Then she swaps them for the cartons she has with her, the seals carefully replaced. You could only tell the difference if you looked closely. The shop assistant does not look closely. She runs to the back of the shop, and again to the till, then to the next customer.

Thank you, says Laurie, I don't think these are quite what I want.

The shop assistant doesn't even look up.

Laurie leaves the shop. Easy, she thinks. Nothing to it. She hardly has to think about it these days. But she can't get all the stuff she needs from the same shop, that would be pushing her luck too far. And she can't visit the same shop twice in too short a space of time. This means a lot of walking around. Already Laurie feels a faint tinge of weariness as she sets off towards the next shop. The sky is wet and silvery, like a trout.

Echoes of pain recur. A trap, she thinks, a trap for the working-class student. She rounds the corner and the traffic thickens. She remembers going into the big university, the kind of displacement she felt, the loss of power, the sense of being invisible.

At the next health shop she buys an ounce of pulsatilla, and as the shopkeeper measures it out, slips the propolis tincture and vitamin-B capsules into her bag. She is sweating slightly as she leaves the shop, but once again no one has noticed. Sometimes she almost wishes someone would. That would stop her, but she can't imagine what her life would be like if she stopped. Fantasy, she thinks, she would lapse wholly into fantasy, like at university. The less power you have, the more fantasy. She turns at the corner towards the flea market.

She feels lighter now, more irresponsible. She picks up socks at the flea market just for fun. But she is ready to go home. All she wants now is something to eat. One of the new soups she saw last time in the local supermarket, Mexican chili, Indonesian sayoran. She will go and talk to Joan, or Sue.

She remembers wanting her tutor to notice her, to recognise and appreciate her unique gifts. It was like there was no other way to express her gifts, they had to be noticed, recognised, or she would remain invisible for ever. When he did not notice her it was like being totally erased.

At the supermarket Laurie settles for cream of asparagus soup and croissants. She talks to Joan about soaking her feet in hot water with oil of cloves.

Then, as she is leaving, there is a hand on her arm. Laurie half-turns, smiling, her heart hammering.

Will you come with me, the man says. The pressure tightens on her arm.

Laurie offers no resistance. She walks back with him through the store, past the astonished faces of Joan and Sue. He takes her to a room at the back of the shop. He asks her to take out of her bag the things she has just taken from his store. I haven't taken anything, she says.

His assistant empties her bag.

What's all this then, he says.

Laurie says nothing. She is thinking, unaccountably, of Joan and Sue.

The manager phones the police.

Then Sue comes into the back room.

Excuse me sir, she says. There's a woman wants to know if we'll order something for her.

She is looking at Laurie. Laurie looks away. She digs her fingers into the palms of her hands.

The manager tells Sue he will be out in a minute. Then he walks round the desk and looks at Laurie. This is a very serious offence, he says.

The manager goes on and on. Laurie stares at the floor and at the smooth polished wood of the desk. His name is printed on a plaque and on a badge on his jacket, Mr Harrop. There is a jagged scar on the shiny surface of the desk. The scar and the surface of the wood are the only things that are real, everything else is a dream. It is all happening with the curious inevitability of a dream.

The police arrive. They talk with the manager as if they are friends, about the price of stock these days. The manager is genial and smiling. They talk as if Laurie is not there at all. She feels like a very small child, listening to a conversation she is not meant to hear. She feels very cold.

The officer nods his head towards Laurie. This the one, he says.

Aye, says the manager. The officer picks Laurie's bag up off the table. Come on you, he says.

There is a policeman on either side of Laurie holding her arms. They lead her back through the store. Laurie looks downwards all the way. She does not look at Joan or Sue. She is taken outside to the car and told to sit in the back. The car is cold, but when she thinks of the police station she feels very hot, with a suffocating, clammy heat. They pull off into the traffic and it is like they are not moving at all but a stream of shop windows and lamp-posts and people is rushing endlessly past. Laurie feels like a snare is tightening about her face and neck. She feels she has been walking into it all her life.

Laurie sits pressed into a corner of the police station. They have taken her fingerprints. When they emptied her bag all the tablets rolled out. They are very interested in all the pills.

They ask her a lot of questions. Laurie says nothing at all. She wants to but she cannot speak. They pierce the capsules with a pin and sniff the contents cautiously. They ask her what other kind of pills she takes.

The policewomen arrive. Get up, they say.

Laurie wants to, but she cannot move. They take hold of her arms and haul her out of her chair, not roughly. As they go along the corridor her feet drag along the floor. They come to a room with a cubicle in it. Laurie is told to take off her clothes. When they let go of her arms she sags downwards but they pick her up again. One of the policewomen helps her into the cubicle. You may as well get it over and done with, she says.

Inside the cubicle Laurie feels cold again, so cold she can hardly unzip her clothes. She pulls her anorak off with the zip only part-way down. She can hear the policewomen talking outside. One of them is going out with someone called Arthur. He is taking her to the pictures tonight. She is wondering whether or not to henna her hair, to bring out its natural red.

Laurie takes off all her clothes and passes them one at a time through the door. Some of them are grubby. There is a hole in her T-shirt and in both her socks. She feels like she is handing over all the squalor of her life. She unhooks her bra and slips her knickers off. She is crying with the cold, her face is wet. The policewoman taps on the door of the cubicle. You can come out now, she says.

*

None of that seems to matter now that she is looking for the last time at the view she has seen so many times from her balcony window. The sky is an even grey, but with thin ribbons of orange where the sun has been. The town is lighting up. Coral is playing on the different landings of the flats, running up the stairs and jumping down. She knows she must not go outside, but Wanda cannot keep her in the flat any more, it is too small and cramped and the neighbours complain if she is noisy. The bath is ready. Wanda looks round at the front room as if trying to hold it all in her mind. She looks at the pink sofa, and the small table with the two chairs, and at the blank spaces where the pictures and the rugs and the telly used to be. She tries to remember the room as it was, before Di came.

Wanda was watching the telly in the front room when she heard a noise in the hall. When she went to look, Di was there.

How did you get in, Wanda says. Di holds up a key. Kev had one made when he fixed your lock, she says. In case you lost yours, like, and were ever stuck. Wanda says nothing and Di says, we haven't seen you for a while, we've missed you, kids and me. So I thought I'd come to see how you were getting on, and why you haven't been round. Can I come in? Di makes as if to walk into the lounge but Wanda stays where she is, in the doorway. I'm not coming round any more Di, she says. Not after the other night. Di takes a cigarette out of a packet. O that, she says, lighting up. That were nothing. Police do that regular round here. Happens to everyone.

Well I don't want it happening to me, Wanda says. They're having me investigated you know. I can't earn any more money. Di gives Wanda a sharp sideways look. At least not regular way eh, she says.

Wanda flinches like she has been hit. The trembling feeling starts in the pit of her stomach. O don't worry, Di says. No one need find out. Not social worker, or anyone like that. She looks at Wanda closely from beneath her eyelids.

You'd better go now, Wanda says. Di inhales.

So you won't be wanting my services any more, she says.

What do you mean, says Wanda.

You know, says Di. Babysitting, mugs of tea, the odd fiver here and there, new door. We'd best reckon up.

I haven't got any money, Wanda says. The trembling in her stomach is worse, now there is a thudding noise in her ears.

Did I say anything about money? Di says. She looks past Wanda, through the open lounge door. I always liked them pictures, she says.

Wanda feels like it is hard to believe this is happening in her own flat. She feels like she must be able to get Di out. So she stands very straight and stiff and says Get out. Now. Di doesn't move. Long shadows flicker in the hollows of her face. Not just yet, she says.

So that was how Wanda came to lose the pictures. Di took them with her there and then. Later she came back with Gareth for the telly and the large plant, the rugs and the clothes from Wanda's wardrobe, including the black dress, though it is too small for Di. Probably she will sell it.

Whilst Di is taking the things Wanda sits at the little table, eating one pill, then another. She feels helpless, paralysed by all the things she has ever done or failed to do in her past. She feels like she does not care any more. She feels almost relieved, like the feeling of debt she lives with all the time has been eased a little bit. Coral runs round Gareth and laughs when he pulls faces at her. Wanda leans back and closes her eyes. She feels like she should hate Di but she doesn't. That night she dreams about a face, trapped beneath the frozen surface of a pond. The eyes are open and the lips move like it is trying to say something, but no sound comes through the ice. When Wanda looks it is Di's face, but when she looks again it is her own. So she can't hate Di. They are too much alike.

Down below Mr and Mrs Whitcombe inch their way across the estate as they do every Thursday. Mr Drayton stands at the bottom of his garden in his shirtsleeves, for though it is winter he never dresses any other way. The bottom flats of Dunkirk Terrace have a small unfenced square of lawn each, with a bush or two. Mr Drayton is trying to make a trampled bush stand up again. When he has finished the gang on their bikes will come back, roaring over his lawn and its tattered bushes, emptying his dustbin over the path. Some time after they have gone Mr

Drayton will clear away the litter and tend to his ripped-up lawn, like a kind of penance. For Mr Drayton was once in court for messing with a little boy, though nothing was ever proved. Before that, a long time ago, he was a pharmacist, but he lost his job for supplying drugs to his wife. He lost his house too, and came to live on the estate. Then his wife died and after that there was the court case. Wanda used to avoid Mr Drayton, pushing Coral quickly by if she happened to see him. When she saw him she always felt a slow chill. She used to wonder how far it is possible to go on the downward slide. Now that she knows she can look at him without feeling anything at all. For Wanda has slid further than she ever thought it was possible to go, especially now she is on the tablets. She cannot leave them alone. Once when she was taking them Coral hurt her arm. Wanda heard the crash of the falling pan, then Coral screaming over and over again, but she felt no urge to move. She stayed in the front room, by the little table, and unscrewed the lid of the tablets.

So Wanda knows there is no limit to the downward slide. She used to think you could go no further than hurting a child, but now she has hurt Coral in every possible way. Worse than hurting her, maybe, she has failed to love her. Without money she has failed to love. She did not know before that money could come between you and love, but she knows it now.

Wanda looks at the lights of the town, the cinema, bingo club, Tandoori restaurant, and the long strands of lights stretching away into the city. She used to find it so interesting to watch the town light up at night, the windows in Trafalgar House, or Dunkirk Terrace, or in the terraced houses off the estate becoming suddenly yellow, or red, or even green, all at the same time. Then she could watch the people inside doing similar things at similar times, making tea, watching telly, like they all live a common life really, but separately, in their little rooms. When she watched them moving around in their rooms, unaware that they were being watched, she used to feel like she was a part of lives other than her own, but she does not feel that any more. As the outside world gets brighter and Wanda's room gets darker, she can only see the lights of a thousand rooms she cannot enter.

Coral will be back soon. Wanda must get in the bath. Still she pauses, one hand on the curtains she has made, looking at the scene she has looked at a thousand times. When she is not here it will still be the same. Then she turns and walks over to the kitchen. Her bare feet make soft flapping noises on the oilcloth. She will not see her front room again. In the kitchen she takes a sharp knife from the drawer, then she goes into the bathroom. She takes off her dressing-gown and gets into the bath, holding the tablets and the knife. Then she eats all the tablets she has saved. She has managed to save half a bottle, but she does not know if this is enough. That is why she needs the knife. She has thought it all out, planned it carefully, many times. At first she thought she would jump. It seemed the obvious thing to do, with her being nine floors up. She thinks of herself tumbling from the sky like a brightly-coloured flower. But then she leans right over the balcony one day and thinks of the ground coming up to meet her in a sickening rush, all the windows of the flats spinning past. She thinks of Lindsay Myers, who jumped from the top of Dunkirk Terrace and was not even unconscious when they carried her away. She goes back into the lounge and sits down shakily. Not that way, she thinks. It is too ugly. Then she thought of electricity in the bath, but there is no plug in the bathroom and she thinks of the sudden violence of the blast, her face twisted and hideous in death. It is not easy, this planning. She has thought of the best way she can, though the knife will not be pretty. It seems like there is no pretty way to die.

It was not easy saving the tablets. Sometimes without them it is like all the voices in her head are shouting at one another. Sometimes she ends up cringing and whining on the bathroom floor. Sometimes she wonders how her life ever got this ugly. She has stopped saving the tablets now, it got too hard, but she doesn't know if she has saved enough. So now she presses the knife to the white inside of her wrist with its blue-green patterning of veins. She presses hard but it does not cut. Then she draws it across her wrist once or twice. Faint scratch marks appear, and beads of blood. She is not doing it right. She closes her eyes. Maybe she should pray, she thinks. But she has forgotten how.

*

Laurie is in the Cozy Caffy. She sits pressed into the wall, as grey as death. Over and over again in her mind she sees what has happened to her. It is worse than a violation. She feels broken up inside, like she is sick and can never be well again.

Brenda shuffles from one table to another serving tea and toast. Her feet in the rubber sandals are short and square, the nails yellow and curving like horn. The customers heckle her. Get a move on Brenda, says a man with a thin red beard.

Hold your horses, Brenda says. The faster you eat the harder it is to shit. She goes slowly between the tables, the soft grey ash from her cigarette flickering onto the tables and floor. Each time she passes Laurie she slops more tea into her mug. Drink up, she says.

Laurie is thinking about what has happened. She sees herself lying on the slab like a corpse whilst they examine her. It is hard to believe that everything she has ever thought about herself and what she does could be so completely taken away from her. In the end it seems that nothing is in her control at all. She thinks about the row of gulls she saw that day whilst waiting for the bus, and of the bird that seemed to be different from the rest, testing the wind to see how far it could go. She smiles, bitterly.

Outside the window Di and Kev are waiting for the bus with some of their many children. Sheets of rain blow into the shelter at both ends and the children press their face to the café window, but Brenda will not have them inside.

There's working-class, she says, and there's rough. And then there's low-life scum. And a long way after that, she says, there's Di and Kev.

Brenda is speaking to her.

Did you hear about that girl that did herself in, she says, in Blenheim House?

She is called away to the other side of the room.

Found her in the bath, she says, walking past again.

How did she do it, Laurie thinks. With electricity? a hair-dryer? Laurie's mind recoils from it, the sudden force of the explosion, the violence of the blast into darkness.

Found her Thursday afternoon, says Brenda, passing by.

Thursday afternoon, thinks Laurie, whilst she was at the police station. The slow trickle of information is maddening. She waits impatiently for Brenda's return.

Slit her wrists, says Brenda. *And* took pills. Her little girl found her, after school. Terrible eh, she sighs.

It is terrible, Laurie thinks. Terrible enough to disrupt the flow of ordinary life, to make fissures on the surface of people's ordinary routines, big enough to make them stop momentarily, to think about what is happening, to be troubled. But then, thank God for individualism, they can tell themselves that she must have been a weak person, a born loser even. They can tell themselves that they would never be brought so low. Fancy leaving a child like that they could say, shaking their heads.

Laurie is thinking of the greenish water, the overhead light floating in it like a broken moon, the curling flow of blood. It is almost like hearing about herself.

Haven't you got any fried eggs, a customer says.

Haven't you heard of salmonella, says Brenda, brushing the crumbs from a table to the floor with her hand.

What about angel delight, says another.

What, with all this listeria, Brenda says.

The events at the police station, the shop manager and the girl in the bath are all mixed up in Laurie's mind, running round like the screening of some terrible film she cannot stop. She groans and her head sinks forwards onto her hands.

Tea bad again love, says the woman on the next table sympathetically. Laurie looks at the tea. It is bad, greyish, with small droplets of grease floating on the surface. I should tell her to change it if I were you, the woman says.

Laurie stares out of the window. She is thinking about Joan and Sue, Phyllis and Marje, all her so-called friendships. She is seeing them all in an unbearably clear light. Friendship is not possible for her, she thinks. It is not possible for her to have friends.

Fat Anj comes in but Laurie takes no notice. She is thinking of the court case that is to come, of how it might be in the papers and everyone will know. They will probably already know on the estate, in her block of flats. She cannot even shit there without people knowing how regular she is. They will certainly know about Laurie's crime.

Fat Anj takes a cup of tea and toast and looks round. There is nowhere to sit except at Laurie's table. She begins to weave her way through the chairs towards Laurie. Laurie looks at the spots of soup on the vinyl table-top. There will be a fine, she thinks, she will have a record. If there was ever a chance of her getting a job it is gone now.

Fat Anj sits down heavily, facing Laurie.

What's up with you, she says. You look like you've been eating your own shit.

Laurie looks up for the first time into Fat Anj's face. Wet tendrils of brown hair cling around her face and shoulders, there is a large damp patch on the grey-black sweatshirt. Laurie looks at her but doesn't speak. Fat Anj pours ketchup from the stained and sticky bottle over her toast.

I heard you'd been in trouble, she says. Laurie's face registers no surprise. Fat Anj picks up the toast and licks the margarine which is running down her fingers.

I had a friend once, she says, got into trouble. Drugs, I think it were. She glances sideways at Laurie but Laurie does not respond. They took her down station and went through all her bags. Then they made her take all her clothes off and searched her. Stuck their fingers right up her the dirty buggers. She said after, I don't know what they thought they'd find up there, a set of encyclopedias or what? Fat Anj grins and Laurie smiles too, she cannot help herself.

Then Fat Anj gets into her stride.

Hello, hello, hello, she says. Is this your turd madam? Only there were one just like it up the vicar's arse last week.

Fat Anj and Laurie laugh, they cannot stop. They roar laughing and stamp their feet. Everyone is looking at them but it does not matter.

I suppose you'll never get to be Prime Minister now, Fat Anj says.

No, says Laurie, and I did hear they were going to offer me the job.

Then Fat Anj stops laughing and looks out of the window. Rain's stopped, she says. I'd better go.

Why, says Laurie. Can't you stay a bit? But Fat Anj is not listening. Already in her mind she has left, Laurie can tell. She swallows the last bit of toast and sucks her fingers. Then she stands up, pushing the chair back noisily. I'd best be going, she says, and she makes her way through the chairs and tables, raising a hand to Laurie as she leaves.

For a moment Laurie thinks of following. She watches Fat Anj until she turns the corner, then changes her mind. She takes her mug to Brenda, who only charges her for one mugful of tea though she must have had at least four.

See you soon, she says to Brenda. Brenda rests her elbows on the counter shedding the ash from her cigarette onto the sausage rolls. Don't let the bastards grind you down, she says as Laurie leaves.

*

Valerie walks all the way to her mother's. The patchwork colours of the hills fade in the haze of light. Nearer the trees shed their colours with great violence, bright brassy gold, blood-red. Valerie's eyes wince away from all the brightness. She looks downwards at the softer colours of the rustling leaves she is pushing with her feet.

She thinks of Marcie saying your mother wasn't always like she is now. She remembers being on a beach when she was very young. When she could in the summer Valerie's mother worked in the holiday camps to give Valerie a holiday and get herself some money. Mostly Valerie doesn't like the camps. They are noisy and smelly, and she is always expected to join in and enjoy herself. In the evenings when her mother works she is left in the dark chalet room, with the bars of light from the shutters and the babysitter patrolling outside. Most mornings Valerie has to play

210

quietly by herself, not disturbing her mother who sleeps till midday. But sometimes Valerie's mother takes her to the beach in the early morning when no one is around.

In and out of the waves she bobs, up and down. She sinks right under the water and comes up again spluttering.

Come on now kipper, calls her mother, you can do it.

The water slaps Valerie's face. It is in her nose, her ears. Her face is screwed up tightly. She wants to call for her mother but she cannot get her breath. She drifts further away in the bobbing water. If she had any breath left she would cry.

Suddenly she is sinking down again, kicking frantically, gulping at the bitter sea. Everything is shifting all around her, then she is caught up and pulled back to the surface. Her mother's hands hold her in a strong grip. Valerie is relieved and angry all at once. Her mother swings her round onto her shoulders. Valerie clutches, pinching, at the wet flesh, the black strands of hair. Her mother dives into the water and comes up again. She throws herself into the waves, leaping in and out of the water like a dolphin, laughing as the waves roll over her. Valerie digs her fingers in hard, squealing in horror and excitement.

Valerie kicks a great heap of leaves in front of her. She remembers her mother supporting her. Perhaps she always expected her mother to carry her. Maybe she always expected too much.

She is nearing the estate. There is litter and dog shit amongst the leaves. Valerie stops kicking them in front of her.

Kids are playing in the square. As Valerie walks past they fall silent. At the back of her neck she feels them staring at her. She thinks of her mother's flat, of petrol-soaked rags through the door, burglary, arson, vandalism. She thinks of radiators stripped down and flogged, windows taken out whole.

It looks alright as she approaches. As she reaches the door several stones whiz past, one grazing her ankle, and there are shouts of laughter. Valerie does not look round. She opens the door and lets herself in.

The flat is in the same mess as before; nothing unusual has happened. There is more litter round the front door, pushed in through the letterbox, but that is all. Valerie treads carefully through the rubbish on the floor to the kitchen. Her head is worse. She needs some aspirin. Her mother keeps her tablets in the fridge, more than twenty bottles rattle as she opens the door; tablets to cheer you up and calm you down, to put you to sleep and keep you awake; tablets for stomach pain, diarrhoea, urinary problems, water retention, arthritis. On each bottle is printed NOT TO BE TAKEN WITH ALCOHOL. Valerie sighs as she searches the fridge. It is a wonder her mother is alive at all.

She finds the aspirin and swallows two with water. She wishes there was food in the flat but she took it all two days ago. She returns to the lounge and stares hopelessly at the mess. There is the same clutter on the floor, the same dishes and mugs around the chair. In the middle of the floor, as before, is the dark blue dress in a crumpled heap. Valerie picks it up and stands with it in her hands. No one owned a dress like this, in all the clubs. Her mother kept saving for another one to change with but never managed it, so it cost her a fortune getting it cleaned at the same-day dry cleaners, and repaired. It has not been repaired for some time now; the zip is split along the seam where her mother has tried to force it up. There are little tears all through the chiffon, and dark patches where the sequins have come off.

Valerie stands and holds it in her hands. What they want for her mother is a kind of death, she thinks. She is too loud for them, too noticeable. They want to wipe her out.

Suddenly it all comes together in Valerie's mind; her own fear, the terror that strikes her in the class-room, or reading her school-books. It is the fear of being erased, wiped out, like they are going to do to her mother. All this time she has been content to be invisible, unheard, without realising what was going on. Her mother is not like this. She will not live like a fugitive or a ghost. She draws attention to herself. Valerie is being wiped out bit by bit, but they must use more drastic measures on her mother.

So they are suggesting a kind of death.

No one has the right to do that to her mother.

But she remembers her mother sitting in that chair, wearing this dress and saying, if I could just die . . .

Perhaps it is what she wants. Perhaps it is the only way she knows of getting what she wants.

Valerie doesn't know. She doesn't want to think any more, her head feels worse. Instead she begins to tidy up.

She hangs the blue chiffon in the wardrobe and clears away the dishes round the chair. She stacks papers and empties rubbish into the bin. She stuffs dirty clothes into the wash and cleaner ones into drawers. As soon as one thing is picked up there is something else beneath. Underneath a pile of papers she finds a small framed pane of stained glass.

Truly the light is sweet, it says, and a pleasant thing it is for the eyes to behold the sun.

Valerie holds it in her hands. You too mother, she thinks. For herself and her mother only the old words will do. Only the old words have meaning.

Valerie wipes the pane of glass and sets it on the window-sill. Then she washes all the dishes and scrubs the cooker. Finally she changes the bedding, stuffing the old bedding into a bin-liner since the washer and wash basket are full.

Valerie is more tired than she would have believed possible. There are white lights in front of her eyes. The flat still needs cleaning, but the light is fading. Tomorrow she will clean the flat.

Slowly Valerie wipes the last cup. She does not know why she is doing this. Her mother may never see the flat again.

Suddenly she is not only tired but sick. She goes into the bathroom and is violently sick. Then she leans back exhausted. Tomorrow she will clean the flat. But for now she must go to bed.

In the bedroom Valerie kicks off her shoes. Outside there are horns blaring, bike engines roaring and the frenzied unfocused yelping of dogs. In spite of this she collapses onto her mother's bed, folds the coverlet around her and falls asleep.

Valerie dreams she is on the beach with her mother. It is evening, or early morning. Long fingers of pink light touch the sand and very far away the sea is silver. Valerie is making a castle with her mother, as they have done many times, but she is older now. She is absorbed in the castle, building ramparts and a moat. Her mother is wandering further and further up the beach looking for shells and stones so they can decorate the castle. It is already beautiful with mother of pearl, mussel and jade. Further and further away her mother goes, then she stoops over something in the sand and picks it up. Look Valerie, she says.

Although her mother is far away Valerie can see it clearly. It is a round jade-green stone. Curled around it in a spiral whirl is the fossil of a baby.

I have to take it back, her mother says, then it can live.

Don't mam, Valerie calls, but her mother is already heading along the beach towards the sea.

Mam, mam, calls Valerie, come back, but her mother is wading far out to sea. It is frothing round her knees. She goes on and the waters lap around her waist, her shoulders. Soon they close above her head. Valerie's eyes fill with tears. She feels an inexpressible relief.

When Valerie wakes up the pillow is damp with the wetness from her face. But it is morning and her headache has cleared. Today she must let them know at the hospital what she has decided. But first she must clean.

As Valerie cleans, wiping down surfaces, dusting, hanging up washing, she notices a feeling so extraordinary she doesn't recognise it at first. It is a feeling of absolute peace. She is watching herself filling the kettle, folding the ironing. She goes outside to feed the cat and all the movements of her hands are steady, skilful. She does not know yet what she will say at the hospital but it doesn't matter. She opens all the curtains in the flat. The light is shining on the frosted windows. She collects her mother's things into bags and puts on her duffel coat and shoes. Then she looks once more at the transformed flat. Her bags are packed, she has the keys. She is ready to go.

*

Already the sky is dark, a deep liquid blue. Laurie's steps falter towards the empty flat. Suddenly she pauses then changes direction entirely, walking with new energy towards the road leading off the estate. She is going on one of her favourite walks, down the long road where the rich people live.

As Laurie walks she thinks of Shelagh and herself and her tutor, and the feeling which was so much like fear. She remembers her first days at university, when the face of her tutor began to assume more importance to her than her own. She felt like he was more real than she was, with his assurance, his command of language. She felt like she had disappeared, like a thin moon when the sun appears. It was like she could only exist by reflecting him. She remembers her mother's awe of the university, how she felt it would 'make something' out of Laurie. Laurie can see the irony in this now. All her life she was brought up to worship power, that was what it was in the end with her tutor, power, not sex. She remembers the man in the subway, flicking open her purse, and the way it felt like a sexual attack. She stops still in the middle of the street. Power, Shelagh, she whispers. I told you it all came down to power in the end.

Sex, says Shelagh's voice.

Power, Laurie says.

She is nearing the big houses. She walks past one set of ornate gates after another and pauses, peering through railings at massive lawns, and squares of light from great bay windows. There is so much beauty in the gardens, in the buildings themselves. For a moment it hurts her that there is so much beauty. Her fingers curl tightly round the railings. She wonders if the people who live there have ever seen the council estate where she lives. It is close by, but they have probably never even seen it. They will not stand like Laurie looking in on it. For a moment she remains at the gates, feeling her own invisibility, their presence. Fine droplets of rain wet her hair until it clings about her face. In the brass plaque on the gate-post she can see her face, an oblique triangle, the eyes glittering strangely. She feels almost like she could slip through the gates unnoticed and invisibly enter their lives. She feels almost that she could ring the bell on the gate-post, and walk in as if she belonged there. It could be done, she knows. Almost any kind of confidence trick can be performed by those with confidence, or power. She presses her face into the iron of the railings. O my soul, she thinks, remember past strivings.

She presses her hands against the railings and pushes herself away as if trying physically to break away from some kind of spell. O my soul, she thinks, remember past strivings.

With an effort she returns to the street, to the lights and cars, the people carrying shopping on their way home from work. She thinks again of Shelagh and herself, and the different paths they have taken. So much has happened, so many changes in both their lives, but in one way they are both alike. They have both broken away from their old lives. Nothing of their former selves remains. They have both been erased.

As Laurie walks down the street she feels a sense of well-being that is almost elation. If she has been erased, she thinks, she is free to be anything at all. She walks along the street and the streetlamps shine in her eyes. The sky is orange, leaking into blue, pouring itself into black, and the street is luminous with glittering reflections. Long stretches of water on the road flare into sudden brilliance as cars flash through. As she walks Laurie feels that the silence within her is more than the absence of noise, it is a force in itself, shaping her life, carrying her along in its stream. It is all one, somehow, with the glinting reflections of the street. Laurie walks, feeling new sensations of weightlessness and boundlessness, as though everything has been peeled and peeled away from her until she is deep and limitless, like the sky. She is floating like music down the street, thinking about the past, the present, the future, and the silent God she half believes in. As she turns the corner she is thinking of the late-night shops, the Asian supermarkets, still open on Harper Street nearby.

*

Wanda remembers a day that felt like praying. She sees herself clearly, sitting on the bench in the square near the DHSS offices. Her hair is permed and bleached so many times it is wispy, like baby hair, but her face is very old. She sits hunched over on the bench. They have stopped her money again, but they can't tell her why.

Besides Wanda, Coral is trying to skip. She has a proper rope, with handles, but she can't skip. The rope hits the ground and then she jumps. Two, she says. Five, four. She can't count either. Wanda stares at the ground. She never felt so bad as this before. Then she straightens, looking upwards, and watches a massive drift of cloud passing slowly over the roofs of the buildings in front. As she watches she notices how the clouds seem to contain light, even the grey ones; they are like soft wrappings of light. Wanda looks at them a long time, like she has never seen a cloud before. Then she lowers her eyes and looks at the buildings in front of her, and notices for the first time the wetness clinging to them from the last downpour. It makes them look different somehow, dark and shiny from the rain. They are glowing and heavy like the day itself. The leaves pushing their way through the railings are also dark and shiny; there are burning berries already on the bushes. Outside the square there is a bright stream of traffic.

Wanda looks at all this, then she looks at Coral. As she looks, something seems to give inside her. She looks at Coral like she cannot look enough. She looks at the darkness of her skin, which is like the ripe darkness of a plum, and the soft, peach patterning on one side of her face. She looks at the stringy muscles of Coral's legs, which tighten as she jumps. Coral is beautiful. It is a miracle, a revelation. Coral is beautiful, and Wanda never knew it before. As she looks Wanda feels the place inside her which is hard as stone becoming warm. She loves Coral. A great sob fills her chest and then comes bursting out of her so that Coral stops skipping and looks at Wanda. Wanda cannot bear it. It is too much beauty, too near. One sob comes tearing its way out of her and then another. Coral runs to Wanda and buries her face in

Wanda's lap. What is it mam, mam, what is it, she says. Wanda shuts her eyes and moves her fingers through the softness that is Coral's hair. She cannot stop crying. The last time she cried was when she saw the ugliness of Coral, now she is crying at her beauty. She does not know how she could have missed it all these years. She picks Coral up and buries her face in her neck and cries.

Then, when she has finished crying, she wipes the wetness off her face and laughs, and tells Coral it is alright. Then she puts Coral in her trolley, for though she is four it is a long way home.

Wanda doesn't care about the long way home. She has never had so much energy. Everything around her is warm and glowing. She runs with Coral into the warm wind and Coral laughs and shrieks as the air rushes into her face. Wanda laughs too. She loves Coral more than she ever thought it was possible to love. It is mercy and grace, all those words Wanda learnt at school, mercy and grace that Wanda can love her child.

Wanda cannot look enough at the day around her. Some grey days are just dull, but this one is glowing. Light floods down from the rolling clouds onto the streets and buildings below. All the colours are dark and vivid. She sees the people around her not noticing the day, looking grim. I used to be like that, she thinks. She used to be worse. When you get shut off inside yourself you notice less and less of anything, till in the end you are moving in a dark, vague world of your own. But now Wanda feels like she felt in hospital, that she has found a new way of looking at everything, except that this time she is not ill. She feels for the first time that she is well. She walks through the streets, past offices and shops and people, loving everything she sees, for now she loves Coral it is like she can love everything. She turns corner after corner and is still not tired. She wants to run and sing but the pavements are too rough for Coral so she walks, looking from side to side all the time and trying to contain it all inside her. It has always been like this, she knows. Somehow she knows it will always be so, if only she does not forget how to look. She has seen beauty in the ordinary streets of the town, she has known what beauty is. That can never be taken away from her, she is sure. She has been terrible to Coral but she will make it all up to her, she knows. From now on she will be different with Coral.

Then when she gets home she is very tired, worn out really, but still happy. She does not mind too much when she has to bump the trolley all the way up the stairs because the lift is not working, but when she has finished her shoulders and back ache and her head hurts. Really she is dead tired but Coral will not go to sleep. She is over-excited like she has caught Wanda's earlier mood. She runs round the flat, jumping and stamping and kicking her toys. The man in the flat below hammers on the ceiling of his flat with a broom-handle and Wanda's front room shakes. She is afraid he will come upstairs and complain so she makes Coral a drink in her special cup. When Coral saw the cup in the shop she wanted it so much that Wanda bought it for her though she had no money. But now Coral knocks it over, smashing it, and there is spilled milk everywhere. Without meaning to Wanda hits out at Coral. Then she cries with Coral because she never wanted to hit her again. But the money she spent on the cup was all she had that week. When you are poor all the little things become disasters, stopping you from being the kind of mother you want to be. Wanda clears up the mess and gets Coral ready for bed. Then she crawls in with her, worn out.

That night she has a dream she has dreamt before. She is walking slowly in the slippy shoes along the banks of the canal. She is trying to hurry because she knows she is being followed, though when she looks round there is no one there. If she doesn't get to the tunnel soon Sim will not be there. But she walks and walks through the tall wet grasses and cannot find the tunnel anywhere. Then when she knows she is going to be caught she sees it, and Sim stepping out to meet her. She hurries towards him, but when she gets up close it is not Sim at all but Kev, taking her arm so that she falls slowly, slowly to the ground. Then she cannot stop anything that is happening, Kev loosening his trousers and lifting her skirt. It is all like a film that is being made by someone else. All she can do is to worry about her hair, which is full of leaves and mud. No matter how often she rakes her fingers through it, there are more and more leaves.

Then, when she has struggled out of this dream she strays hopelessly into another. It is Jim this time, the suffocating weight of him on her so she can hardly move or breathe. Jim takes her face in his hands like it is a ball of clay, and wipes out her features one by one with his great blunt fingers. Her nose is gone in one smudge, with two prods out go her eyes, then he is rolling her lips up together in his fingers. When there is nothing left of her face he laughs, sticking his tongue out. It is thick and red. Bylo baby bunting, he says.

When Wanda finally wakes up she is threshing round the bed like a great fish. All the bedclothes are knotted round her in a rope. They are damp with sweat. She lies still a moment looking at the ceiling. There is a terrible taste in her mouth. Slowly she sits up and lets her head rest in her hands. She is overwhelmed by the ugliness of her life.

Coral is already out of bed. Wanda can hear her singing to herself in the front room. All she wanted was some beauty in her life, Wanda thinks. It can't be wrong to want beauty in your life. But then how could everything have got this ugly?

Wanda needs her tablets. She gets up slowly, dragging herself across the floor towards the kitchen. All the time she feels like Jim is there behind her in the room. He has never left. The half hour of lying still and pale and crumpled underneath him has never ended. She fills a glass with water and takes her tablets. She is overwhelmed by the ugliness of what has happened with Jim.

She feels like he has raped and beaten her.

She feels like he called her names and threatened to turn her in.

In fact he did none of these things.

She feels like he did all of them.

She does not know why she should take it all so badly, why still in her mind it has never ended, she is always trapped beneath him on the bed. It is like he has taken her apart and put her back together again his own way, so badly she can hardly move. She wonders why Mabel never felt like that, or, if she did, how she got over it. Then she thinks perhaps Mabel was always like that anyway; put together in the interests of those with money.

Wanda goes to make herself a cup of tea, then she remembers that there is no tea. She presses her head into the cupboard door and gazes out at the scene below. It is grey. Grey drizzle on the grey slate roofs. Narrow grey streets. Wanda closes her eyes. She feels the silence pressing in on her. She feels all the beauty she saw just the day before draining away from her like dishwater from a sink, down a hole she cannot see. It is like being poisoned.

Wanda sits down at the table and opens the bottle of tablets again. She feels like she cannot live with this slow draining of beauty from her life. She has abused Coral in every way. It is hard to live with, very hard, but it is not so hard as this. Even as she sits the things she looks at become squalid and sordid in her eyes. There is no beauty in her life. She does not know how she could ever have thought that there was.

When Coral comes in Wanda closes her eyes. Mam, Coral says. Wanda sips the water. Mam, Coral says again. She comes over and tugs at Wanda's skirt. Mam, mam, she says. Wanda keeps her eyes closed. She does not want to look at Coral and see the beauty draining out of her as well. She does not want to see her ugliness again. Mam, says Coral, mam, mam.

Just a minute, Wanda says, not yet, not now.

But mam, mam, Coral says.

Please Coral, just a little while, please. But Coral will not go away. She will not go out to play. She clutches hold of Wanda's skirt and follows her from one room into another. Wanda feels the walls pressing in on her. There is no place she can go. She hums to herself to make some room. Jack and Jill went up the hill, she hums. Jack fell down and broke his crown, but Coral will not be put off. Mam, mam, she says louder, mam, she says, mam, mam, mam. Wanda goes into the bathroom and fills the glass on the side of the sink with water. She has told Coral she mustn't ever follow her in there. She unscrews the lid to take another tablet for now the doctor has reduced their strength she has to take them all the time. Then Coral comes in, pushing the door so that it knocks against Wanda's hand and the water spills out. Wanda turns her face to the wall, so Coral can't see what she is thinking. She presses her fingertips into the wallpaper. Go away, she is thinking, go away go away go away go away go away . . .

*

Coral pours the tea and drinks the first little bit. Outside great drops of rain gather and splash down, intermittently at first but soon there is a furious downpour, rain bouncing off garage roofs and car windscreens, and streaming down the kitchen windows until Coral can only see blurred ribbons of the scene outside. The pounding on her wall stops. Coral is tired of all this thinking. I will go to bed, she thinks.

Coral lies down on the bed. Soon she sees herself entering the basement of the flats where she lives. She is carrying the shopping. She is going to make pizza for Larry's tea. She looks up and there is Larry on the stairs! He looks down at her and smiles. She hurries after him. Up and up the stairs she goes, and as she climbs higher and higher her bags get heavier all the time and she is smaller now. The door of the flat is open but she does not think she will ever reach it. But at last she gets inside in time to see Larry disappear through another door she did not know was there. As she reaches it, it clicks shut. With a pang Coral sees it is the bathroom door in her mother's flat.

Coral struggles to wake up. The objects in the room around her are dim and vague. Her eyes close again and flutter as she tries to open them.

She stumbles into the kitchen. Her mouth is very dry so she runs some water into a beaker. When she turns round her mother is there.

Coral's mother stands by the table humming a tune she has often hummed to Coral. In the distracted way which has always driven Coral crazy she is gently touching the typewriter keys, not pressing them, just touching.

No – shouts Coral – No – No – No –

She shuts her eyes and shouts as loud as she can. When she opens them her mother is gone.

Coral sinks into the chair moaning softly. She is weeping, her face is wet. This is it, she thinks. She has gone mad. When she closes her eyes she can still see her mother, close enough to touch.